JURASSIC DEAD 3
CTRL-Z

Rick Chesler and David Sakmyster

Severed Press
Hobart Tasmania

JURASSIC DEAD 3

ISBN: 978-1-925342-78-9

Prologue

The moon was engorged but not sated, nearly blood red and staining the wispy clouds. The night had only just begun, but already the world below seemed weary; sycamores twisted, slouched and motionless, willows along the riverbank drooping, exhausted and meek.

The Mississippi, whose waters had ushered in exploration and commerce in centuries past and had borne witness to epic adventures and nourished nearby farms until great cities had arisen, whose tributaries and vessels had been old before *homo sapiens* had even struggled to emerge upon the earth, now shuddered in the wake of something far older.

Not the mighty 74-ton sternwheeler riverboat gracing its surface, the vessel retrofitted with Pratt and Whitney engines to complement its mighty ferry wheel—harkening to the bygone illustrious era of Twain—not this mighty floating fortress which currently held as its captain the most powerful man in the country, if not the world (if what he was now still qualified as a 'man'). What caused the waters of this ancient river to tremble, to part and break with the shadowy hint of reptilian scales and crustaceous fins, in fact was something far more ancient than the river itself. Much older still than this young land upon which, until very recently, a great civilization had grown to immense heights. Something moved in those shallow depths, something that had died out along with its kin 95 million years ago.

It had no business, no right even, to be around, much less swimming. It should not have been snapping at and devouring crocodiles in its path, those modern threats, so dinosaur-like in their own right, that suddenly found themselves far down on the food chain. This semi-aquatic prehistoric beast's time had come and gone, but to William DeKirk, master of this vessel—and master of that which dutifully swam along like a pet behind it—the past was the future, and if he wished it, death was just the beginning.

And nothing that was extinct had to stay that way.

#

Standing on the aft balcony outside the captain's quarters, DeKirk licked his lips, tasting the humidity and the salty heat, the iron tinged with blood from his recent meal. The nearly insatiable hunger stirred again, grumbling and tearing at his insides. As he watched the ripples in the vessel's wake and saw the spinosaurus' spiny sail fin break the water then submerge, he reached out with his thoughts, honed after months of fine-tuning. He let his mind seek it out and felt the sympathetic proteins in the dinosaur's blood-addled brain, swimming around the microchip he had implanted there two weeks ago. A melding of technology and biology, he had perfected a viral super-communicator that served to enhance pheremonal, instinctual and neurological impulses, allowing DeKirk mastery over the beast as if he had become its Alpha.

He blinked and looked up at the moon as he thought about it some more. In effect, he was the Alpha. To this creature, and all of those now sweeping over the planet, evolved and enhanced far above their weak predecessors upon whom they fed, all un-life itself, this zombie plague he had single-handedly unleashed upon the world--for all of them--he was their master. In moments, he would go back inside the captain's stateroom, where from his mobile control center he could monitor the state of the world, access his cabinet of ministers back in their Springfield, Missouri bunker—those he delegated to run the operations and prepare for the next stage of his plan; from here he could keep the limited remaining military forces staffed with human soldiers loyal to their Commander in Chief. He could also combat the Resistance and continue to seek out more ancient creatures from the time of the great extinction, to bring more and more elite creatures into his service.

His previous life as a billionaire innovator, geneticist and public enemy-slash-biological terrorist now seemed a vague, distant memory belonging to an unfamiliar ancestor. He bore no more resemblance to that man, owed him nothing, no more than any successful person would thank a forefather seven generations dead. It had all been going so perfectly, these past three months. Since the fall of Washington, D.C., since his masterful coup that brought down not just the mightiest nation, but all the nations on Earth. Europe and Asia had offered little resistance beyond what he'd expected. And realistically, what could they do? This was no mere invasion force. It was biological warfare for which there was no defense. No immunity, no pills or shots could ward off this onslaught.

One zombie, one raptor, one pterodactyl getting through the defenses was all it took. One bite led to a geometric infection progression, and the beauty of its advancement was a thing to behold with wonder and respect.

Even though DeKirk was the enhanced, living embodiment of the zombie prion's full evolution—the control, the alpha—he was still ever in awe of its basic microscopic force, the relentless, unstoppable inertia once it got going. A parasite in name only, it was magnificence made tangible. Nothing could stand in its way, nothing but extinction of all life. And that unfortunately was its only weakness. That's what did in the dinosaurs, for when there was nothing left to eat that wasn't like itself, then only one route remained to satisfy the hunger. The prions weren't wired that way, and apparently had genetic safeguards against it, much like human mores about cannibalism, but just the same…when all alternatives were gone…

That was a problem, but DeKirk was working on it. He didn't intend to become a god only to rule over nothing but a skeletal wasteland. He wanted a living, hungry world, and wanted to be its master. There was time, and with a blend of science and nature, tweaking one with the other, he would find a way to turn off the mindless drive for hunger, the natural progression to reproduce—the only way this prion knew how, through violence and consumption.

He'd get there, but in the meantime this pesky resistance—so human, so inferior, so primal and lacking in vision—had to be snuffed out. Not until all the isolated pockets of humanity could be found—and his satellites, survey planes and methodical bands of human-zombie seekers were working on that—only then could he move on to the next phase.

His stomach rumbled, and at a thought—barely registering as conscious—an order was sent. Moments later, his meal arrived.

Dragged onto the deck from the oppressive storage room-turned-brig below, a once-beautiful young woman stood before him. Eyes nearly vacant, her pupils contracted in the moon's sliver, reflecting its bloody glow. Her clothes were tattered and stained—the letters of a New Orleans football team barely visible beneath the gore and sweat.

DeKirk nodded to the zombie aide—a beast of a man who might have been a linebacker for the very team this sacrifice had, a lifetime ago, cheered on during many a lazy Sunday. The zombie's skin was already layered with scales, more reptilian than human, its eyes lizard-like and cold, desperately cold and DeKirk could sense its hunger, its agony at refraining from taking this meal itself.

DeKirk licked his lips, both in anticipation of the feast, and in the knowledge that he had this power over both the living and the dead, that they all had to obey his whims.

Me first, he thought as he reached for the woman's throat.

She offered no resistance.

DeKirk kept his eyes on the zombie servant—the man who in that previous life could have crushed him like a twig but now had to stay motionless, starving and helpless but to watch as his master lavishly feasted: tearing away flesh and muscle, gorging on spurting blood, devouring bone and gristle, brains and cartilage and then—when the screaming and thrashing had stopped and the victim was a limp collection of unrecognizable features, DeKirk stepped back.

The creature trembling before him looked on hungrily, like a dog waiting patiently for the last scraps…or a bone at least.

Instead, DeKirk lifted the bloody carcass, still with wisps of bloodied blonde hair hanging down, turned and then threw it over the rail…

…into the rising maw of that monstrous prehistoric creature, his sleek pet that was all teeth and rotting scales, hideous eyes, an elongated snout, ragged sail fin and short stubby limbs.

Then it was gone in a huge splash that reached the upper deck, and the Mississippi again rolled over the bloody carnage and once more took on the reflection of the crimson moon.

#

Inside the cabin, more spacious and stately than his corporate office back in Geneva, with plush carpeting, elegant tables, lighting and impressive artwork, and with an amazing stained glass skylight overhead, glittering from the sternwheeler's rooftop lights, DeKirk assembled his generals.

"It's time."

He addressed the four warriors, carefully selected from the strongest, fastest and most ruthless of all those he had converted and then trained in the arena back in Antarctica, when this march to glory had begun.

Each had their own microchips in their brains, in the temporal lobes, enhancing DeKirk's suggestive abilities, tracking capability, and further cementing his dominance over their loyalties.

His elite four were standing ready like armored warriors preparing for their glorious crusades. Three males and a female. The toughest of all, she was like a golden-plated Amazonian warrior. He had even brought in military-designed armor for them—the latest in Kevlar body suits (just because they looked cool, and well, would protect their regenerative flesh from wear and tear), and most importantly, helmets designed to withstand and deflect most lower caliber bullets, and certainly sword and knife attacks.

Looking a bit like sleek, frightening hockey goalie masks, these things—his elite commanders—stood at the ready, poised like starving wolves ready to launch after prey as soon as he gave the command.

He had even given them each names of ancient deities from major mythology. Loki, Baal, Anubis, and Hecate.

"It's time," he repeated as he moved to the nearest console and pressed a button, releasing the upper cargo doors. "Ride forth into the night on your prepared steeds."

Four magnificent pterodactyls—crimson-black with enormous wings and monstrous beaks, each outfitted with leather and metal saddles—rose from the shadows, snapping at one another and screeching into the night. They leapt and scrambled and alighted on the railings on either side of the ferry, rocking it back and forth with their weight.

"You each have your orders, your targets. Go, slaughter and report back to me. I want to see through your eyes, I want to taste the bloody flavor of victory on your lips as you feast on our enemies."

Their hunger was palpable. Their desire to please even more so.

"Do not fail me." He stepped aside, and let them rush past, up the stairs. On the monitors, the four figures were blurs of speed and precision, racing to their mounts, which then rose up in a rush of wings and dust.

Licking a spot of blood from his lips, reliving the sweet taste of his last meal, he sighed and pulled up a chair. *Time to get back to business.*

He had a world to run after all. A minor rebellion to crush. Some pockets of isolated humans left about the world on islands and remote areas—places that hadn't yet received his blessing. Their time would come, and for now they were unfinished business.

Much like his meals of late, he hated leaving anything unfinished.

This last phase had lost a bit of the fun he had relished in the past year: the thrill of conquest and the challenge of a decent foe. This was the mop-up phase: annoying but necessary.

There were still thorns outside that needed to be burnt away. Thorns that he had history with, but now finally, he knew where each of them were.

Alex Ramirez. Veronica Winters. Commander Remington, and Dr. Arcadia Grey.

Four generals. Four thorns.

It wouldn't be a fair fight, but DeKirk was never about fighting fair.

He pulled up the satellite maps of the United States, then superimposed the crimson bands, much like those showing severe storms on a weather map, but this program tracked the spread of the prion transformation.

Like the moon outside, everything was almost all red.

1.

Cheyenne, Colorado

The road to NORAD was paved with corpses.

Covered with a late October dusting of snow, skeletons lay strewn in scattered heaps, flesh picked clean, bloodied icicles clinging to eye sockets and teeth. Ragged strips of cloth whipped in the brisk winds, and skulls seemed to turn aside from the Humvee that took a slowing approach to the mountainside rising up from the cracked pavement.

At the gate—twenty feet high and crowned with barbed wire, the vehicle came to a stop, the front tires just beyond the shredded chain-link entrance.

"So much for that," said Veronica Winters, inside at the wheel. It had been a long cross country trip, and she and Dr. Arcadia Grey hadn't held out much hope for even getting this far, so she counted her blessings. Many, many others hadn't been so lucky.

"It can't be," Arcadia whispered. Eyes wide, she fearfully scanned the damage to the fence, then peered beyond. The road ahead, as well as the vast area leading up the mountainside entrance to NORAD, were bleak, but not unpopulated.

"How many do you think got through?"

"Right now I'm just thinking about what smashed through that fence."

"Yeah," Veronica sighed, getting ready to put the HV in reverse. "I'm not up for another game of 'can our car drive faster than a pursuing zombie *T. rex*?'"

"Do you think anyone's still in there?"

"I don't know. It's all underground or in the mountain, so we could hope so, and hope they had enough supplies to last three months, but I don't know. If even one of those things got in there, there might be no one alive."

"Or if DeKirk sent in some phony-ass soldiers..."

Veronica nodded. "Surprised he didn't just bomb the place to be sure, but we know as Commander in Chief he could have shut it down—evacuated the whole place even, or ordered an airstrike with just a keystroke."

"But he didn't." Arcadia scanned the mountain and the nearby areas, looking for signs of launches, attacks, or nuclear fallout.

"Probably wants to keep everything here nice and intact in case there's a need to use it as a command center or something in the future." She tapped the radio, the UHF on the dash, and again tried tuning in to a frequency that had worked before.

"Nothing in days," Arcadia said, not even looking. "They've gone silent."

"Hopefully it's just so they don't give away their presence. It's what I would do." God, she hoped it was true, otherwise, these three months of nail-biting terror, battling, sneaking and racing across the country, were all for nothing. The road might just as well end here.

At least for them.

Arcadia met her look, and after three months of being constantly together, they pretty much knew each other's thoughts. "You're still hoping Alex made it."

She made a pained face, as a cloud darkened the sky and the eerie shadows ahead all merged into one blanket of gloom. "There's been no word for so long."

"I'm sure he's safe."

Veronica shook her head. "I'm not. You don't know Alex like I do. He's impulsive, thoughtless, overly high on himself. Even worse, he attributes his survival to skill when in fact it was either pure luck…or me being there to save his ass."

"And now you're not, you're halfway across the country. I know, but you have to hope."

"Oh, I do hope." She gripped the wheel tighter, and for a moment, right before the sun re-emerged, she was back there, back in Atlanta three months ago, right after the bomb exploded and everything went to hell.

#

"Bunker buster," someone said. Matter-of-fact. Like observing the weather outside.

Veronica braced herself for more, for pain, for something to fall and crush her. It was a devastating combination: the ringing in her ears and the complete darkness around her eliminated any warning her senses might provide, and now her imagination and fears were running crazy.

No control, no time to react. Who was alive? The doctor? Alex? What about the zombie patient they had just worked a miracle on?

She had to regain control, had to see. No generator power, no lights...that was bad, but somehow the infrastructure down here, and the depth had kept them from the worst of it. Maybe...

A flickering, then a spark and a narrow band of illumination appeared above. One of the lights worked, still powered by a feeble backup generator.

A thought crept in: what's keeping all the killer germs and samples safe?

The answer: What does it matter, when the ultimate super-extinction maker is already loose out there, running on two (or more) legs and devouring anything alive?

"Alex?"

She couldn't even hear her own voice above the ringing in her ears. She screamed when someone touched her wrist, again in the darkness not knowing if the things had broken through in the rubble, and fast as raptors had found her, easy prey pinned for their dining pleasure. She couldn't hear her own scream, but the touch...

Something familiar about it, and then a hand—gentle and rough at the same time, found her face, and touched it everywhere, feeling for her lips, her eyes, probing, making sure...

"...breathing."

Finally, she heard it.

Alex's voice.

"Alive," she shouted, and this time heard it, and then saw a little more come into focus as another light sparked into life, or maybe the dust had just settled enough to see it.

Cell phone.

"It's me." Alex's voice. "You hurt?"

"I don't think so. Where's Dr. Grey?"

"Here," came her voice, shaken and sounding like she stood at the bottom of a deep well. "God, what was that?"

"Bunker bomb." Alex helped Veronica up and waited until her dizziness passed while she reassured herself that, other than some rough scrapes and bruises, she was all right.

"No one else hurt?"

"At least not in this room," Arcadia said, shining her flashlight phone app around and toward where the door had been. "The others..."

"Don't think about them now."

"But if we can help, I have to—"

Veronica looked at Alex and nodded. "Doctor, all you have to do is survive. With that research and with your brain, you are our top priority."

"No, I can't leave..."

"The world's top priority," Alex emphasized, scanning the rubble and what was left of the lab. "Now let's move. Need to find another way out of here."

"There's an access tunnel," Arcadia said absently, still staring at the thousand tons of brick and rubble. She pointed behind Alex. "Through there, an exit hatch. Emergency escape route, normally floods with water as a decontaminant, it will lead to the surface, an exit point a mile south of the central hub."

"And then what?" Alex asked, and for all his calm and his appearance of leadership, Veronica knew he was still just a kid, an activist-turned-hero thrust into a world of hell. Not unlike thousands of other boys his age who had gone off to fight (and die) in countless wars throughout history. Their mettle tested way before their time, forced to show what they were made of, to hide and die or to stand and fight.

Nevertheless, Veronica was still the one in charge. This was her mission, entrusted to her straight from the president himself. She had to call the shots, and everyone and everything depended on her.

"Then," she answered, "we do what we have to. We do what our last orders were, and damn the new boss."

"Damn him to hell," Alex intoned, with the hint of a smile on his dusty face.

Dr. Arcadia stood there motionless and trembling.

"Doc, we have to move."

"All my friends…this…this was my life. All gone…"

"There's a lot of that up there too," Alex said. "Life will never be the same, even if we pull this off and somehow stop the spread of these things. If we can prevent…"

"Extinction?" Arcadia turned around at last. Took a deep breath and looked for anything that could be salvaged, taking a few crumpled notebooks and dented hard drives and stuffing them in her purse.

"Doc…"

"There could be a follow-up strike." Veronica eyed the gaps in the ceiling nervously, especially one jagged hole, and furtive shadows darting about up there, tricks of the light…"Or something worse.

Alex was at her side in a moment, also looking up, following the trail of rubble, broken pipes and sparking electrical wires flashing in the dust from the upper level. He aimed his light up there.

"Hear something?" Veronica asked, touching her belt, feeling for her 9mm.

Alex took her arm and led her back, away from the hole, and his grip intensified.

"Doc? The exit?" Veronica had the gun out now, aiming above at a spot in the hazy darkness beyond the wire that sparked again and left a residue of light smearing across what may have been an optical trick, a remnant of the blast and her disorientation, but it also could have been something else: the rigid outline of a curved snout, a set of spiny demonic-like horns and a single yellow eye blinking, closing and cunningly blending in with the darkness. Stalking them.

"I'm just about ready," Arcadia said from beside a toppled cabinet. She finished rooting through a drawer and stood up with an armful of files—just as the wall behind her exploded like a phony barrier in a Hollywood set piece. Arms burst through and one hand gripped her shoulder and spun her around. Head-butting through the wall, a hideous face—female, with enormous incisors and crazed reptilian features—closed in on Arcadia with jaws that never had a chance to close.

A single shot from Veronica and the thing's forehead popped back in a spray of blood out the back of the skull. It dropped and thrashed once in the rubble as Arcadia's files and papers all fell and covered the body and the debris.

"Now are you ready?" Alex shouted.

Arcadia screamed them, a loud piercing wail of frustration, disbelief and primal rage. She looked about her office in utter exasperation, and Veronica knew what she was thinking: all this for nothing, and the only thing that mattered was getting out of here alive.

Veronica was about to rush over and shove the doctor and make her get moving when she finally did it herself. Assumed a straighter pose, hands clenched into fists. She turned and pointed, then took off, leaping over some rubble and vaulting a desk, getting to what looked like a closet door.

"Help me clear the entrance. It's in here, stairs and then..."

The rest was lost in a screeching, thrashing and violent cacophony of chaos and motion from above.

"Oh shit." Alex turned and rushed to the closet door.

Veronica spun around, gun aiming, staring up at the form lodged halfway through the opening from the upper level. Its monstrous lizard head, the bony protrusions, the twisted yellow eyes and powerful jaws that kept snapping and snapping at empty air as the neck twisted and lunged this way and that.

The raptor-zombie smelled prey. Smelled fear, and smelled them. Its little forearms, covered with light feathers, clawed and scratched at the section where the jagged concrete had caught in the creature's belly, and its ribs were breaking apart, its muscles splitting, making room so it could slip through and get to them.

Before Veronica stepped forward and emptied the clip into the trapped dinosaur's head, making a neat star-shaped pattern from its eyes to a point in its forehead, down to its snout, making sure she could hit every possible entrance point to the brain, she felt those eyes lock on hers. Felt the certainty that what looked out at her wasn't the prehistoric animalistic-turned zombie mind, an alien and ancient thing with no connection to Veronica's present nature, but instead was something...someone else.

Someone she was intimately more familiar with.

DeKirk, is that you?

One or two bullets, well-placed from point blank, might have suffice, but now... If it's you watching me, *she thought,* take this asshole.

"We're coming for you."

The echoes of the gunshots still ringing in her ears, taking the place of the muffled bunker blast from earlier, she barely heard Alex and Arcadia screaming for her. Screaming to run.

"They're coming!"

The others, the zombie horde that must have broken through after the blast, driven by their own bloodlust mixed with DeKirk's ravenous orders to find and exterminate all threats. They were coming, floor by floor, descending, following a few dinosaur scouts, decimating all who had survived and searching for them in particular.

"NOW!"

She turned, had a glimpse of a crowd of forms pressing against the hole in the eastern wall, scrambling to get through, and then she ran. She slid through the partially ajar door, which Alex then hauled shut and locked and barricaded with something heavy, something loud. She couldn't see in here either, just a frenetic flashing of the phone's light bounding ahead, down the stairs and ultimately, she hoped...to freedom.

#

"They're coming!"

Arcadia's voice brought her back and it took a moment for her surroundings to slip back into place. Feeling like one of those old Viewfinder toys with the slides all jumbled and caught between two frames, Veronica finally shook herself into the present—and wished she hadn't. A wave of forms ran toward them, loping and hopping, some on all fours, across the lot, toward the broken chain fence and out of the gloom.

"Shit." She put the HV in reverse, felt it jam, heard the gears stick and the engine sputter in fear, maybe terror even of something moving in that midst ahead. Something larger and clouded in mist. A huge tail and short arms, and humanoid forms atop it, clinging to the sides, riding along like inebriated teens for the sheer thrill and something far more primal and symbiotic.

"Oh God," Arcadia whispered, then her voice cracked. "Please get us out of here, please... All for nothing, they've overrun everything, we have no hope. We have—"

The transmission caught and they rocked backward, launching over a straggler zombie, one they hadn't even noticed until the rear fender smacked it in the head and then the back wheels crushed it, dragging and pulverizing the body over the next fifty yards. They roared back, just as the mob surged against and then through the fence, which split apart in an instant as the *T. rex* charged through it like it was a final race marker, meant to be broken through by the victor.

Veronica had a moment of pure admiration, as if appreciating a beautifully rendered CGI action sequence, a melding of creature and human all captured against a backdrop of the rising sun and the steaming frost in a surreal slow-motion moment...

But then she shielded her eyes, let out a scream of surprise and slammed on the brakes.

The world had erupted into light, then fire and a concussive sound that shattered their windshield and lifted them back on the rear wheels for a moment before dropping them hard.

They rolled another twenty yards, coming to stop at a guardrail overlooking the serene snow-capped peaks at their backs.

"You okay?" Veronica asked, blinking, never taking her eyes away from the sight ahead, even to check on her passenger, who sat in a pile of shattered but contained glass shards caught in protective mesh and the deployed airbags.

"I...don't know," Arcadia mumbled. "Did we just get nuked?"

Veronica shook her head. "No cloud, no blast wave, but man that was something. Something big, maybe some kind of ballistic missile."

"DeKirk? He tried to get us?"

Veronica stared harder, willing her eyes to pierce the raging fires and the smoke and to look past the raining debris—concrete, flesh, bone, and...was that a *T. rex* head, falling end over end, rolling toward them? Half in flames, eyes burnt and bubbling, teeth shattered?

"I don't think it was DeKirk," she said at last.

"Why?"

Veronica let Arcadia's question hang out there as the head rolled and collected a layer of snow that snuffed the flames until it came to a stop, gazing at her from ten feet away with hollowed-out eye sockets and crisped interior.

The radio lit up and static crackled.

"I think," said Veronica, suppressing a surge of hope, "that all may not be lost."

"NORAD to Agent Winters," came the voice on the UHF. "About time you and the good doctor got here."

2.

Atlanta, Georgia. Three months ago.

His parachute ended up somewhere in a pile of glass and tangled over a row of printers and cabinets. His flight helmet, dented and cracked, came off slowly as he worked himself into a seated position. He propped his back against a cubicle wall so he could see back through his entrance point.

Thirty stories up, maybe? Major Casey Remington couldn't tell, and after the landing where his head struck something after his body crashed through the window, things were a little hazy. He remembered the battle over Atlanta, taking down pterodactyls, laying cover fire for the National Guard and the fleeing refugees below, and then…seeing that damn thing straight out of a cheesy Japanese horror movie.

The *dreadnought.*

They were coordinated. Those prehistoric bastards actually had a battle plan. Distract and attack from the flanks. He had been outmaneuvered by near-mindless beasts.

Or were they?

He couldn't think about that now, but certainly had to figure this in to future strategies if he survived this day, that these brute creatures were being controlled remotely. Ordered and given intelligent instructions. If he made it out alive, he wouldn't underestimate them again.

He struggled to his feet. Slipped out of the flight suit and stretched, checking for broken bones and testing his body's ability to flex and move. Before he knew it, he was at the window, looking out over the twilight spreading over Atlanta.

A war zone.

He swallowed hard, tasting blood, smoke and pain. From this vantage point, the world seemed lost. This city, just days before a normal metropolis bustling with families and business and sports and leisure, was now caught in the grip of a pure fight for survival. He couldn't think any longer in terms of casualty rates or limiting civilian deaths. This was a matter of protecting the few, the remaining lucky (or unlucky) ones. They needed a win, and if that meant sacrificing everything to save a last contingent and prove that humanity wasn't about to go down without a fight, then he was ready for that mission.

Except, standing up here alone, far above the fray, it seemed hopeless. And this was only one city. He couldn't even think about the rest of the world. About what had happened back in Washington, so quickly, or what was happening in Kansas City.

Oh God, he hadn't thought of Olivia in hours. His wife—and his unborn daughter, due any moment. Waiting for word. He had promised, just twenty-four hours ago. His last tour, one more mission before coming home to her. Could they have made it? Were they holed up somewhere in the farmhouse (just like in a Romero movie), waiting for help that might never come?

An explosion below and to the southeast…near the Georgia Aquarium and the Coca Cola Museum. Smoke billowing into the sky, looking so surreal from here, as the giant behemoth thundered down Central Ave, leading what looked like a small army behind its tail.

Another sortie flew overhead and a shock wave rocked him into action.

He had to get down there.

#

An hour—or five minutes, ten, thirty—later, Remington was back in the thick of it, in the worst firefight he had ever experienced, something that made his Afghanistan operations look like peaceful exercises on some island beach.

He had caught up with a contingent of National Guard and local residents, all armed as best as they could be, not far from the armory which they had managed to empty before the first airstrikes.

"They're bombing their own goddamned people!" Captain Henry Ellis had cursed at Remington when he caught up with them behind a barricade on 7th Street. "Not answering our communication attempts, and damn, they even took out the bridges and highways."

"They want you trapped here." Remington left it at that. The captain could infer this was a tactic to aid in the quarantine of

Atlanta, and that the president was merely making the difficult choices, but he had a feeling that Ellis was no idiot. He could see this was an extermination, and if the bombs and bullets didn't get them, a worse fate was headed their way.

"We're not in charge anymore," Remington told them during a break in the assault, as the first line of zombies—their recent neighbors, friends and citizens—were mowed down by the defenders behind a wall of crashed cars, rubble and barbed wire. The Georgia Aquarium was just to their south on Baker Street, and until just before Remington joined the defenders, it had been a safe zone, a place of peace and comfort, with the soothing marine life swimming calmly as if the world hadn't just descended into hell. Then a missile strike took off the domed roof and rained death and debris on thousands of refugees inside—and let a couple of cryolophosaurs inside, thrashing and biting their way into the midst of those who had thought they might be safe in there.

Fortunately, Captain Ellis and his squad of seven well-trained ex-SEALs had been in there as well, doing what they could to coordinate a rescue and evacuation, and to design a plan. The cryos ran right into a buzz saw of precision bullet strikes, and had their fan-head crowns nearly blown off their bodies, along with their heads.

A few dozen permanently dead human zombies later, and the exits at least were secure. They could begin moving out the survivors and the wounded.

So many injured and so many heroes stepping up, Remington noted proudly of his fellow Americans. His fellow humans. Men and women, even teenagers and kids, helping out, rising to the occasion and leaving no one behind. Despite the shock and the trauma, despite the inability of so many to grasp just what the hell was happening, they were doing the impossible.

Or, Remington thought, simply doing whatever it took to survive, knowing that at the moment when nothing matters but yourself, that's the moment all is lost. They had to help each other, and only together did they have a chance. Whatever that might be.

"What the hell can we do against these things?" Ellis asked, catching his breath and reloading. He checked their ammunition crates with a wary eye. His men reloaded and met his glance, shaking their heads.

"Too many of them," Remington said, agreeing with the unspoken assessment. "But that doesn't mean they have to overrun us. Contain them, trick them, trap them and rely on the environment for your defense. Get these people out, stay in tighter alleys and narrow fighting lanes where they can't flank and you can mow them down before they get close."

"As long as we don't run out of ammo."

"Yeah. Aim for the heads, be precise, and…" Remington stopped just as all the sound from this side of the barricade went dead.

"Oh crap. Company coming."

The dark draconic head rounded the edge of a Bank of America building. Horns and jagged cheek plates, eyes of crimson-yellow, and even from this distance, as the neck emerged and the first of the enormous forepaws, Remington could see the figures clinging to its throat and to the scales and the horns. It had a convoy, and a full contingent of warriors.

Remington stood up, holding out his arm to the men as he scanned ahead, then up. *But we've got something else,* he thought, scanning the evening sky.

"Tell me," Captain Ellis asked, for himself and the benefit of his men, "that these bullets will pierce that thing's skull."

"We've got grenades…" Someone chimed in hopefully.

"Won't get close enough to use them," Remington countered. "But good thought. And yes, we may get its brain, given enough shots and precision, but I'm thinking those damn riders might be clinging to its head for more than just transport."

"Infernal things," Ellis said. "Strategic even though stupid."

"A bit of a hive mind thing going," Remington said. *Or they're being controlled…* Either prospect chilled him. More gunshots to his right, then above: from the two snipers—or best shots they had among the guard. He kept his eyes up though, scanning through the thick clouds and the jet trails.

"What are you looking for, Major?" Ellis's voice was a distant hum in Remington's ears. "In case you haven't noticed, we've got a serious problem coming our way, and unless you've got reinforcements coming, or can put me in touch with air command…"

"Hang on, I may have a way out of this. Silver bullet time." He looked around the supplies, the crates and piles of ammo and items on tables at the front of the aquarium.

"What do you need?"

"UHF you said you tried, but without the right codes, you'd get nowhere with those pilots."

"Right."

"But I'm one of those pilots…"

"And you know the codes?"

"I do, but voice commands on some amateur frequency won't cut it. If you had a laptop…"

"Here, sir!" One of the other guards came forward. "Civilian back there had one, doing a school project. It's undamaged…" The man offered it over, even as his expression fell. Remington sadly knew not to ask about the condition of its owner.

"Firing it up," he said, quickly popping the lid and being grateful for the lack of a password screen.

"How are you going to get access, or email or whatever the heck are you doing?" Ellis glanced over nervously, then flinched as more sniper shots blasted from above, and a few other men began firing.

"Wait for it," he hissed. "Too far."

Remington lifted his eyes. The enemy was about three hundred yards out but would be gaining on them fast. The only thing on their side so far was that their zombie pterodactyl air support had been either decimated or reassigned as the last couple of local F-18's remained around to do the job.

"I've remotely accessed our birds time and again, and we all need to know how to reach our friends in the air in case of rescue or other covert signaling." He brought up the access page, searched for the nearby signals—found one, then held his breath as he typed in the access codes, hoping President DeKirk hadn't bothered to go about changing things at the lower levels yet. Believing in himself and his absolute control, and with a million other things on this mind…

"Yes! Signal acquired. Now..." He dared to look up, and wished he hadn't. The dreadnought had gained ground, rumbling and stomping down Baker Street. It roared into the night, challenging anything and anyone, and settled on its target.

"It looks really freakin' hungry," someone said. It might have been a civilian, who was then ushered back into the aquarium lobby, to take shelter in the rubble and water leaking everywhere, from above and the sides, and rolling over the floor. The stink of marine life was nearly overpowering the fumes and the smell of carnage floating over the city.

"Well," said Ellis, "we're not going to be its next meal." He cocked the AK and sighted, and Remington had a moment of respect, as well as almost feeling like he couldn't blame the guy for trying to capture a sound-bite, no matter how cliché. This was it, their one stand to take back a chance at survival, to stop the invaders and to live to fight another day. This was war, all out, no-reprieve madness, against an enemy that fought by no rules but its own primal hunger.

Remington typed as fast as he could to bring up the appropriate interface, then thought carefully and selected: TARGET: NEW, SIGNATURE: HEAT (Order: Descending), LOCATION: BAKER ST SW. He input the access codes and pressed enter.

"That it?" Ellis shouted over another volley of gunfire as the first wave of zombies neared; they were cut down with something less than precision. Then the shadow of the dreadnought fell on those in its path. They scattered without glancing back, giving room to some of them, others hopping along to the rotted, ancient flesh and muscle for a ride.

"Come on," Remington whispered, listening, trying to hear about the roaring and the gunfire. He wanted to tell the men to hold their fire and not waste ammo on the dreadnought, but he knew he wouldn't be able to hold back in their place, not when trusted to defend his city, his family and friends.

Can't think about them now, don't...

Another stomp and the thing was gaining speed now, barreling downhill, past the World of Coca Cola Museum, with its huge red sign shattered and the dome ruptured. The dreadnought screeched now, a hideous cry of hunger and insatiable need, and the zombie-things on its hide seemed to echo with their own voices, forever tortured and changed into a language a half billion years old.

Come on, Remington urged, and now he could hear: the distinctness of an engine. Change in course, a dipping, a turn, and now coming in fast over the aquarium, toward the creature.

Would it be in time?

"Can't wait!" Ellis shouted, aimed and fired.

The shot—and the barrage of firing from his men—was drowned out in a concussive thump of a sound that blasted out the remaining windows on Baker Street.

Remington felt a moment of pure joy and pride at the marksmanship of his fellow aviator, nameless though he was and most likely just responsible for following previous orders that caused mass civilian casualties. Then he had to duck and look away as the burst of hot white light exploded dead ahead.

He heard a multitude of shocked cries, a cacophony of voices and cries, of shouts and finally, thrilled whelps of joy. He stood, shaking his head and still wincing with pain from the glare. Now the image was coming into focus, the only problem was, it wasn't something he could quite force into a recognizable anything.

Bunker Buster, he thought, or maybe said aloud. He couldn't hear anything above the shouts and the ringing in his ears. Dimly, he was aware of men cheering and someone slapping his back, but there ahead in smoking clumps and pieces of debris that looked like a mountain of tires he'd seen once in a dump, on fire, was the dreadnought. Flaming chunks of it, twisted and fused and pulverized and mixed in with human flesh and bone and concrete from where everything had been pounded into the pavement.

A few legless human zombies were dragging themselves out of the pit, on fire still and charred. A large one walked out of the smoke, then seemed disoriented as to its mission. Turned, revealing half a face just gone, seared off completely; it stumbled back toward a large boulder-shaped mass, with a single recognizable horn sticking up, above a torn section of the dreadnought skull. The zombie moved in and reached for the gooey pink insides, cooked and shattered and ripped apart in the blast.

It would feed one way or another, but for now...

"Looks like we're safe for the moment," Captain Ellis said, still with his arm on Remington's shoulder. "We can't thank you enough."

"Just get these people out. Somewhere safe, if there is such a place."

"What about you?"

Remington was about to tell him he had other concerns. A wife, a soon-to-be-born daughter. He had to get back to them, and damn his station and his duty and everything else. "The armed forces are compromised, and everything we thought we could depend on is gone or turned against us. I hate to say it, Captain, and all of you, but we are on our own."

He saw them staring at him with expressions that lost a touch of the previous victory, the jubilation rapidly transitioning to fear and hopelessness. They were looking to him, as the one who had just rained down salvation from on high, as the one who might now lead them into safety and peace. Wherever that might be.

As his ears cleared and a brisk wind blew away the lingering remnants of an oppressive fetid smell from the heated carcasses down the road, Remington tried to see a way out.

"I have to find my family." It was honest, and as direct as he could be.

"Then you'll fit right in with the rest of us," Captain Ellis said, and now there were others coming out from the rubble of the aquarium's interior. Lost, desperate faces emerging from the shadows. So many of them, so many in the same condition: looking for family, for friends, for a way back to a life that had been torn from them.

"It will be a long trip," Remington said. *And I would be much better on my own, and actually have a chance of making it.*

"We can do it," Ellis said. "And maybe along the way we can amass other survivors."

"Build up an army," someone said from the shadows.

"A *resistance*," said another, voice tinged with determination.

Murmurs of assent, excited sounds of agreement.

"We're not going to lie down," Ellis said, shaking his head. "We're going to fight this, fight them. Find our loved ones. And rebuild." He reached out to take Remington's hand.

Major Remington knew he had just been conscripted. He could almost see the future, maybe a couple months out: a diverse force under his command, with delegated commanders running missions in separate parts of the country, moving ever north and west, liberating cities and towns in their wake, converting other members of the armed forces if possible, acquiring weapons, tanks, bombs and vehicles. Building up a force to be reckoned with, an army that could be everywhere and nowhere at once. Maybe it would start as a thorn, but grow into a massive impediment to DeKirk's plans, to the spread of extinction and chaos.

Ellis was still shaking his hand, smiling as the others cheered, even as the visions of a violent future faded into a hazy, flickering glory.

"We need a leader."

3.

Springfield, Missouri – the Present

The urge to gag was insufferable. For the last twenty minutes, with every exaggerated motion, Alex Ramirez regretted his foolish decision. Stumbling through the woods, drenched in blood from the fresh human zombies he had battled back on Route 65 just north of Freemont Hills, he made his final approach to the bunker.

It was a trick he should have remembered from *The Walking Dead* and used a long time ago, but it only came to him after he had been ambushed by three of the things while holed up for the night after a long, grueling day of travel through the zombie human and dinosaur-infested wasteland. Fending off two of the female creatures, freaky-fast and catlike as they lunged for his throat, he was able to slip away, roll and close the distance to the third—a huge brute of a man whose bulk never impeded his newfound speed; big as he was, he wasn't prepared for Alex's quickness. Or his machete. One upward swipe and the head was gone, then on the downswing Alex spun and slashed—burying the blade in the first girl's skull. The third leapt on him and bit at his wrist, but thanks to the metal forearm sheaths he had duct taped there and on his thighs and shins, she had no success. Two of her teeth crushed and shattered. Backing away confused, she could only hiss out a defensive cry before he sideswiped her with the bloody blade, hacking off the top of her head.

When he lowered the machete and stood over the carnage, he started to curse out the fact that he had just found a new change of clothes this morning at a deserted mall—a loose-fitting grey sweatshirt and relaxed fit Levi's, when he realized being soaked with zombie blood and gore might just work out in his favor where he was going.

Now, with dawn still an hour away, the darkness stretched over the sky in a blanket rolled thick with clouds to conceal the stars. The half-moon was not enough for any chance of real light, and he was more than ready for a stealth approach.

Every step toward the single bulb burning down at the end of the long unmarked drive was an exaggerated effort. Alex had seen enough of these things during the past three months, had studied them and knew their movements and motions—both at rest and during heightened hunger activities. He matched those of a couple others that were shuffling toward the door and that light.

Not just any door, this was a large garage type door he sure hoped would open. He had actually seen a *YouTube* video a couple years ago, a covert filming of this very facility for a conspiracy website. A truck driver filmed his delivery through this same door and into the enormous, city-sized space below.

Alex had watched this site for almost a half hour, standing and shifting about as nonchalantly and mindlessly as he could imagine, and with the darkness, hadn't drawn any attention. He hadn't seen any activity to speak of, but then a few minutes ago, movement through the trees caught his attention. A small group of zombies, led ahead by a sleek, small and feisty dilophosaurus, hopping about like a monstrous and diseased sparrow, marched to the door.

Alex quickly shambled and loped along with them. Careful not to betray any signs of his humanity, he matched the movements of the two banker types on either side of him. Both were still in their power suits, Italian loafers torn and scuffed with gore, but otherwise they could have been on a brisk walk back from work denying loans to farmers or small business owners. He did his best not to react, but to ignore the snarls and the unnecessary snapping of jaws these things were prone to, the jerky motions and the random lunges, even toward each other. This prion thing was obviously hard-wired for the ultimate sense of self-preservation, ready to attack anything and everything so long as it either presented a possible threat or constituted sustenance. As Dr. Grey had described it, the protein-turned-invasive-evolutionary-predator would hunt and kill and spread itself on all those not like itself, driven to change the host's chemistry. Like keeping an accelerator down with a brick, this thing turned up the hunger nodes in the brain, overriding everything but the most basic functions.

On the approach that felt like a mile, Alex had too much time to think. Somehow DeKirk had found a way to interrupt the process and alter the chemistry, at least a little. Take the pedal off the metal, so to speak, and insert an overriding obedience function. Able to command these things now, even the dinosaurs, he could force them to hold off on their hunger just enough to first obey his requests. For example, go out and forage or undertake certain missions. Alex imagined that this regiment he now pretended to be a part of was just returning from some targeted strike. Perhaps they had just wiped out a local enclave of survivors or resistance members seeking sanctuary in some barn. Or perhaps they were new recruits, answering the call to come and join the elite, serving the shadow government.

Whichever it was, Alex was about to find out.

After nearly three months... *Has it been that long?* Three months since he'd seen or even heard from Veronica? Since Atlanta where they split up. Did she make it to Colorado? Was the doctor safe, did the cure still stand a chance? Had they given up on him to do his part?

He approached the door, which rose at their approach, as the dilophosaurus fanned out its cranial crests, normally bright and colorful extensions of its nasal and lachrymal bones, subdued now in the dark. It screeched a bubbly, high-pitched sound that overcame the echoing hisses and excited answers from the bankers and the other dozen or so zombies packed in around Alex.

In a moment of sheer fright, Alex nearly betrayed himself. One who had been an older woman, perhaps in her eighties and in an old folk's home previously, suddenly spun around, stood up on her toes and shoved her face into Alex's. She cocked her head and took a big, deep sniff.

Apparently I didn't make the right response, he thought at the same second his reflex kicked in and he reacted. Swift and just as he had seen these things do a hundred times or more. He shoved her, hard and fast, with all his momentum behind the thrust that would have knocked an ordinary old woman down and broken her bones. This one launched back, got her footing and was about to spring when Alex screeched at her, the same as he'd been practicing for weeks.

Got the damn thing mimicked by now.

The other zombies scattered, riled up and looking for a fight. Might have been enough to override their modern signals to the contrary and this could have turned into a frenzied bloodbath, but the noise of the rising garage door jarred their concentration. The old zombified woman, her eyes seething yellow and her claws out, was still undeterred and had a scent of something and she wasn't going to stop.

I'm done for, Alex thought, getting ready to reach behind him for the trusty machete strapped to his back—or for the 9mm on an ankle holster—but then the dilophosaurus leapt into the air, landed between Alex and the woman, facing her, and it puffed out its crest, thrust out its neck and screeched in the woman's face. Alex waited for it, shrinking back, expecting that stream of vile acid he knew these things were capable of expelling—but whether it was holding back, or no longer produced it, it didn't happen. Fortunately.

She shrunk back, rebuked. Shook her head, rubbing her eyes, then she turned, head down and shuffled into the bunker with the others.

Thank you, dino-critter! Alex lowered his head, too, and followed, jostling along with the other zombies, shuffling after the skittering, hopping dilophosaurus, who had apparently been trained like a shepherd dog. The door creaked and began lowering just as he crossed the threshold.

#

Immediately, he was struck by the immensity of the pillared area within. It had the scope and feel of an enormous underground parking lot, except with higher ceilings, and indeed he saw some semi-tractor trailers parked in a few spaces up ahead. Tire marks everywhere. The fresh scent of diesel tried to cut through the grime and the blood, and he would have relished that, along with a hundred other smells, but at this moment all he could think of was a nice hot shower, with citrus body gel and some frothy herbal shampoo. *When was the last time...?* Maybe three weeks ago at a deserted mansion on a Tennessee farm. That was incredibly nice. The bed...

Snap out of it and focus!

They were approaching the center of the open space, with innumerable pillars supporting an immense roof of rock and concrete. Loading docks and a multitude of doors led off to God-knows-where in every direction. It had the feel of a modernized mine, hollowed out and expanded and equipped with every modern convenience.

They were being led by the dilophosaurus toward a distant entrance point, a glowing sign with a number, simply displaying: 3.

For some reason (and Alex's imagination could come up with several dozen), he did not want to be part of this group any longer than necessary, and certainly didn't want to find out what was behind door number 3.

So he slowed his pace, head kept down and shuffled slightly to the right as the others jostled and hissed and shoved and pushed past him, still ruled by the herd mentality. Soon enough, he saw his chance. At the next pillar, after a quick glance behind and to the right to verify he was last in line and no one—man or dinosaur or even a camera within sight to catch him—he ducked behind the next pillar.

Waited, counting to ten, then he made himself revert back to zombie gait and shuffled purposefully toward a stack of crates and an idle forklift. He flashed on driving one on Adranos Island, shaking his head at the close call. Walked between the crates and the lift to an unmarked door he had noticed earlier.

No key card access. No key. It was open—which meant either they didn't care about security once you had gotten this far in, or this door didn't lead to anything too important.

That didn't bother Alex at the moment. All he cared about now was getting out of the open and inside the facility proper. One way or another, once inside, he'd find some way into the heart of this place.

Now he could smell and taste something other than the foulness about himself and his disguise. He was close, and his enemy within striking range.

He opened the door and pushed his way in.

4.

Natchez, Louisiana

DeKirk replayed the video feed one more time. Not so much for his benefit, since he was convinced, but for those watching the same eighty-seven seconds back on their screens in the Springfield facility.

He knew there would be some rumblings that after three months it was time. They could and should leave the protected bunker and return to the real world that they were set to rule, but like every meeting lately, DeKirk shot down that proposal and urged patience. They were far too important to risk exposure. The Resistance wasn't finished, and like any change of government, uncertainty bred violence, greed and a power vacuum that sucked in any fool who thought he had a chance to take over.

No, they could come out when this was done, when humanity was beaten down and when it had accepted its fate. When only the weak remained as fodder for the new and evolved prion-enhanced humanity. The race for whom death itself was not a threat.

DeKirk let his attention wander during the last twenty seconds, and gazed out the set of large windows beyond the captain's wheel and the control panel displays. Beneath the soft glow from the stained glass domed skylight above, he watched the proud expanse of the mighty river, where the moon—now lofty and crowned in a cold throne of light—manifested as a silvery reflection of itself in the currents. Again DeKirk imagined Mark Twain, with his pipe, glass of whiskey and a notebook, observing the state of humanity and nature from his stateroom.

How the times have changed...

This time for the better, DeKirk thought. He would make sure of that. No more strife, no more inequality, race wars, riots, poverty or shame. Nothing but the one constant that bound all life together: *hunger.* And that was good. A most basic instinct that drove behavior. Hunger could be understood. Sated. Fed. Hunger led to progress, to enhancement, and hunger would save the world. He would see to it.

A quick check of the radar, showing the way clear ahead, and then back to the map of the country and other displays of Europe and Asia. DeKirk sighed. He was far more relaxed than he would have imagined, but really, there was nothing to fear.

Hunger, once he released its full potential upon the world, would do its job. There was nothing and no one to stop him. Just a couple of speed bumps, like this Colorado issue that annoyingly demanded his attention.

Back to the screen, he paused the feed an instant before the white burst of light—the explosion that took out one of his favorite *T. rex* specimens. The very one that he had implanted with a microchip—and an ocular camera that recorded everything the creature saw. DeKirk had spent many enjoyable hours watching the *dino-cam* as the creature disembarked from a carrier in San Francisco and made the trek over to Colorado, picking up a convoy of hunger-crazed zombies along the way, a veritable army to secure NORAD—which had gone dark shortly after he took over power.

"What do we know?" Jules Norris asked from the bunker cabinet room, appearing on the teleconference screen as the camera tracked her voice. Forty-seven, with a severe haircut and her typically bright pastel suit that DeKirk was none too fond of, she was—as the rules of succession decreed—next in line should something happen to DeKirk.

Something like what? he wondered. He was already beyond the known limitations of life and death, his body toughened and enhanced even more so than the speed, strength and scaly thickness the regular zombie transformations provided. However, he had to be prudent, had to take steps to preserve the legacy he was building here if the impossible were to happen. He could do worse than have this one take up the mantle when he was gone.

Jules had an impressive resume. She had headed up a multinational pharmaceutical corporation and she displayed an admirable balance of ruthlessness and efficiency when it came to dissecting companies after mergers and acquisitions. She would do nicely as his second-in-command, and would bring the others in line.

"We know what we can surmise from the video feed," DeKirk said with a heavy emphasis on 'surmise.' "NORAD received a visitor around oh-eight-forty this morning. From the video enhancements, I would say we are more than safe in arguing that the tourists in this case were our own Most Wanted: former CIA Special Agent Veronica Winters and CDC Chief Dr. Arcadia Grey."

"Now we know what their destination has been all this time," Jules commented.

"Must've taken the scenic route," said Charles Wilford, a relic in his own right, a political has-been who never made it past the state assembly, but who had a truly brilliant economic mindset. Currently sitting as treasurer on this cabinet, he'd come in useful soon. *Or not*, DeKirk thought. Finance and science were two of DeKirk's own specialties, and there was no real need for redundancy there. DeKirk had built up his own financial empire without any help, and was sure he could more than manage over a sovereign autocratic system in the future.

For now, at least he was reasonably sure this team, those that he had spared after careful research into their backgrounds, would be safe bets to follow his commands and to get on board with the new world order. Of course it helped that he promised them and their families a stake in immortality. They would get a similar brand of enhancement and join the elite in the next stage.

"It's a big country," DeKirk said. "We had a lot of eyes and ears, but still these two got through."

"At least now we know where they are," Jules said.

"We know that, and one more thing." DeKirk played the last second of the video again. The bright light, the loss of the feed. "NORAD. It isn't as dead as we had assumed."

He sighed. This is why he had sent the *T. rex* and the zombie contingent to check it out. "For three months, that mountain has been utterly silent. Not a single heat signature even, but of course, given the depth of the facility and thickness of the reinforced walls, that was to be expected. Now we know, someone's still down there, someone survived—and chose this moment to launch a defensive strike."

"They knew Winters and Grey were coming?"

"Obviously," DeKirk said. "Primitive communication measures most likely. They must have gotten the word and waited, biding their time." He sat in the comfortable leather captain's chair and sighed again, tapping his fingers on the desk beside the monitor showing his Cabinet members.

"Options?" someone said on the other end, and the camera panned over to a dark-skinned man in a uniform. Head shaved, rigid jaw line, eyes too close together. The perfect example of a military specimen, DeKirk had figured. Another reason he had chosen the Springfield shadow government site, knowing that Neville Hughes would be an imposing enough figure in public, and even more so once 'enhanced'; he would have the faith and trust of the armed forces.

DeKirk just hadn't been sure why that trust hadn't extended to NORAD. Something else must have happened there to throw off the chain of command and to lead to either a loose cannon down there, or something else.

"Part of me would damn sure like to know what's going on in that mountain, and what happened three months ago," DeKirk said. "But the other part? Well, it doesn't give a shit. I want to level the goddamn thing."

Neville Hughes didn't bat an eye. "I'm assuming we are still keeping the nuclear option off the table?"

"Correct. I don't need decades of fallout and wind patterns to deal with, never mind the worry about mutations and shit. No, what else do we have?"

"ICBM from the San Francisco carrier. Could launch within an hour."

DeKirk nodded, not even bothering to look at the rest of the Cabinet. "Do it, but send in some drones first. I want eyes on Grey and Winters. If they're in the blast zone, all the better, and if not, I damn sure want them tracked, hunted and killed."

"Done." Hughes stood, saluted, and left the camera view.

DeKirk met the eyes of his VP, and for a moment he saw something in her dull green stare that he didn't like. "Everything under control there, Ms. Norris? Something to say?"

"Everything is under control, sir," she replied. "Although I would like to reiterate my objection to your refusal to allow us to know your location."

Wilford nodded his head, as did a few of the others. "You're mobile, that's all you've told us, but it's not enough. We need to know. In the old days, you'd have Secret Service, a documented travel plan, researched ahead of time, and—"

"And I'm safe. That's all you need to know." *Safe from them. Safe from you, safe from anyone, in the last place anyone would look.*

He stood, stretched, and felt his stomach grumble. "Now, if there are no other objections, you have your responsibilities. A country to run and all that. Get back to work, and leave me to my own location, and to handling this resistance and a few personal loose ends. We'll meet again soon. DeKirk out."

He pressed the button to deactivate the live feed, and then closed his eyes, sending out a summons below.

Send up dinner...

He licked his lips, deciding they were a lot closer than ever to ending any opposition and finalizing his dream. Time to celebrate.

Make it a double serving.

5.

Cheyenne Mountain Complex, Colorado—NORAD

"Doesn't look like much." Veronica Winters leaned against the HV as she appraised the entrance to the underground fortress. Beside her, Dr. Arcadia Grey, briefcase in hand, also studied the property which had been the goal of their grueling journey west. Now that they had finally reached it, Arcadia had to admit that Veronica was right. It didn't look that different than the rest of the country they'd seen, ravaged and desolate, up to this point.

They hadn't known exactly what to expect, but NORAD conjured up visions of gleaming, state-of-the-art military defense installations. The barren, corpse-littered ground in front of them just wasn't that. Or at least it didn't look the part. Maybe inside that massive cave was all the high-tech salvation they'd been dreaming of for the last few months, but they'd have to see it to believe it.

"Hopefully the inside hasn't been compromised. Only one way to find out." Arcadia strode toward the entrance to the cave. A huge tunnel large enough to drive several commercial vehicles through side by side was open on their end. The pair walked into the part of the tunnel still open to the outside and immediately detected foul odors. Veronica produced a flashlight and aimed its beam to the far sides of the tunnel. Bodies lay here and there, mostly single but the light also picked out a pile of three.

"Human or zombie?" Arcadia wanted to know.

"Can't tell from here. I could take a look…"

Arcadia grabbed the former CIA agent's arm. "Let's not get sidetracked. Don't forget about how far we've come already. The key to solving this thing could be within these walls. I need a lab, materials and sanctuary enough to finalize a cure. We were so close back in Atlanta…"

She nodded toward the end of the tunnel, where a stout-looking metal roll-up door, now shut, was plainly visible. They continued on down the tunnel, which grew darker the farther inside they walked. When they reached the door, Veronica played her light beam around it, looking for a keypad or some sign of an entry point, but she saw only smooth metal. She looked up, checking for cameras, seeing none. Arcadia put her ear to the door and listened. After a few seconds, she pulled back from the barrier.

"Don't hear any activity in there."

Veronica rapped on the metal door with the butt of her pistol. They waited while the sound reverberated throughout the cavernous space, but still no one answered.

Veronica swept her beam along the door's bottom edge, which appeared flush with the tunnel's concrete floor. "I don't see a good old fashioned handle anywhere, either. Because if we had to we, could probably roll this thing—"

Suddenly they heard a sharp *click* and floodlights bathed the tunnel in harsh white light. The two women took frantic steps back, unsure of what was coming next.

Then they heard the clang of iron on concrete, whirled around and saw a fenced barrier barring the way back outside, trapping them in the tunnel.

A male voice issued over a loudspeaker. "State your intentions."

Veronica exchanged glances with Arcadia, then Veronica shouted toward the still-closed rollup door that blocked the way into the complex. "My name is—"

The voice cut her off. "That's not what I asked. We don't care who you are, only what it is that you want."

Veronica led off. "We've come a long way specifically to get here."

Then Arcadia continued, holding up her briefcase, assuming they were under some sort of video surveillance even though they couldn't see any cameras. "I've brought key elements of my research from CDC-Atlanta in the hopes that I could complete my work here on a cure for the scourge."

"The *scourge*, is that what you call it?" The voice held the tiniest bit of sarcasm.

"That's what it is, isn't it?" This was met with silence during which Veronica looked around for signs of anyone approaching.

At length, the male voice returned. "You must be two tough cookies to have made it all this way from Atlanta."

The two women remained silent.

"Unfortunately, I'll wager you're tougher than you are smart, because the top experts in immunochemistry, prion science, infectious diseases, you name it—they all say—those who are still alive anyway—that it can't be done. This...*scourge*...cannot be reversed."

Arcadia held her bag up higher. "I have evidence that shows otherwise."

This was met with a beat of silence, followed by, "I can only hope you are as talented as you have been lucky."

"Me too. But there's only one way to find out." Arcadia glanced back at the locked outer gate. "You going to let us in? Why'd you trap us in here?"

"We closed the gate not to lock you in, but to lock them out."

The words forced a chill over the spines of both women. "Undead?"

"Oh yes. Lots of them. Entire armies of those a-holes still roam the land, with quite a few under some kind of remote neural control. We have to seal the entrance of the tunnel before we open the inner door, otherwise they'll all come running the second it's open."

A couple of seconds ticked by while nothing happened. Arcadia stared impatiently at the sealed door. "You going to let us in or what?"

"Yes. But...a little word of warning: they're in here, too, although most of these don't seem to be under external control. Just garden variety zombies. Still, there are, well...hundreds, leftover from when we repelled the initial waves of attackers. They knew about this place, that it represents a bastion of hope, and they tried to take it out."

"DeKirk," Veronica spat.

"How do you work if they're in there with you?" Arcadia asked.

"We have a subsection of the compound walled off and fortified with defenses."

"How will we know where to find it?" Veronica heard the first disturbing sounds of the undead outside the gated tunnel. Wheezing, groaning; the dragging of feet.

"Just follow the yellow brick road. Get your weapons ready. Door opens in ten seconds. Remember: once it does, you'll have no choice but to fight your way to us inside. The throng outside has grown now, too much for the two of you to deal with on your own. So don't start crying and change your mind once we let you in, okay?"

Veronica said nothing but Arcadia looked panicked. "Hold on. Is it doable? I'm not looking for a suicide mission."

"It's doable if you're careful, skilled with weapons, and have some more of that luck on your side. That's all I can promise."

Arcadia was about to object again, to ask for more time to prepare, but they were out of time.

The rollup door creaked as it began to crank up.

"Good luck, ladies. See you on the inside."

6.

Arcadia held her Beretta 9mm at the ready in a two-handed stance, while Veronica favored her Taurus in one hand and a fixed blade knife in the other. She'd lost track of how many kills she'd had with each, so many zombies put down they were all a bloody blur, but she was most impressed with Arcadia's progression. Her training had paid off and she had more than pulled her weight these past three months, overcoming her initial terror and disgust, and becoming almost mechanical and ruthless, the way a scientist would terminate an experiment that had lost its usefulness.

Artificial light flooded out of the interior space as the door rolled up. Veronica took it as a good sign. At least they had power on in there. The door finished rolling all the way up, reminding the women that they now had only one way to go. They stared inside to their new reality as the first wave of zombies piled against the locked gate behind them.

Corpses lay huddled on the white tiled floor ahead, but so far they saw no living beings of any kind. Stepping over the bodies, it was apparent they had all been dealt serious head trauma of some type, whether by gunshot, stabbing, or unknown blunt force. Some of these dead wore military uniform while others still had on white or blue lab coats.

Veronica smiled as she pointed to a yellow painted line on the floor.

"He wasn't kidding," Arcadia said.

"Yeah. Come on, Dorothy."

So far there was only one direction in which to go. The walls were smooth with no doors on either side. They moved cautiously down the hall at a pace that was somewhere between walking and running. They reached the end where it opened up into a room with a bank of elevators on the right side and a single door on the left with a panic bar and no window. A trio of shambling undead milled about here, sniffing the air and coming to life as the humans entered.

Suddenly, the voice from the entrance jarred them from their grim thoughts. "Don't bother with the elevator. You'll have to take the stairs down. We're on floor four. That's four floors underground, not four up."

"Can you hear us?" Veronica jabbed at a zombie's neck with her blade, but it managed to be just fast enough to avoid being sliced.

"I can't hear you from where you are, can't even see you, so I hope you're there. You should be there if you walked straight back. Keep following the yellow line."

Taking a precious second to glance down at the floor, Veronica could see there were several colored lines painted—red, blue, black, and yellow. One of each led to a different one of the elevator cars, while all of them led to the stairs door.

"Stairs, four floors down." Arcadia sidestepped past a confused-looking dead soldier and pushed into the stairway door. It opened partway but then stuck, meeting resistance. "Something's blocking it!"

Veronica dispatched a second zombie with her knife, afraid of having a bullet ricochet around the concrete room were she to use her gun. She moved to the stairs and threw her weight against the door. It opened this time, sending her body stumbling into the top of the stairwell, which fortunately had a wide landing before the stairs led down. Unfortunately, four more undead occupied that landing, making it clear that one or more of them had been stacked up against the door which then flew open with Veronica's weight.

She scanned the space while kicking the closest of the four walking bio-threats down the stairs. The back of the creature's skull impacted with the concrete wall half a flight down, momentarily knocking it senseless. Its eyes remained lifeless but open as it slowly slid down the wall into an off-kilter seated position.

Arcadia, meanwhile, took a chance and discharged her firearm at near point blank range into the eye socket of a second zombie, dropping it instantly as a river of blackish ooze issued from its orbital cavity. She leaned over the waist-high railing. The drop to the stairs below was scary-high.

"Help me!" Veronica was backed into a corner by the two remaining dead ones, slashing with her KA-BAR. Arcadia jumped over and pistol-whipped one of the mindless assailants hard enough to cave in the top of its skull. She had to pull hard to extract the butt of the gun from the dead thing's head. By the time she did, the remaining Z was ready to do battle, lunging at her with festering jaws agape. She slipped on a blood slick and went down on one knee. The monster made its move, diving onto Veronica, but a shot from Arcadia's gun exploded its head like a melon, as if the hole in the skull had released the pressure of massive amounts of pus waiting to be released.

Veronica shut her mouth an instant before she felt the gore splatter across her face. She shoved the corpse off of her and wiped her lips with her sleeve. The two women took stock of the situation. Four formerly undead, now dead for real, littered the landing and stairwell. Veronica put a finger to her lips, indicating they should listen for more approaching, but they heard nothing save for their own labored breathing.

Veronica made eye contact with Arcadia. "Thanks." Then she waved an arm and led the way down the steps. A huge pile of rubble and debris blocked the way at the bottom of the next flight down, but thankfully there were no undead here. They labored for some time to clear a path, cursing a lack of gloves, and then continued down. At the bottom of the next flight, where a giant "2" was stenciled on the landing door, three more zombies waited for them.

"Let me stab them if I can." Veronica moved in with her blade. "Don't want to draw any more attention, or worry about ricochets."

"If I have to shoot, I'll try to make it point blank."

But it didn't come to that. Veronica's efficient blade work stabbed the brain stems and through the skulls of each zombie in turn, dropping them in heaps.

They moved down another flight, this time having to step over a couple of dead zombies which had clearly been dispatched with permanence in mind—metal rods through the brain. The pair of fighters leapt down the stairs until they reached a landing with the numeral "4." The door here was ajar.

"This is it."

Veronica nodded. She pointed at the floor where the yellow line curved off to the right, into the door to level 4. "Cover me."

Arcadia moved to the side and aimed her pistol while Veronica pulled the door wide open and stepped back. A tiled floor, lit by a muted fluorescent bulb, greeted them, but no zombies or people they could see in the corridor.

"C'mon." Veronica followed the yellow line inside. This hallway had rooms off to either side. Most of them had doors open, and they paused at each one to look inside. One was a conference room, chairs overturned around a table where a bloody, rotting corpse lay prostrate on the table, conference phone handset still clutched in fingers stiffened by rigor mortis.

They continued on. In another room, they found a group of copy machines. On one of them a dead zombie was positioned such that it kneeled on a chair in front of the machine, with its face plastered on the glass, the lid flopped over the back of its head. A pile of printout pages had spilled out of the machine onto the floor, as if someone had run off a large print job and left. Veronica picked one up. It was a graphic close-up of the undead's face, a neat circle in its forehead marking the bullet hole that had ended its miserable second life.

"Somebody was having some fun in here?" Arcadia looked around, weapon held in the ready position. Veronica tossed the paper to the floor and returned to the main hallway, where the yellow line snaked off deeper into the building. They followed it, stopping occasionally to blast a zombie's head over the top of a cubicle farm or to stab one under the chin that turned suddenly around a corner. By the time they reached the closed door the yellow line disappeared into, they had lost track of how many undead encounters they'd had. Their clothing was spattered with blood, hair and pieces of decayed skin. Their faces were grim masks of determination.

Dr. Grey sighed. "Once this is over and we're safe, please let this place still have running water and a damn shower..."

They stood at this new portal, a regular office door with a knob, set into the left-side wall. The hallway continued on past this point. Veronica reached out and turned the handle.

"It's locked."

Then they heard the voice again. "If that's you two, give two knocks, wait three seconds, and then four more knocks. To make sure you can follow directions and that you're not one of those mindless fuckers."

Veronica and Arcadia exchanged glances and then Veronica rapped on the door as instructed. A few seconds passed during which they heard footsteps approaching on the other side of the door. They held their guns at the ready, but not pointed at the door, as it opened.

7.

"Greetings! I see you managed to follow the yellow brick road. I guess you could say I'm the man behind the curtain. Please come in."

Veronica and Arcadia lowered their weapons. They weren't sure who exactly they were expecting, but the man standing before them looked nothing like the average government scientist or lab worker. He was dressed in baggy cargo pants and a T-shirt with the sleeves cut off reading, "Colorado: I'm in a Higher State," featuring a marijuana leaf graphic. His hair was longer than shoulder length, sculpted into thick, dirty-looking dreadlocks. He peered at them over slim profile reading glasses. He wore a government issued ID badge of some type on a lanyard around his neck. In the picture his hair was still long but without the dreadlocks. It was definitely him, Veronica noted, the possibility not escaping her that this guy could potentially be a street person who had somehow managed to infiltrate the besieged facility.

"Name's Zephyr," he said, stepping to one side of the doorway and waving an arm inside. He held his hands up to show he was unarmed. Still, that didn't mean he couldn't have cohorts hiding somewhere in the room waiting to ambush them, but they'd come this far in order to seek help here, and so it was a risk they had to take. What did they have other than a hope for a cure? And they needed them alive for that. Or at least Arcadia, Veronica reflected grimly.

Veronica entered the room first, head on a swivel, with Arcadia close behind.

"If you don't mind, I'll close the door now," the man said. "From the looks of things, you cut down quite a few of those aberrations, but there's bound to be more out there wandering around, and we like to maintain a dead-free zone in here." He shut the door softly and then engaged a deadbolt, a doorknob lock and a security chain, before turning around to address the newcomers.

Both women stood aside and stared at Zephyr. He blushed a bit, looking down at his disheveled outfit. "Sorry, I know I must look a bit strange for a NORAD employee, but hey, water's been shut off since the shit hit the fan and so it was easier just to grow dreads and a beard..." He held out one of his dirt-caked locks before continuing. "Besides, I always wanted to play in a reggae band and so I told myself that when this is all over and if I get through this..." He choked up a little on the words, "Yeah, I'm going to do that."

Veronica nodded. "Well, Zephyr..." *If that's your real name.* "We're here to see that you get your chance." She pointed to Arcadia, who still clutched her battered briefcase. "This is Dr. Arcadia Grey, a CDC expert on the prion agent responsible for the plague."

Arcadia reluctantly shook hands with Zephyr. "What happened here?" she asked. "How did the infected get inside?"

Zephyr shook his head as he remembered. "We were all so buried in our work. So consumed with trying to maintain a safe command center, to be on active alert status for the president, that we..." His eyes took on a faraway, distressed look as though he'd seen a ghost. He continued after a brief, disconcerting spell. "It only took one. One of those things got inside during a shift change at the outer gate—that one at the end of the tunnel."

Veronica nodded, picturing the mass of undead flesh eagerly pressed up against that metal barrier. Zephyr went on.

"It wasn't like that solitary zombie went on a rampage, either, or that it overpowered us. It had stealth. Somehow, it remained undetected inside the compound for weeks before it struck. Bit a janitor in a supply closet, and then *he* made the transition. So we had two of the things walking amongst us. Meanwhile, the president was urging us to ready our defenses, that something big was about to happen..."

Again, Zephyr seemed to quake with a PTSD-like combination of fright and depression. He took a minute to compose himself while Veronica and Arcadia exchanged concerned glances. Then he continued.

"They just slowly infiltrated us. Overwhelmed us. In retrospect, it was so stupid. We all had our heads up our asses, going about our jobs like it was just another strategic battle situation."

Veronica got the point. "How many more of your staff are left in here?"

At this Zephyr looked up, as if from a trance.

"How many?" Arcadia echoed.

Zephyr met their eyes in turn before speaking. "It's just me."

Both Veronica and Arcadia were so flabbergasted they had no response. Arcadia's briefcase slipped from her sweating fingers and hit the floor. Outside the door they heard the shuffling of feet and indiscriminate crashing into things.

"Just me and those things," Zephyr added. "It's been pretty nerve-wracking being stuck in here with all of them inside. Talking to the walls, and sometimes my reflection."

Veronica ignored this latter statement. "But before you referred to the facility as 'we,' as in, 'We had to lock ourselves in...'"

"Well it was 'we' at first, for a while. But gradually, after three months..." His eyes took on that faraway look again. Veronica knew that he must have been through unspeakable things, horrible events, to have remained alive. Committed them, survived them. He was little more than a shell of a man, a kid even, not even Alex's age. She could see it now, holding onto the last vestiges of his former life by still wearing the ID badge and hunkering down in his former workplace.

Veronica placed a hand on his shoulder, and a tear coursed down his cheek.

Arcadia picked her briefcase back up from the floor. "So, the laboratory—is it still functional? Tell me we didn't come all this way for absolutely nothing?"

Zephyr looked up. "Yes, it's mostly functional. It—"

Static crackled from a speaker somewhere in the room. Veronica looked around. "What is that?"

Zephyr moved to a table against the wall with a host of electronic equipment. "Shortwave radio." He put the headset to his ear. "It's a Major Remington...he's been calling periodically, warning of something about to happen but so far with no specifics. Let's see what he's got now." He transferred the audio to the main speaker.

Veronica and Arcadia followed him to the radio table, where Remington's voice was now distinguishable through the still considerable static and squelchy noise. "...come in, NORAD..."

Zephyr snatched up the transmitter. "Copy, Major Remington. Zephyr Simmons here, go ahead with your message, over."

When the major spoke, it sounded as though his voice was weak—not only due to the long-distance transmission, but also because he was speaking quietly.

"Are your defense systems operational, over?"

Zephyr shook his head as he replied. "Negative, sir. Used our last perimeter clearing munitions a short time ago. Skeleton crew here, quite literally I'm afraid, but we do have two distinguished guests. However, we don't have the juice to power anything but life support systems—air handlers, water pumps, a few lights, food refrig—"

Remington cut him off. "Got it, now listen up: NORAD is about to come under attack. I repeat: we have intelligence that NORAD is being targeted. You need to evacuate all personnel and essential equipment immediately, over."

Zephyr, Veronica and Arcadia stared at one another, eyes widening. Zephyr gripped the mic again. "Major, a CDC expert has just arrived here to complete work on a prion cure. We have a lab here that has everything she needs…"

"I understand, and I'm sorry…Dr. Grey. You have to forget about it and evacuate if you want to survive. Take whatever you can in the next few seconds, but get out. Get out now!"

Dr. Grey was shaking her head, looking around in hopeless confusion. "No way, not after all this…"

They heard a faint rumbling, seeming to come right through the very walls of the complex. Then Remington's hard voice again.

"I'm sorry, you're out of time. I need to get going, things are bleak at my location as well. Get out now!"

8.

Veronica and Arcadia looked to Zephyr as he let go of the radio transmitter. He grabbed a backpack off the table, disconnected the main radio unit from the antenna wire and shoved it inside, before looking at his guests.

"C'mon, there's a contingency exit deeper underground that lets out some distance away from the complex, in the woods."

Arcadia clutched her briefcase tighter. "Wait! What about the lab specimens? Can we get some of the stockpiled medical kits? A centrifuge? Anything?"

A deep *boom* shook the walls.

Zephyr shook his head. "Not unless you want to be here for the bombing run."

Veronica nodded. "He's right. DeKirk obviously knows this place is a threat to his new empire. We're too late. We've got to face it and move on. Any more firepower laying around?" Veronica looked at Zephyr.

"The real goodies are downstairs, but let's see..." He moved to a file cabinet, hurriedly produced a set of keys and unlocked the bottom drawer. "Just these up here, I'm afraid." He pulled out two 9mm lugers, handing one to Veronica and tucking the other in his waistband. Then he reached back into the drawer. "Extra clips." Again, he handed one of these to Veronica and kept one for himself.

"Which way?" Veronica looked around, hoping the only exit wasn't through the door by which they'd entered, where the sounds of scratching and clawing came from the other side of the reinforced metal.

"C'mon." Zephyr ran the other direction, thankfully away from where they'd come in. They reached a door on the other side of the room. Zephyr flung it open apparently without concern for what might lie on the other side of it. But Veronica could see right away it was simply an adjoining office. More of the same. Cubicles, a couple of workbenches with assorted electronic equipment. A now useless bank of displays meant to track incoming missiles. No dead, undead or living.

"This is still part of my secure space," Zephyr breathed as he ran through the room, "but on the other end there's a door that leads out to the rest of the complex, and out there, we'll have to be very careful."

The wary trio moved through the room until they reached the mentioned door. Veronica and Arcadia stood on either side of the doorway with their guns aimed where the door would open.

Zephyr turned the handle and flung it wide. They looked into a concrete stairwell that led only down. No bodies of any kind were anywhere in sight. Zephyr took off at a run, jumping down four and five steps at a time, the two women close behind. They passed two more levels, 5 and 6, but Zephyr continued below them, not stopping until they reached a door marked "8."

From outside, they heard another ground-shaking tremor. Zephyr yanked the door open in a hurry. Veronica pulled him back onto the landing before he ran headlong into two former humans standing there silently with dead eyes and hungry mouths. As soon as Veronica and Zephyr were clear, Arcadia blasted a round into each of their heads.

Another blast rocked the compound, this time sending puffs of drywall dust raining like a snowy mist. Zephyr ran through the door and Veronica and Arcadia squeezed through side by side right behind him. This room was different. Warehouse-like, cavernous, it featured a smooth concrete floor leading off into the roughly rectangular space. A pair of electric carts were parked nearby. Zephyr got behind the wheel of one. Veronica took the front passenger seat beside Zephyr while Arcadia jumped into the back. Zephyr pressed the start button and the little vehicle hummed to life. He floored the pedal and they took off with a jolt down the cave-like space. To their right and left, the uncoordinated movements of zombies caught their eyes. So strikingly different from the purposeful motion of a normal human. So hauntingly lifeless, they meandered aimlessly against a backdrop of stored armaments and other wartime machinery.

"Nothing that could help us now, unfortunately. We'll have to settle for something a little more manageable."

Veronica waved her 9mm. "This is pretty manageable."

Zephyr shook his head while he swerved to avoid two zombies lunging for them, a little too close for comfort. "Not to take down enemy aircraft, it's not." As if to underscore his point, they heard a sharp, prolonged whine followed by a dull thud that sent the cart skidding on the smooth floor.

Zephyr glanced in the rear view mirror at a cadre of five zombies ambling directly after the cart. "It sounds far away but we're eight stories underground. There must be bombs or missiles striking the grounds above us now."

Zephyr veered left into a path created by two stacks of shelving that reached high towards the multi-story ceiling. The shelves held various machine parts, including motors, wheels, and unrecognizable electronic equipment. High overhead a blinking light fixture dangled and sparked.

"They're following us!" Arcadia faced around to look behind them, where four zombies turned down the corridor created by the shelves. Up ahead, two more turned in, blocking their path.

"Why did we turn in here?" Veronica shouted. "We'll be trapped!" She checked the action on her pistol, ready for another fight. Zephyr pulled the cart to a stop and got out.

"I'm pretty sure there's something here that will greatly increase our chances for survival once we get outside." He walked to the shelves on his left side and craned his neck to look up.

"Pretty sure?" Arcadia's voice was a couple of octaves higher than normal.

"What are you looking for?" Veronica asked.

Zephyr moved a few feet to the right, farther away from the cart. "Here we go! Rocket launchers. To a place like this, RPGs are just toys, but right now they might be enough to take down an aerial threat. If I can even find them..." He sidestepped to the right some more, closer to the pair of zombies that now accelerated down the corridor, sensing prey. Veronica saw Zephyr turn to look at the undead. "I'll cover you, just find them."

"Okay!" He pulled a wheeled ladder for the purpose of accessing the higher shelves closer to him and started up. "I think I see them!"

His words were drowned out by two shots from Veronica's gun. A pair of undead slumped to the floor midway down the corridor. Something heavy crashed from a shelf that Zephyr knocked into.

"How we doing?" Veronica asked, reloading.

"Got one!" He pulled a rocket launcher from a high shelf and rested it on the ladder in such a way that he could slide it down. Grabbed a case with several shells, then came down and placed it in the back of the cart with Arcadia and the RPG. He then looked back up, but Arcadia grabbed his arm.

"One's good, we're out of time."

Veronica fired off another round at the growing crowd coming their way. "It'll have to do, Zephyr. Let's go!"

That settled, Zephyr climbed back into the front of the cart and started it. The four zombies from the other direction had by now almost caught up to them. Arcadia took them out with six shots, cursing at the two that missed.

Zephyr floored it, racing to the end of the shelf corridor and making a right turn. More zombies up ahead. He made another sharp right down another route just before reaching them. At the end of this one, he turned left back out onto the main floor, heading for the opposite end of the building from where they'd entered.

"Where's that damn exit?" Veronica wanted to know.

"Up here on the left," he shouted over a muffled explosion from somewhere far above.

He swerved around a zombie wearing a tattered lab coat with several hypodermic needles sticking out of its midsection and arms. Veronica shot it in the head as they passed and it fell onto the floor face first, landing on the stuck needles.

"That was...F'd up," Arcadia said as they left it behind, then was almost jarred out of her seat as Zephyr deliberately rammed the cart into a zombie which had been standing in place and walking into one of the shelves, like a hamster on a wheel. He hit the undead speed bump at around twenty miles per hour, felt it crunch and bones break under the wheels, hopefully getting the head, but he wasn't going to take the time to check.

"We're here!" Zephyr said after another few seconds of driving, leaving bloody tire tracks until squealing to a stop. He got out and pulled the RPG from the back seat. Strapped it over his shoulder and then motioned for his guests to follow along the wall to their left.

Veronica and Arcadia looked up ahead to Zephyr, who stood in front of a normal-size metal door with a panic bar. He glanced back, eyes worried. "Shit."

"What?" Veronica caught up to him first, then Arcadia.

"I hear movement on the other side."

"Weapons ready." Veronica had her pistol out, but she switched to a one-handed grip and drew her knife also, wielding that in her right hand. Arcadia assumed her favored two-handed stance, gun aimed at the door. Zephyr held a 9mm and reached out to the door.

"No time to waste." He unlocked it and turned the handle slightly to remove the catch. "On three I'll kick it open, and you two start shooting."

Zephyr took a step back from the door. He turned sideways to it and then landed his sneakered foot with a flying kick. The door opened about a foot before stopping suddenly against something solid. Grayish hands with yellow-streaked skin reached eagerly through the open door. Arcadia shrieked at the sight of so many rotting fingers with split or missing nails, all seeking something, anything alive, to feed on.

Zephyr tried again, this time with his right shoulder. He collided with the door after a running start. It opened another foot and a sea of hungry hands marauded over his body as he slid along the door while it opened. Arcadia's gun was popping off rounds, dropping zombies mere feet from Zephyr's head, while Veronica grabbed him by the belt and yanked him back. Once he was safe, she added her bullets to Arcadia's and together they drilled the dead things back enough that Zephyr was able to shove the door open without resistance.

The three of them stared into a tunnel of hell. A dark place, full of lethal motion. Unseen bodies and shapes moving in the background, beyond the front row of rotting attackers.

"Are there lights in there?" Veronica spit out just before her finger squeezed the trigger, loosing a slug into the cranial cavity of a zombie missing both arms.

Zephyr called out, "There used to be small ones just enough to see by, but they must have been taken out in the air strikes." As if on cue, another deep rumbling shook the building. Arcadia balked at the entrance to the infested tunnel.

"Is there any other way out?"

"Negative." Zephyr's response was free of any hesitation. "We either fight our way out through there, or we stay in here and hope we somehow survive the bombing. But even way down here, there are bombs that can take us out, especially given enough time."

"Damn, then we fight. And pray." Veronica handed a flashlight to Zephyr. "You hold the light so I can lead the way with both hands free." She held up her gun in one hand and the KA-BAR in the other.

Zephyr agreed and Veronica led the way into the tunnel. Zephyr lit the way from behind her and Arcadia brought up the rear. The sound of their gunshots was deafening in the close confines of the tunnel, where the reports echoed madly, bouncing off the concrete walls to mingle with the unintelligible wailings of dozens of walking corpses. But they were advancing through the passageway, fighting their way to freedom step by bloody, gore-splashed step. Reloading and repeating.

The tunnel sloped upward, almost imperceptibly at first but at a gradually steeper angle the further they went. Zephyr estimated they'd gotten almost halfway through when Arcadia announced in a deceptively calm voice that she was out of bullets.

"I've got some party favors!" Zephyr called out. The meek technician seemed to have awakened something of a bloodlust within himself, almost enjoying grabbing the monsters, pulling them up close to his body—closer than he needed to, really—so that he could jam his gun barrel under their chins, feel the dead hand grasping, latching onto his clothing, seeking purchase. Pulling the trigger while staring into those dead, unnaturally yellow pupils. Too dark to really see the wet stuff explode from the zombie head, but he felt it shower him, like a pulpy mist of terrifying truth.

Only a few months ago, he'd been a trained technician working in one of the most vaunted facilities on the planet, making a good living, able to plan a future. Now, his reality consisted of a series of death-defying escapades, often with only the most mundane goal as a reward. Get from point A to B, or procure basic survival items. Even more confusing, it should have frightened him (*What if things stay this way forever? What if this is it?*). Sure, he could die at any moment or become one of those things. But if they survived this, he was at least in the company of two other women, neither of them what he would call unattractive. That was something he'd never had happen before, ever. Who knows, maybe…he had a laughable moment, thinking about the apocalypse, about rebuilding and maybe becoming the new Adam and having the enviable job of repopulating the world.

"Zephyr! Snap the fuck out of it!"

"C'mon man, shine the light over here!"

Veronica and Arcadia continued to do battle while they tried to get his attention. He'd spent too much time on one zombie, relishing its destruction by his own hand, allowing his thoughts to wander. He dropped the smelly, wet corpse and shined his light in the direction of Veronica's voice. She was back to the left side wall, where he saw her slice a zombie's throat and shoot it in the head simultaneously, obliterating its head from the neck up.

Arcadia swung the corner of her hard briefcase into the temple of a small zombie, an individual who was probably a teenage boy when he died. Then she stomped on it hard, several times, with her heel.

"Arcadia! Here!" She turned to look at Zephyr, who flashed a box of shells in his palm. "Party favors!" He tossed her the box. It bounced off her midsection and she almost caught it as it rebounded, but her fingers were not quick enough. She knelt down and passed her fingers across the floor in search of the ammo. She felt blood and entrails, and then finally, the box.

"Got it!"

Veronica's pistol spat and an undead fell at Arcadia's feet. She saw an opening ahead, with no zombies for quite a few feet. She moved fast, reloading as she went. The others followed suit, recognizing they had better take advantage of any opening, no matter how small. When they reached another group of zombies, Veronica called out from her point position. "Daylight! Up ahead."

She shot a zombie that walked fast towards her from ten feet out. A bloody hole formed in its pasty forehead, and then it fell forward in a dead faint. Veronica broke the thing's fall with her knife in its throat. By the time she kicked it off her blade, Arcadia and Zephyr had dispatched two more ghost-like assailants, clearing a path to the exit.

"Run for it!" Zephyr cried. "Let's get out before they pin us down." The three of them set their legs into motion, jumping over fallen dead as they literally sought the light at the end of the tunnel.

An explosion rocked the grounds nearby, so close that a shower of dirt hit them like desert wanderers in a sandstorm. "Don't stop!" Zephyr urged. "This way..." He led them at a full run up and to the left, away from a dazed group of stumbling dead, where the dirt ground immediately in front of the tunnel exit transitioned to flatter, forested earth. Ferns whipped their faces as they trammeled through the undergrowth. They reached a large tree with a hollowed out trunk and sat inside it to rest and take cover.

"No zombies out here, so far, at least," Veronica said.

Arcadia and Zephyr were too tired to give a response.

Zephyr got to his feet and exited the tree hollow. As the women got to their feet, they heard noise from somewhere ahead, not far away. Like feet on the ground, but very loud and fast.

"What is it?" Arcadia whispered.

The noise grew nearer, lying to rest any doubt as to what it was. Veronica recognized it first, her body freezing with a flashback to Adranos Island, to her and Alex crashing in a helicopter and running from those horrid animals, doing anything to keep them at bay...

"Oh God."

"What is it, Veronica?"

The footfalls intensified, became even faster.

"Something bad. Get ready."

Zephyr appeared doubtful. "How do you know it's—"

No sooner had he began his question than an adult velociraptor burst from the foliage not twenty feet in front of them.

The bipedal lizard halted in its tracks and cocked its head as it processed the fact that it was very near to warm-blooded prey. Its nostrils flared, seeking the scents. The three humans froze in place, just outside the tree. Arcadia was trembling. Zephyr stood stock still, holding his breath.

Veronica spoke softly. "We all shoot it in the head at once and it should drop."

"Crazy!" Arcadia hissed.

"If we don't kill it now, it's over." She took a calming breath. "On three, then. Headshots. Aim for the eyes."

She gave them a few seconds to aim and then counted down. Near the end of the count, the raptor started to bob its head up and down in rapid fashion, detecting scent. Veronica held a hand out. "Wait. It'll stop. Then shoot."

They waited as it continued to move its head, then, when its skull came to the top of its arc, it stopped. Frozen in place, it seemed to home in on the source of an odor it had detected. Veronica fired first. Arcadia and Zephyr let loose next. The raptor began to dance in a hail of lead, the percussive sound of the shots instantly triggering it into motion. But many of the bullets found their marks. The reptile's narrow head was nearly shorn in two by the close-range salvo. When it opened its jaws to screech in rage, they split apart, the lower one breaking away at a right angle to the rest of its face. Then it dropped to the ground on crumpled legs, no longer receiving proper neurological instructions from the walnut-sized brain. It lay there in a non-functional heap, bleating out empty sonic threats.

The bullets stopped. "No time to celebrate." Veronica led the way past the ruined beast, giving it a wide berth lest it summon some last burst of coordination sufficient to lunge at them. They made it past the fallen dinosaur into the next copse of trees, and then the mountain took a direct hit from a massive bunker buster bomb dropped from one of DeKirk's airplanes. The three of them were knocked to the ground, half-dazed.

"Good thing we weren't still in there." Zephyr's eyes were open wide as he looked back toward his former workplace, where robust roils of black smoke billowed skyward.

"Now what?" Arcadia examined her briefcase. It was still with her, still intact. But would she ever get the chance to use its contents?

"We keep heading away from here." Veronica looked back at the chaotic, fire-laced smoke clouds now enveloping the mountain. "And hope they think we were in there."

Zephyr agreed. "We need to put more distance between ourselves and this place. Let's go."

The beleaguered trio headed deeper into the forest, away from the burning conflagration that was once one of America's most sophisticated military installations. As they disappeared beneath a canopy of greenery, they failed to notice a small, consumer-sized drone no larger than a toaster. Outfitted with high-definition cameras, it followed them into the forest.

9.

Outside of Kansas City, Missouri

Major Remington concentrated on the vision of the farmhouse he could just make out between the rows of corn stalks. It was a property he knew well, since it was his, or had been at least. Now, caution was not only a watchword, but the only word. In this new world, being away from a place for any length of time at all meant that you could no longer be sure you still knew that place. It was a thought that depressed him, since this house, this home, held so many cherished memories for him and his family...

Olivia.

Where was she? And...the baby? If she had survived, she would have given birth almost three months ago. He would have a daughter, a child born into this hell. Not a day went by he hadn't thought of them, hadn't sacrificed knowing about their safety in order to serve his larger purpose. To build the resistance, to lead, to save so many along the way and organize chapters to carry on in each place he stopped. He had sacrificed so much for this country. *Former* country, he corrected himself with no small amount of bitterness. After the fall, he led the charge in disobeying direct commands, conscripting others where he could, which hadn't been difficult in the face of obvious horrors committed by the man in charge. He continued to fight, reuniting kindred patriotic forces whenever and wherever possible. He had done this selflessly, without putting himself first, thinking only of his once great nation and the mind-boggling fall it had experienced.

But now, it was time. He left a burgeoning resistance group, his own stalwart militia he had trained and given orders to expand to nearby regions, liberating as much as they can while keeping a low profile. He had established a complex system of coded communications through shortwave radio, and the word was getting out: that there was hope, that we could fight back.

It would happen. And for now, for at least a few days, they could manage without him.

He had to do this now. He hoped his family was safe. He recalled the contingency plan while he continued to survey the residence from his place of concealment in the cornfield. If their house became unsafe or unlivable, Olivia was to drive up to her mother's house in Illinois. All phone lines and cellular traffic had been down since the outbreak, with very few sporadic exceptions, to the point that it now seemed strange to him to communicate long distance any other way other than by radio. If they weren't here then he'd have to make his way up to Illinois, unless he could use the ham radio nets to try and reach someone in his mother-in-law's neighborhood. There were still a few old guys hunkering down with their base stations, making brief transmissions now and then lest they be ferreted out by DeKirk's techno-savvy militants, but their network was also spread thin. The chances they could reach anyone in a specific neighborhood within a reasonable amount of time were slim to none.

Please be here. Remington stowed his field binoculars and emerged from the cornfield with the barest whisper of stalks against his jumpsuit. The faint scent of fertilizer rode on a light wind as he crept toward the farmhouse. He looked for vehicles as he neared. Didn't see his wife's sedan. He went to the garage first, to the rollup door with windows in it. He peered through one of them. No car. Everything else looked pretty normal. His workbench against the back wall, his rack of tools. On second thought...Remington cupped his hands against the glass to block the glare. Were some of his tools missing? Where were the bolt cutters? His sledgehammer? He passed it off as unimportant for the moment. It's not like he spent a ton of time here even when things were normal, and he was far from the pinnacle of organization when it came to domestic matters. He left the garage and walked over to the main entrance of the house, a two-story wooden affair built eighty years ago but with modern additions.

His sidearm was drawn as he climbed the short flight of steps leading to the wraparound front porch. He avoided the soft spot of wood on the right side of the second step from the top, knowing it would creak horribly. He pulled open the screen door and paused with the front door key in one hand, pistol in the other while he listened for any signs of activity inside the house. Hearing none, he keyed his way in.

He was relieved to see the home in remarkably mundane condition. While watching from the cornfield, he had steeled himself for the scenes of destruction which had become all too common: looted buildings, ransacked belongings, torched residences. Everything here was in the comfortably disorganized state that typified the way he and Olivia lived. Pillows strewn about a sectional couch, a couple of them on the floor. DVD cases scattered about the coffee table and entertainment center, where the TV was currently powered off and would be for a long time, if not forever. A crib in the corner choked him up. This is what he had missed. He had helped her set it up weeks before he left for his last assignment. Had it been used?

He thought about diapers, bottles and baby food, but had to force himself to stop doing that, to focus. Checked the clock on the kitchen wall, its second hand frozen into oblivion when the power was cut months ago. 6:18. He wondered if it was A.M. or P.M. and where everyone was when it happened.

Quickly, Remington searched the rest of the house, room by room. He found no one and no signs of struggle. Back in the living room he breathed a deep sigh and ran his fingers through his hair. *Where were they?*

His gaze shifted around the room yet again, where it lit on the coffee table and the objects scattered atop it. At first he had dismissed all of the electronic devices there as TV remotes or game controllers, but on more careful examination he saw that one of them was a Smartphone. Remington moved to it and picked it up.

The screen was dead. He pressed the power button and then swore softly when nothing happened. He went to the kitchen counter and found what he was looking for. The power cord was already plugged into the outlet, which he knew was no good. He needed the cord. He grabbed it and pulled a portable USB battery from one of his cargo pockets. He'd been relying on them almost exclusively lately to power cell-phones (searching for the occasional pocket of service or to take surveillance photos), and small computing devices, charging the portable juice packs from vehicle batteries.

He plugged the phone into the USB battery and powered it on. No service as expected, so checking recent voicemails and texts was not an option. But he knew that "phones" likes this were more than just phones. He navigated to the image gallery and scrolled through the pictures. Most of them were old, snapshots of better days, before the hell that DeKirk unleashed on the world broke loose. He and Olivia, some of their favorite moments she saved for her gallery. That trip to Cabo, then the follow up: skiing in Aspen. A shot of their dog, the golden retriever, Zappo. No sign of him now, hopefully they took him with them where they went. And there…Olivia smiling with a weak, ragged smile, holding a swaddled baby to her chest.

Relief and joy flooded over him. Remington wiped a tear from his cheek and clicked out of the photos. There were no others, that was it. He was about to see if he could read the old, already received texts when a video folder caught his attention. He opened it. Immediately, he sucked in his breath. Only one video occupied the folder, with a file name of DAD PLEASE WATCH. He checked the date in the video's file properties: a little under three months ago. He clicked open the video and brought the phone closer to his face.

On the small screen, a close-up of his baby's face. The background of the video was unremarkable, just the kitchen wall. She was asleep, peacefully dreaming dreams of innocence and a future that might never come to pass.

Then Olivia's face appeared in the lens, those deep blue eyes he loved so much, that little crease under her lip; she spoke softly. "Casey, we're leaving the farm. I hope…I know you're alive. You're fighting this, you're out there kicking ass somewhere. You're alive." She broke into a sob and then raised her head again.

Remington touched the screen. *I am, Olivia. I am.*

"So much to say, but I have to make this short. People are being rounded up and taken away…" She began to sob again but visibly composed herself and then went on. "It's hard to get decent information, but we heard over one of your old radios we found in the garage that people are being taken to Alaska."

Suddenly a loud crashing noise distorted the phone's speaker and Remington heard his wife scream from somewhere off camera. She spun around and then ran, abandoning the phone but leaving the video running. He could see nothing dramatic in the frame, but the audio told him all he needed to know. DeKirk's army had come for his family. He didn't yet know if they were specifically targeted because Remington was leading the resistance movement, but he shook with rage at the possibility.

He heard an even louder commotion, surprised at the vivid output from such a small speaker. Then he realized with a start the video had stopped, yet the sounds continued.

Someone's here!

Remington wasted no time cursing his lack of awareness. He drew his service pistol and crouched behind the kitchen counter.

#

The smell of the intruder gave it away. Remington supposed that stealth was not the interloper's chief concern, seeing as it bashed straight through the back door even though Remington had left it unlocked. The zombie's wheezy rasp preceded it. Remington stood and aimed his pistol at the thing's head, and then hung his hand limply in the air, stunned at the appearance of his target.

This zombie wore a helmet. Not just any helmet, either, Remington could see. This one was the sleek, streamlined shape of army special forces, black in color and made of Kevlar. Lightweight and made to stop bullets, the face area was exposed, leaving the monster able to bite while also making its face the only available kill shot. A miniature camera was mounted atop the front of the helmet now pointed at Remington.

The armored zombie—huge and muscled like a gladiator from Sparta—faked a move to the left, remaining standing. A blur of motion through the windows outside distracted Remington. He kept his gaze fixed on the zombie while also monitoring what was outside. Two large pterodactyls landed on the grass and strutted toward the house. This zombie had come with escorts.

Remington knew from experience that without heavy artillery the ptero's were most difficult to kill indeed. He would dispatch the helmeted zombie first, and then try to escape the winged predators.

He thought it odd that the zombie had been stationery for so long, that it wasn't moving toward him, but he considered it a minor piece of luck. He could use a little break, not having to chase this thing around the room in order to put it down.

*Now let's see, only a direct hit to the face will do...right between the eyes, let's do this...*Remington steadied his pistol and began pulling back on the trigger.

"I have something you want to hear, Major Remington."

Remington opened the eye he had closed in order to sight through the pistol. *What the—*

The zombie slowly raised its open hands in the air in the universal gesture of surrender.

That alone was weird enough, but was he hallucinating or did this thing just *talk* to him, actually speak English? The voice was grated and strained, air forced through a rotting cavern unused to the effort.

"Your family—your wife and daughter."

Remington felt a creeping numbness come over his entire body. *It can't be...* His eyes alighted on the helmet camera. But he knew the voice wasn't issuing from that piece of equipment, even if it had a speaker. The zombie's lips moved as it said the words, in perfect sync, even while the eyes still held no expression whatsoever. Yet it was *talking*. But how?

"We've spoken before, Major. I am speaking to you now through the body of one of my generals in the New War. We have been awaiting your arrival here for quite some time."

Suddenly, it hit Remington what was happening. He knew the president had been able to control the zombies, directing their movements—both human and dinosaur—but he had no idea the extent to which he had mastered the remote manipulation.

"DeKirk?"

"In the rotting flesh." A gob of festering pus leaked from the zombie's mouth as it uttered the word, plopping onto the floor with a wet smacking sound.

Remington had trouble processing the fact that words with any sort of intellect behind them were issuing from the throat of this undead monstrosity. "What in the hell is this goddamn circus? Where are my wife and child?"

The zombie trembled a bit before speaking, as if its body were being pulsed with some kind of energy so that it could do something it was not meant to do. "At ease, Major. Most of these dead folk still retain perfectly functional vocal cords and larynx, it's just that they lack the mental capacity for the formulation of language itself. So I am merely instructing it how to speak again by activating the relevant brain regions and... Ah, why bore you? Let's get on to business."

Remington had to breathe deeply in order to remain calm while watching the lifeless corpse spew out DeKirk's end of the conversation. Outside, the pterodactyls screeched as they scrapped over pieces of a hawk one of them had taken down. The zombie's neck momentarily convulsed, then smoothed into a regular breathing pattern.

"As for your family," it began with a hiccup, "I can assure you that for now they are safe in our Alaska breeding facility." The dead humanoid seemed to go slack after delivering the statement. It remained standing but grew very still while Remington replied.

"Breeding facility? You mean, you've figured out how to make these damn things *breed*? Like there aren't enough of them already, you crazy bastard?"

Laughter, or what Remington guessed was supposed to be laughter on DeKirk's part, emanated from the zombie, but it sounded completely off, more like some piece of machinery malfunctioning than even a strange version of human laughter. "No, no, no—there's no need for that! To make more of them, they need only to bite one of you, and you'll eventually turn—or rise from the dead."

"Well, you said you had—"

"The breeding facility is for the humans, Major."

Remington had heard the standing corpse parrot DeKirk's message, but he couldn't help himself; he had to hear that again. "What?"

"Do I really need to repeat myself?"

The iris inside the camera lens mounted on the undead's helmet moved a little. Remington guessed DeKirk was zooming in on his facial expression, no doubt taking great pleasure in his shocked astonishment. He pre-empted Remington by making the zombie talk before Remington could reply. "Humans are becoming more and more rare with each passing day. Finally, the planet's ultimate apex predator has met its match! The undead army grows exponentially, neutralizing the human race. But, of course, I can't let the entire *Homo sapiens* species die out. They must be preserved, only in a more manageable way. Kind of like a zoo."

"You're sick, DeKirk, you know that?"

"Sssssssssick?" the zombie rasped. It whipped its head side to side in a frenzied manner. "Would a sick man offer you the deal of a lifetime that I'm about to?"

Remington shut up and listened. DeKirk's vocal proxy went on.

"Your wife and daughter, as I said, are safe for now, but you and I...we need to chat."

"You sonofabitch!" Remington raised his weapon and was about to let loose a rage-filled torrent of lead at DeKirk's undead general when the thing voiced, "Listen before you act. I fully intend to allow all of the humans in the Alaska facility to live out their lives in safety and with proper care. An entire community. A human society in miniature to be studied, remembered, reflected upon, and of course...fed upon should the need arise..."

Remington held back his anger. How could he even respond to this? "Cut the shit, DeKirk. You said you had an offer for me."

DeKirk's undead speech synthesizer went momentarily slack again before perking up with a new vocalization. "End your involvement with the resistance movement immediately, Major Remington. Give me the locations of the various factions. Do this, and your wife and child will be released to you unharmed, untouched."

Remington took a step closer to the camera. "How do I know they're still alive?"

The thrum of a helicopter became audible in the distance, as the pteros screeched, shook their wings, and then got out of sight.

"Because, Major, we're going. Come, see them yourself."

10.

Alex Ramirez thought his zombie integration might be a little too successful. Once behind the access door into the secure bunker, he found himself in the facility which currently housed the ranking members of the interim United States government, the entire elite leadership.

Alex chose the right moment, carefully noting the movement of the one guard who patrolled at the end of the hallway. He paced, bored like he'd been doing this for months without any action, back and forth beyond the corner.

Got to chance it, ease out and start checking doors. He counted six of them here, three per side, and he'd have about two minutes' time before the guard returned. One last glance up and out either side. No cameras that he saw, but that didn't mean they weren't there. Maybe farther back near the end of the hall. Stay in character, he thought: another wandering zombie, and he'd seen a few of them from the passages and his surveillance through the ventilation shafts. He had only made it so far, but what he had seen only charged up his resolve. He had to end this place, take them down and sever the jugular.

Experimentation rooms, caked in blood and gore, where zombie corpses lay in heaps beside shredded raptors and half-consumed cryolophosaurs. At one point he saw down into a huge warehouse type area, except there were stations and barricades, and bloodstains everywhere as well as a stage with computers, cameras and speakers. Monitoring stations where human loyalists of DeKirk probably thought they were doing honorable work, monitoring the state of the world, the transference of the outbreak and the loss of millions of lives. Civilization was in collapse and these people—some of them not more than college age—sat here in front of screens like they were playing some apocalyptic video game and racking up high scores and barbaric achievements.

Alex could only get so far in the vents though, as fans and other blockages barred him from further progress into where he could only guess the inner sanctuary lay. The interim Cabinet, and hopefully President Zombie Asshole DeKirk himself.

Alex reached down and reassured himself of his trusty machete's presence, secure and snug, strapped against his outer calf, then made his way out.

#

First room on the left: storage, boxes and more boxes. Probably grain. *Or brains*, Alex thought giddily. Next door, locked, but through the window he could see dozens of black body bags, full and stacked high. He hoped they had a crematorium of some kind and these poor souls, either rejects or failed experiments, would find peace in the end.

Hurry. Next door, locked again. Check the window... A face appeared at the glass, a twisted grouping of features, reptilian and human, bright yellow eyes and razor teeth that snapped and chipped the glass. Ruthless pounding on the other side of the wall. Alex jumped back, heart thudding, and almost reached for his blade.

Nothing to worry about. The thing was confined on the other side and he wasn't about to fight through that one to see what it might be guarding, or simply confirm that it was just there for lockdown. What was it with these things? He wasn't sure how it worked yet, but most zombies seemed to be under intelligent control in this facility. Perhaps micro-chipped, or more of DeKirk's remote instinctual control. Still unsure how that worked, Alex didn't quite care. He had to stick to the mission. All the more reason to take out DeKirk and return the bastards to their mindless state of instinctual hunger. That, he could understand, and that could be dealt with far easier.

He turned, remembering the guard. Had to get to concealment, but—damn, he was back already!

And not alone. Alex saw another man in a white lab coat: tall and lanky like a bone yard skeleton, rounding the corner, striding fast. His gaze caught on a tiny blinking red light in the corner. A camera.

He'd been spotted.

#

The guard had him in his sights, M50 raised, but the skeletal doctor with horn-rimmed glasses and a bad comb-over restrained the soldier. "Hold up. This one is either lost or…" He came closer, and as Alex stood, teetering and uncertain, trying to appear hungry and undead and everything like he had studied these creatures to be for so long.

"Perhaps," said the mad scientist type, moving in and narrowing his unnerving slate-blue eyes, "he is something else."

I'm screwed, Alex thought, keeping an eye on that soldier and the M50. What were the chances he could grab this Dr. Freakenstein and use him as a shield, draw his knife and take out the guard? And then what? Trapped in this underground prison, with how many zombies, dinosaurs and human guards armed to the teeth? Could he get out, forget his mission and just save his ass? And then what? Face the inevitable? Veronica might be gone, and he would truly be alone, facing a drawn out end, where the rest of the world fades into undeath and he alone hides out in caves and on the run until he eventually ends it all with a bullet to the brain?

He had to move, couldn't let this guy touch him and feel the lack of undead cold, or whatever test he might fail. This disguise fooled the other mindless zombies, but it wouldn't fool a suspicious human. It was time, now or never.

Behind him, the door barring the nightmare zombie thumped hard and cracked. The soldier raised his weapon and the doctor-scientist jumped back behind him for protection. Alex turned, made an instinctive snarling sound to stay in character, and then the door exploded.

It's got my scent, Alex thought. *It's pissed, and it isn't alone…*

Three more ravenous, crazed and huge zombies shredded what was left of the door, and then burst out, spun and raced for the three humans.

#

"Kill," Alex heard someone say. It dawned on him that it was the doctor, and then he realized he was talking to Alex, not the soldier. Giving a command. Him? Fight these three? Is that what they did here? Is that why all those bodies were in the other room? And that other huge area he had seen? Maybe it wasn't an experimentation room so much as an arena?

Have to obey, Alex thought, or he was dead. One way or another. Bullet or teeth. At least with teeth, he had a chance. Not much of one, he thought, seeing these brutes converge on him. But he'd go out fighting. He lunged and ducked one swipe and slammed his fist up into the first one's jaw, knocking his head back, then spun around the other's charge, ducked and flipped the third one over his back—landing almost on the doc, as he hoped.

One chance, scare them enough and maybe…

He got up, kicked one in the face, snarled and made a mock snapping attempt with his teeth, then leapt on the one he had tossed and before it could recover, Alex charged the guard.

After months of boredom and probably no combat, the soldier reacted as Alex hoped. He raised the M50 in a jerking motion and out of reflex and self-preservation, started firing just as Alex ducked and rolled to the side.

Bullets strafed the lead zombie, the monstrous brute who had broken the door with his first assault. One caught it between the eyes, and despite its size, it went down hard and fast.

"Stop!" the scientist doc shouted, but it didn't make any difference to the soldier who wasn't going to cease firing until the magazine was empty.

Alex just hoped the other zombies would soak up the remaining bullets, before he got around to Alex. One more went down, then the third had its temple shattered along with gaping holes peppering its neck and ribs.

The fourth launched itself onto the guard, below rifle point. It moved so fast and suddenly the soldier's throat had two sets of nasty teeth gouging and tearing and ripping through muscle and crunching through the windpipe, nearly severing the head.

Two more shots rang out from the spastic death throes, and then the guard was down and the zombie was lost in its bloodlust, so preoccupied it didn't notice Alex leap onto its back. He brought his head down—hopefully out of the doc's line of sight, and made a motion like he was biting into the zombie's skull—at the same moment he grabbed the thing's chin and twisted hard clockwise and up, snapping the neck and brain stem.

Alex lifted his head and made a triumphant gargling noise.

"Enough!" the doc said, and Alex dutifully stepped back, lowered his head and stood trembling in the midst of the carnage. The soldier's body still twitched (how soon until it rose?) The other three zombies were reduced to mere carcasses and a whole lot of blood and bullet holes.

The doc moved closer and Alex tried not to stare into those eyes, where his own reflection stared back in the glass panes.

Two other soldiers suddenly rounded the corner, guns raised, but the doc held out his arm in restraint. "Under control here, men. Bring the corpses to the morgue, and here..." He pointed to their former comrade, whose blood still oozed out from the shredded throat. "Bullet to the brain please." He stepped back, and again Alex sensed a closer scrutiny coming.

"This one here," he said after the shot rang out and the dead soldier was now going to stay that way, "escort to the arena. And prepare the next trial."

"One isn't scheduled until tomorrow, Dr. Nietzman."

"I don't care, I'm rescheduling. This one shows some free-thinking abilities I haven't seen before. Perhaps the evolution DeKirk has promised is on its way. I have a job to do, men, and schedules were meant to be broken. You and I," he said, eyes close and dangerously searching Alex's, "are going to enjoy a lot more time together."

#

In the arena, the great warehouse area Alex had seen from above, he was led into the center. Doors on the sides he hadn't noticed before slid open, and he had the sudden sense that he was in the Coliseum and the Roman legions waited outside as the gladiator slaves poured out to do battle for their emperor.

Those cameras and microphones... Would this be broadcast as well as recorded? Was DeKirk already watching? If so, his cover was blown. The gore and the messy hair and bloodstained, tattered clothes were not a good enough Halloween costume to fool his arch enemy, a man on the lookout for him for months.

But he couldn't worry about discovery right now. At this moment, it was all about survival.

Dr. Nietzman emerged, climbing the few steps to the stage area where two other white-dressed technicians—a middle-aged woman and a young nerdy man—were already at their posts, clicking away on keyboards and checking screens. Nietzman spoke a few words to them, pointed to Alex, and then nodded in the direction of the doors.

Out came the living embodiment of gladiators and monsters. Three muscled, scaly warriors, complete with exotic metal helmets and... *Zombies with weapons?* That was new, and unsettling.

But what was even more unnerving came hopping-skittering out of the next door to open, on Alex's left: what looked to be the same dilophosaurus that had escorted him inside earlier. Bright blue, predatory, nasty and playful all at once. It bounded up to the first grouping of creatures, spread out its fanlike crown and screeched at them, then did the same toward Alex, and turned about, screeching even more at its scientist masters.

Calm down, Alex thought. The show hasn't started yet. And what exactly was the show all about this time? Fight to the death most likely, and as if these three warriors out of a Spartacus episode weren't enough to deal with, throw in an acid-spitting undead dinosaur to boot?

Alex fumed. This, he didn't need, but he had to focus. For Veronica, for the sake of whatever could be saved out there, he had to get through this, had to survive and do whatever it took to leave this damn arena of death.

"It's time!" Nietzman shouted and his voice boomed over the speakers. Like he was preparing a crowd before a rock star's entrance, the doctor worked up the nonexistent observers, unless it was just for the recording, or the live feed to whomever else was watching this spectacle. "But first...the new arrival needs to be brought up to par with the competition. Assistants, please prepare the microchip for insertion. Latest iteration, please. DeKirk will be very interested in how this one works, and we have to test all the parameters versus the prior model."

"Ready," said the woman. Dark hair, a little on the heavy side, she might have been a model in her younger years. Skin like it was too tightly stretched over her features and she had been trying too hard to retain her youth.

The younger man walked down the steps behind a crate and returned a moment later with a gurney, complete with straps and clamps. He joined the woman, pushing the gurney to Alex's location. They took a wide berth around the dinosaur and the three gladiator zombies, who fixed Alex with their hideous stares. One wore a horned helmet, another something like a black knight's guise and the third a skull cap with a spike at the top.

Alex sized up the chamber again, noting the location of each and every enemy, and they were all enemies. Make no mistake about that. These two attendants—scientists, interns, whatever they were, wrong place at the wrong time or just duped by DeKirk's charm—there were no civilians to save here, no good guys or girls.

It was go time, and he couldn't let them insert a chip into his skull. Forget what it might do to a living, breathing human; he was pretty sure that wouldn't be a pretty sight no matter what, and he wasn't about to endure surgical pain without any anesthesia. *This shit has to end now.*

Glancing past the two nervous-looking docs coming his way, one wheeling the gurney and the other sliding over a cart with some sharp and shiny instruments, Alex saw his chance. Only problem was the other characters he needed to play their parts weren't in the right positions yet.

His attention snapped from the dilophosaurus back to Nietzman. *Got to bring him closer...*

"Hop on the gurney now, sir," the nerdy guy spoke, a little nervously, from his left while the woman fidgeted with the surgical equipment. He reached out and hesitated, about to take Alex's arm and lead him to it, then looked back at his boss.

Nietzman, impatient, glared back. "This is taking too long."

Alex grumbled, flinched as the man reached for him, then made a mock-snapping motion. Sudden and vicious, and the attendant slipped and fell and scrambled back, nearly knocking over the gurney.

The other zombies hissed and started, almost breaking off their mental restraints.

"He's not under control!" the kid yelled, rushing to the woman's side and actually moving behind her as a shield.

Great, Alex thought, *as if I didn't care if he survived before...*

"Christ, man. I'll handle it," Nietzman's raspy voice echoed from above. Labored now, he rushed down the stairs, bringing along a laptop which he set up quickly on the gurney. "Just need to recalibrate the levels of pheromone triggers in the air…" He looked up, and Alex risked a glimpse, catching the air vents on the western wall, up high above the hanging fluorescent lamps.

So that's part of it, at least for those in range. And out there…? He glanced back at the dilophosaurus hopping erratically on each foot, bobbing its head like a chicken as it faced the three gladiator zombies, as if herding them, keeping them in line.

Maybe that's it.

"Come here, my little wayward specimen." Nietzman backed away and forcefully spoke to Alex. "On the gurney, *now…*"

Okay, Dracula. Alex resisted the impulse to yank out his knife and stake the bastard in his black heart. Had to bide his time. He shuffled ahead, then in awkward movements, to the best of his mimicking skills, he eased onto the gurney, sitting first, then allowing the doctor to move him back.

Again Alex took stock of the room: the nerdy assistant emerging from behind his partner who was still all business, now wheeling the tray of scalpels and suturing supplies in reach. The dinosaur arching its neck, taking an interest now in this area of the arena. *Did it smell something out of the ordinary?*

Nietzman leaned in and his big magnified eyes locked on Alex's as he reached for a scalpel. "Now, my friend. You will get the chip, and I must tell you the procedure—digging into your temple, prying open the skull plate and inserting it against the temporal cortex, it's a procedure that will kill any living human. Quite painfully, I would imagine."

He leaned in closer, and in the same moment Alex shifted ever so slightly, allowing his free right arm to move, stretching so he could reach the machete handle strapped to his leg.

Those eyes seemed to smile, and Alex knew…knew this was it, knew the crazy doctor knew it as well.

"The gas I just released? Just increased oxygen concentration." He leaned right to Alex's ear, above the scalpel's tip now pressed against his temple. "I congratulate your effort, but I will enjoy killing you now, twice."

The point broke the skin—but no more. Alex lurched forward, smashing his forehead directly into Nietzman's, shattering the glasses and the bridge of the doctor's nose in a vicious head-butt. Up came the machete in a purposely wild swing—which Nietzman happened to avoid by sheer luck and panic as he dropped the scalpel and held his hands to stem the blood from his gushing nose.

Alex hadn't expected to connect with that swing, although it would have been nice. Instead, he prepared himself.

Only one shot at this. In moments, the alarm would be blaring, Nietzman would call in dozens of soldiers with M5's, and he'd have no chance. As it was, he had a few other major threats to deal with, and fast.

The first—the dinosaur burst into action like a guard dog awakened to an intruder. Obeying its mandate, unleashing its aggression, it bounded to the gurney in three swift hops, then launched onto Alex's chest, rearing back and preparing to strike.

Only, Alex was prepared too, his right arm over his face and throat protectively, hand holding the knife blade tight, then shifting it to a downward thrusting grip. He avoided the monster's talons and ignored the shrieking from the lab assistants, who now both cowered, stepping back in the blood of their leader. The woman seemed numbly professional still, reaching for gauze packets to offer him—right before the first of the three gladiators came roaring forward.

They were unleashed from their control as well, wound up for aggression levels even above the normal for their condition. *They're coming,* Alex noted in the same breath as he thrust with the blade—the exact moment the dinosaur reared in attempt to bite into Alex's face.

Blade point met scaly reptilian throat, and effortlessly slid through and out the other side, but lodged in, even as the creature gagged and spastically shook and twisted its head and tried to escape. But Alex sat up swiftly and with his left hand encircled the thing's neck. He twisted his body like a wrestler and got around his attacker—and onto its back.

Hanging on now like a rodeo star, keeping the knife lodged into what he hoped (he knew) was the dilophosaurus's primary defense gland while gripping its throat tight under the chin for balance and directional control, Alex had a moment of pure thrill.

He was riding a damn dilophosaurus, and all the studying of his father's notes and books were paying off! Now to hope the rest worked out and these undead things still retained their other biological capabilities.

The arena was in chaos. Nietzman had acquired some gauze or a cloth at least, and held the bloody thing to his face while he stumbled back to the stairs, seeming to root through his lab coat for something. The female attendant had her scream cut brutally short as the horn-helmeted monstrosity tore through her like she was a wet paper towel, his claws and teeth shredding her from the inside out. It shook its head after burrowing into her back below her neck, then spread out its arms at the same time, and her torso split, guts and marrow flying all over her partner, who could only stand there mute as the other one, with the spiked helmet, leapt on him and pulverized his ribcage before razor-fenced teeth went to work on his skull. The third zombie approached Alex—but cautiously and in battle stance, recognizing a superior threat, perhaps—a rider on a mount.

Alex squirmed and tightened his grip, locking his legs around the giant lizard's torso. *Come on, stay on...* Now the zombie circled to the left while waiting for its blood-soaked comrades to rise from their feasts and join in the assault.

"Attack!" Nietzman shouted in a nasally voice, as if the gladiators needed more prodding.

"Yeah," Alex said, gasping for breath over the fetid stench of the dinosaur's perpetually rotting flesh as he looked over the menacing, deadly opponents, "attack!"

Horned-head moved first, throwing caution to the wind, trusting maybe in the pack mentality and their protective headgear which made this fight anything but fair, but as soon as he lurched forward and prepared to leap, Alex shifted his free hand to grip the dino's ridged skull, then ripped out the knife.

Come on, work—

If Alex had been unprepared for the force of the stream that gushed from the lizard's throat, the zombies were even more taken by surprise. A thick gout of steaming yellow acid struck horned-head first in the chest, then up as Alex directed the beast's head like a turret. The stream cut right up the zombie's chin, bisecting the face and drilling through the helmet.

Horned-head stopped in his tracks, then dropped, hands to his face—where putrid steam and bubbling metal dissolved along with his fingers as the acid ate into the brain. Alex didn't stop there, and the acid supply was far from emptied. Digging his feet in, Alex reared up, and with the knife hand he plunged the blade into the dinosaur's skull, fairly certain he would miss the tiny brain but just needing the extra steering traction. He used it to perfect effect, tugging the skull this way and that, directing the acid stream first to pointy-German helmet gladiator and whipping the acid across the head and chest in two successful X motions. The last zombie— bloodied and still with a huge lumpy meal lodged in its throat— cautiously pulled back, raising its arms and crouching.

Alex didn't give it time to spring, but twisted the dino's head fully and held the thrashing beast in place, moving the head in slight circular motions, spraying the zombie and splashing acid around its arms and head and chest until it was a steaming, dissolving mess.

Not entirely sure enough had hit the brain or dissolved the helmet, but sensing his ultimate weapon was nearly out of juice, Alex turned and tugged one last time—and just in time.

Dr. Nietzman had pulled out what looked like a shiny replica Luger, but apparently it was quite functional, and only user error and a bloodied vision had saved Alex from a direct shot to the back. Nietzman fired wide, then shot again, stepping forward with some misplaced confidence. Two more shots, and Alex felt the dinosaur twitch with the impacts of the slugs somewhere in its body, but fortunately shielding Alex.

Alex wanted to say something like 'Eat This' or 'Open up and Swallow,' but with the screeching dinosaur, the echoes of gunshots, the sizzling of acid and the horrific stench pervading the arena, all he could muster was a choking gag reflex as he directed the last few spurts of acid toward the doctor.

He heard a satisfying scream and the luger dropped as Nietzman backpedaled, his arms sizzling and the front of his chest looking like termites were devouring the white sleeves.

Nietzman tore off the jacket as he looked up, then a sick smile appeared on his face when he saw the acid stream dwindle to a trickle. He picked up the gun, but Alex wasn't about to give him the chance, or a clear shot. He wrenched the knife free from the dino's skull, then stood up and kicked back, launching off the dinosaur's spine even as the effort kicked the lizard forward—right into Nietzman.

The gun went off twice, and any measure of control the mad doctor might have had remaining over the beast was lost in a mode of self-preservation and extreme hostility. The dinosaur roared and thrashed its talons and teeth and shredded the doctor's throat and burrowed its snout down into the hole, slurping up the esophagus and pulling up chunks of lung while Nietzman made his last gasping and wheezing sounds.

Alex, still half in disbelief that his gambit worked, took a look at the carnage: two devoured humans, a third in the process, two dissolving zombies, and bodies thrashing in death throes and a third...

Damn, not quite finished.

The last one, his helmet half-burnt away along with half of a face, looking like an undead Phantom of the Opera, rose up, enraged. It rushed Alex.

Now it was a fight fit for the arena...

Except it was still two against one.

The spitter dinosaur spun around, sensing live prey and the chance to get revenge. The two of them converged on Alex, who was left holding only his blade.

Oh and it just got worse, he thought, seeing Nietzman's twitching corpse take on a new motion—that of rising, his head almost but not quite severed, the body thriving now with the prions coursing up the spinal fluid pathways and reinvigorating the brain.

You've got to be kidding me!

Alex backed up slowly, picking the biggest threat to counter first, although holding out little hope.

Phantom-of-the-Opera zombie launched himself just as the dinosaur sprang, and Alex ducked and rolled toward the zombie, raising the knife and waiting for the collision.

#

He waited, curled up, swinging the knife at the air. And then opened his eyes while it took it a second to register the popping sounds echoing through the arena were not sounds of carnage and breaking bones—not his, at least.

Gunshots. Multiple automatic weapons fire.

Phantom-face was face-down in a heap, the back of his head exploded, and the dinosaur had been spun around with multiple impacts, taking more and more now, its skull getting peppered with rounds, its eyes popping and crest shredded and finally—its brain penetrated and it dropped, motionless.

Only Dr. Nietzman remained standing, making a disturbing gurgling sound from his shredded throat as pink bits of lung flapped in the air. His glasses somehow were still hanging on from one ear, just for a moment before two soldiers in black came running down the stairs, guns trained on him.

"Orders?"

"Take him out," said a female voice from above. "Looks like his service is done."

One more gunshot and the glasses split apart, the bullet blasting between them and exploding out the back of Nietzman's skull.

He dropped and thudded to the floor and Alex instinctively let go of the knife, and then raised his hands. *The only move.* "Don't shoot," he mumbled. "I'm…"

"Still human?" said the woman, and Alex looked past the soldiers' black boots, avoiding the gun barrels trained on his face, and saw the tall brunette in a bright blue power suit, flanked by a dark-skinned, grey-haired man in a camouflage suit decorated with a crapload of medals.

"Yeah," Alex said, arms still raised. "Despite my disguise, and yes, I'm—"

"In a hell of a lot of trouble."

But still alive, he thought. "You…?" He got to his knees, looking closer. She was familiar, he had seen her face on the news once or twice lately. "Madame…Vice President?"

She nodded. "Welcome to Shadow Facility Alpha." Without a trace of a smile she added: "And don't thank us yet. After we extract every last bit of information that President DeKirk asked us to retrieve from you, through whatever means necessary, you'll wish we had mistakenly shot you as a zombie."

11.

Outside NORAD, Colorado

"What's our game plan?" Veronica slumped against a tree trunk, exhausted. Arcadia and Zephyr followed suit on nearby trees. They'd trekked deep into a pine forest, and although they'd gone a few miles without seeing any zombies or dinosaurs, the chilly air, fatigue and general sense of despair about their situation combined to weigh on Veronica. "How much farther do you think it is to this road?"

Zephyr waited for the thunder of another distant explosion to dissipate—the tail end of DeKirk's NORAD bombing run—before responding. "Like I said, I haven't actually gone this way before so it's hard for me to be sure of the exact route, but I know for a fact there's only one main road down from this mountain, and this trail meets up with it. I've heard guys at work talking about it, some of them mountain bike…" He became sullen and paused for a moment of silence before continuing. "…*used to* go mountain biking up here. They used to go."

"Guys! Listen. You hear that?" Arcadia's head was on a swivel as she craned her neck to look up into the tree canopy. The three of them listened and watched. They didn't see anything out of the ordinary, but after a few seconds a faint but distinctly unnatural noise became apparent.

"I do," Veronica said. "A humming."

Arcadia nodded. "Getting louder, too."

Zephyr looked confused as though he hadn't heard it yet, but suddenly his eyes widened and he pointed up into the pine trees off to their left. "There! What is that?" He bolted up from the ground to a standing position and took out his pistol.

"Drone!" Veronica moved around the tree trunk, putting its bulk between her and the aerial threat, which continued to approach as it descended among the pines.

"Can it shoot at us?" Arcadia, taking a cue from the ex-CIA agent, hid behind her tree.

"Some of them can," Veronica said, taking aim at the drone from behind the pine, "but this one is very small. Most likely its mission is reconnaissance."

"Shit," Zephyr grumbled. "They know we survived. Now we're screwed!"

"Settle down." Veronica flipped the drone the bird and then fired a shot at it, which missed, thudding into a pine trunk a few yards past the intended target. A startled raven winged away with a squawk.

Zephyr squeezed off a round at the airborne intruder. This one hit, as evidenced by the metallic *ping* of a bullet ricocheting off the metal frame, but although the mini-drone wobbled in mid-air, it was able to stabilize itself and then scoot off to the right, where it maintained altitude behind a closely spaced grouping of trees.

"Only thing to do is hope it hasn't confirmed our position yet, and we take it out first." Veronica ran to another tree from where she could take aim at the flying camera. Zephyr also moved to a better vantage point, and together they fired off a volley of rounds at the drone. They heard some of the shots find their mark, and a few seconds later came a thud as the sky robot crashed to the forest floor.

The trio remained motionless in the silence that hung over the pine forest. At length, Arcadia asked, "Should we go look at it?"

Veronica shook her head. "It could be rigged with plastic explosives. We should just—"

At that moment, a new sound became audible through the woods. "Is that a motor?" Arcadia reloaded her weapon. Zephyr nodded. "Sounds like a motorcycle."

"Drone must have already got our position out to DeKirk's forces. Let's move!" Veronica took off running into the pines off to the right side of the trail they'd been following. "Stay off the path, maybe that vehicle won't be able to follow through the trees."

They moved off the hiking trail they'd been following and into thick foliage. The buzzing of the motor grew louder until they ducked into some bushes, watching as flashes of camo-green paint whizzed by on the trail.

"It's an ATV!" Zephyr whispered. "Yeah, quad-runner. Basically a motorcycle on four wheels, built for terrain like this. Looked like two guys on it. If they see us, there's nothing to stop them from going off trail." Zephyr shrunk deeper into the stand of plants.

They heard the engine slow and then rev again, growing louder. "They've turned around. Coming back this way," Arcadia said.

"Maybe they don't see us and they're giving up," Zephyr said. But no sooner had he completed the sentence than they heard a voice—strange and gravelly—shout from the path, "That way!" followed by the whine of acceleration.

"Hurry." Veronica started to climb a nearby pine tree, jumping to the lowest branch, pulling herself up onto it with an arm stretch, and then standing on the branch close to where it met the trunk. She began to climb higher.

Arcadia jumped up also and started to climb as the ATV turned off the path into the underbrush not fifty feet from them. Zephyr looked at other nearby trees but none of them looked as climbable, so he ran to the same tree next and leapt for the branch, but he missed, his hands not closing over the top of it. He crashed to the ground in a heap as the ATV roared closer.

Shots rang out from above as Veronica squeezed off rounds from high in the pine. Both ATV riders wore motorcycle helmets, also painted in a woodland camo pattern, as well as full camo suits, making it difficult to tell if they were human or modified zombie. But one thing became clear: they were coming for the humans.

The driver of the ATV pulled the quad-runner to a stop near the base of the tree. The passenger, riding behind the driver on the seat, was the first to dismount. Veronica and Arcadia blasted the figure with multiple rounds to the torso after a couple ricocheted off the helmet. The pursuer stumbled in place, dropped to one knee, but then stood and kept coming.

"Zombie," Veronica confirmed.

Arcadia looked confused. "But the driver must be human, right?"

Veronica shook her head before lining up the driver in her gun sights. "Not necessarily. Something off about them."

"But one spoke!"

"I don't know, worry about it later. They could be remote controlled. The fact that they're wearing helmets suggests they were prepared for battle."

Arcadia wanted to make sure, so she called down to the figures. "What do you want?"

If they understood, they paid her no mind. Instead, they ran for the fallen Zephyr, who staggered to his feet, weighed down by the RPG he still carried. One of the riders drew a knife from a sheath.

"Zombies can't do that!" Arcadia said, popping off another round at the humanoid's chest. It struck, but seemingly had no effect.

"Aim for the neck." Veronica held her breath and then squeezed the trigger. A slug ripped through the helmet-wearing zombie's collarbone, flinging it back to one side as it reached down for Zephyr. It hissed and reared its head back, and Veronica took the opportunity to place another shot high on its neck. A fount of blood geysered from the stricken undead's carotid, and it went down on both knees, where Zephyr promptly yanked its helmet off in one swift, two-handed motion.

A zombie revealed. The thing's hair was missing in random clumps, and what remained were bloody tufts atop a grime-covered scalp. One eye was missing, as was most of its right cheek. When it groaned, the tongue was visible inside the mouth, waggling around uselessly.

"Zombie!" Zephyr shouted. "Look, it's a—"

The rest of his words were drowned out by the additional rounds from Veronica's gun, shots to the head of the undead soldier that put it down for good. But by this time the second ATV rider had wheeled up to Zephyr, reaching for him with a motocross-style gloved hand. Before Arcadia could wonder aloud, *How can they attack if they can't bite with the helmets on?* The creature also produced a fixed blade knife and proceeded to thrust its blade deep into Zephyr's left side.

Veronica and Arcadia peppered the remotely controlled beast with a frenzied volley of shots. Some of these should have found their mark, but the helmet and Kevlar and whatever else seemed to protect the thing enough—but in another uncharacteristic move, it seemed to sense it was outmatched. Ducked, scampered and ran fast into the woods to evade them.

"Zephyr, you okay?" Veronica hustled down from the tree, but Arcadia, who was a couple of branches below her, reached the ground first. She ran to Zephyr, who knelt on the ground in between the two fallen zombie warriors, pressing a hand to his side. He lifted the hand away and held it up to his face to see it dripping with his own blood, very dark in color.

Veronica reached the ground and walked out onto the path they'd been following to make sure no other threats were on the way.

Zephyr started to mumble incoherently, sort of half-crying, half-talking. His face paled even more when he saw his hand.

"Guys!" Veronica called from out of sight on the path. "I think that unkillable asshole's coming back—with reinforcements!"

#

Arcadia gripped Zephyr by a shoulder. "There's no time for me to give you proper first aid right now, but I've got something that'll stop the bleeding until we can get you somewhere I can work on you." She unslung her backpack and pulled from it a small first aid pouch. From that she took out a spongy package and quickly began tearing the wrapper off.

Zephyr started to shiver. "What is it?"

"Quick Clot. It's like a sponge that will adhere to the wound, soak up the blood and help it to coagulate." She began to apply it as the cacophony of multiple ATV motors grew louder by the second. She could even hear the slight change in pitch as a rider went airborne off a bump in the path before the wheels touched down again.

Veronica came crashing through the tangle of plant growth. "Guys, we have to get away from the trail. I see at least four more of those things heading our way." She eyed the ATV and then Arcadia, who finished up the patch job on Zephyr's side and stood.

"Let's get out of here." Veronica moved to the ATV and mounted it in the driver seat position. "Can you lift Zephyr onto the middle?"

The off-road vehicles were made for two riders, not three, but they managed to fit. Veronica wanted Zephyr in the middle in case he lost consciousness, so that he didn't fall off the back, and she certainly didn't want him driving.

The former technician grunted and supported himself with his legs while Arcadia helped him onto the vehicle. Meanwhile, Veronica started the engine, knowing that as soon as she did their cover would be blown, but to stay here on the ground was akin to suicide.

"Hold on tight!" She felt Zephyr's arms encircle her waist, his grip weak. Arcadia, well aware that Zephyr could fall off the bike at any moment, kept one hand on the seat to support her weight, and one arm wrapped around Zephyr's midsection.

Veronica twisted the handlebar throttle forward and they jolted to a start, rocketing out of the underbrush onto the path. She veered right, fishtailing until she brought the vehicle under control, then gunned it and sped off down the path.

Arcadia whipped her head around in the back. "I see them! They're a ways back, but they're following."

Veronica kept her eyes forward. There were no rear view mirrors, which she was just as glad for. It allowed her to keep her focus exclusively on the irregular road ahead of them, both twisting and turning as well as unpredictably rising and falling. A few sharp turns later and the pursuing ATVs sounded farther away. Just as Veronica allowed herself the faintest glimmer of hope, a new threat appeared, this time from above.

A massive pterodactyl swooped down below the treetops and leveled out mere feet above the ground, coming straight for them. Veronica steered with her right hand while she gripped her pistol with the left. She took aim at the winged predator, tracking it as it weaved and rolled. She fired two shots, both passing underneath the creature's belly, but the next three found their mark in the reptile's skull. It screeched and veered from the path, breaking its neck on impact as it collided with a tree trunk.

She had slowed the ATV while shooting the ptero, though, and now Arcadia's voice, fraught with worry, carried to her from the back of the vehicle. "They're catching up! Automatic weapons!"

Veronica throttled up, white-knuckling the handlebars as she followed the forest trail. She had seen no forks in the path, only the single dirt trail winding its way through the trees. While reducing options, it also reduced concern she had taken a wrong turn somewhere; eventually, this path had to lead to the main road. Zephyr had said so, and he knew the area. Which reminded her...

"Zephyr? How much longer until the road?"

No response.

"Zephyr?" She nudged him gently with an elbow. He groaned in response, loud enough to be heard over the whine of the motor. Then he uttered a single word.

"Someday."

Veronica swore. They were losing him. Shots from Arcadia's firearm, and she resumed her focus; she coaxed more speed from the little vehicle. A gouge appeared in a tree trunk to their right just as they crested a hill, a reminder that they were now within range of their pursuer's bullets. Their ATV went airborne as Veronica gunned it over the high point, seeking the temporary cover the downward slope would provide.

She could feel her two passengers slamming up and down on the seat as she descended the trail at unsafe speeds. The path continued down, flattening out after a while, the trees still thick on either side of them.

From the back seat, Arcadia popped off more gunshots. Veronica heard a joyful trill when one of her rounds gave a pursuing ATV a flat tire, causing the driver to lose control and roll the trail bike, tumbling off into the woods. But more riders on other vehicles quickly took up the chase. The ride was bumpier than ever as Veronica accelerated over the slightest patch of straight, level trail, rocks and roots be damned.

Arcadia called up to Veronica. "I don't know how much longer I can hold them off." The ATV launched off a protruding boulder and slammed hard onto the path fifteen feet below. Arcadia's jaws slammed together with the impact, jarring her teeth. And then, ahead...

The trail opened up.

"I see it!" Veronica shouted. "I see the road."

More evidence of human—or undead—occupation littered the area. They began to see parked vehicles—a Jeep here, a camper there, a motorcycle... But behind them the pursuing convoy refused to let up. With the wider path came additional opportunities, and they attempted to flank the target quad runner. The first attempt was aborted when the ATV on the left nearly struck a tree on the edge of the path, but it was clear to Veronica as she stole a sideways glance at the attempted sandwich maneuver that most of these had human riders, skilled soldiers, but they were carrying undead along for extra support. She knew they would not be able to fight off two ATV loads of undead jumping on them at once. They needed to do something to change the game, and fast.

Veronica saw the path transitioning into the road in a few more yards. For now, there was still thick forest cover on either side of them, but once they hit the road proper they'd have to move far to one side or the other to reach the cover of the trees, and it appeared somewhat thinner, too. She slowed ever so slightly while veering off to the right of the wide road, compensating for the feel of pavement under the wheels now instead of dirt. Ahead, the sight of a blockade—a checkpoint manned by armed soldiers in uniform— sent a jolt of adrenaline through her body, nearly causing her to lose control of the ATV.

For a split second, she contemplated barreling through it, but curbed the impulse as the suicidal mission it was. They'd be cut to ribbons before they even hit anything. Instead, she swerved further to the right, where a not-so-solid tree line butted up against the road shoulder. She whipped her head back and yelled to her passengers.

"We need to split up. They're going to get us if we stay together." She studied the battlefield again, coming up with no alternatives. "Arcadia!"

"Yes?"

"I'll slow down enough for you to jump. Take your briefcase. Run into the trees and keep running. Find a way to get to somewhere safe, somewhere with the Resistance, and I'll contact you."

"What about you and Zephyr?"

"We'll act as decoys so that you stand a chance. The world needs for you to make it, Dr. Grey."

"No way. There has to—"

"Get ready!"

Veronica felt Zephyr's hand slip from her waist as Arcadia shifted her position in the seat, apparently realizing the discussion was over and preparing to jump. Veronica deliberately steered the ATV to the edge of the forest along the side of the wide road, where an opening led into the trees. She decelerated to give Arcadia a decent chance at not rolling into a tree and breaking something when she jumped, and that's when a zombie bullet took out the left rear tire. The ATV swerved erratically and forced Arcadia into an early bail out. Veronica managed to get the vehicle under control, turning left back out into the main road.

She couldn't help but turn her head for a glimpse at the departing scientist. *Was she injured in the dismount?* No, there…she saw the woman slip into the trees at a healthy-looking run, briefcase clutched in one hand.

Good luck, Arcadia.

Then she turned her attention back to her own problems, which were many, in the form of multiple ATVs, motorcycles and foot soldiers converging on the now crippled ATV.

Looking at the barricade about fifty yards ahead of them, blocking the main road and manned by an unnerving combination of walking dead and what appeared to be cognizant human soldiers, she decided that way was hopeless. A quick look to the left showed the convoy of ATVs pouring out of the forest path from which they had just emerged, closing off that option. Her best bet was to vanish into the forest as Arcadia had, but in another direction.

She squeezed off a couple of rounds at a contingent of oncoming zombies off to her right, farther down the roadway, then eyed a promising spot on the opposite side of the road from where she had dropped Arcadia. She headed for it full throttle, concerned that Zephyr might not be able to hold on in his weakened condition, but having no choice. She craned her neck back for a quick look at him.

Zephyr's body was slumped backwards on the seat so that he was lying down on top of his RPG, one arm dangling haphazardly in between the two left wheels. Veronica reached back and tapped him on the leg with her handgun. "Zephyr! Zephyr, get up."

But the ex-NORAD technician didn't move. Veronica turned her attention back to the road in front of her. She veered away from two undead coming at them at a fast ramble. Beyond those two were dozens more, and beyond those were human riflemen taking aim at the ATV.

She aimed the ATVs nose for the opening in the pines she had identified moments ago. The ATVs on her left were rapidly eating up the remaining distance to their quarry. Veronica knew that by the time she reached the edge of the woods they would have precious little head start to get lost in the trees, to have any hope of evading their hunters. But at the same time she had no better alternatives.

She heard a frightful voice yelling at her through a megaphone: *"Stop and you won't be harmed."*

Veronica throttled up and rocketed the ATV off the lip of the road into the forest, landing on a bed of spongy pine needles between a cluster of trees. She braked in order to figure out which way to head next. Glanced through two different tight groupings of trees. It would be difficult to squeeze the ATV through them but she thought she could do it. Then she swiveled and looked back to the main road, where the enemy ATVs and motorcycles had converged, their riders dismounting in preparation of apprehending her and Zephyr. Or simply slaughtering them where they stood. They had heard her ATV stop and figured she couldn't penetrate the forest any deeper.

Veronica turned to Zephyr. "The RPG! We've got a shot now while they're all in one place. Take it!"

He only lay motionless on the seat.

"Zephyr!" She reached out and touched him on the face, slapped him lightly. His eyes were closed. She placed a finger under his nose. No breath. She put two fingers on his carotid artery.

No pulse.

#

He shouldn't have expired already. The gauze and the clot... She gave a quick check, and something stopped her short. The gauze—it was perforated near the original wound, but from this side, as if...

She was suddenly chilled.

Arcadia? Was it possible?

She was back there, maybe...

The examination into his death—the spreading loss of blood from the knife wound—was cut short as a burst of gunfire opened up from the edge of the road, shredding the greenery around her. A confetti of plant bits drifted through the air. "Sorry, Zephyr." She shoved the corpse off the bike and picked up the rocket launcher. Hefted it on her right shoulder while swinging it around to face her attackers, still grouped together at the side of the road.

She could hear the soldier with the megaphone, still urging her to surrender. Eyeballed a trio of zombie-riders atop an armored ATV, encircled by various troops, vehicles and undead. Suddenly, she didn't just want to stop them, but she hated them. Hated them all. Each ugly dead thing that refused to stay dead, the brainwashed soldiers fighting for that billionaire freak...she wished she could annihilate every last goddamn one of them forever and for good, wished she could punish them for what they had done to the world. The closest thing she had to channel that rage into was the RPG.

Her hands flew over the weapon to undo the safety and she slid her finger inside the trigger guard. *Here you go...*

The muscles in her hand contracted and she felt the heat from the barrel as the mortar launched with a rushing *whoosh*. A second later, the projectile exploded in a fireball, obliterating the assemblage of vehicles, zombies and humans that had congregated on the side of the road.

Veronica let the RPG fall to the ground. She was about to turn and run when she decided to grab Zephyr's gun. Thankfully he wore a holster in plain sight on his belt, so she wouldn't have to pat him down or rummage through his clothing. She knelt and grabbed the dead man's 9mm. She stood and jammed it into her back pocket, a spare for when and if she ran out of ammo for her own piece, now brandished in her right hand like life itself.

She took off at a run that would be reckless under any other circumstance, ducking her head below low-hanging branches, high stepping over exposed roots and rocks, crashing her way through brush without knowing if a tree trunk waited on the other side.

She'd had a great opening salvo to the battle, but knew she had a long way to go to win. No way had she taken out all, or even most, of the undead soldiers back there. And too bad she missed that first one they had tangled with. More were coming, just as more people around the world were dying and joining the undead ranks with each passing hour.

Her job—her duty to her country which she had formerly served proudly as an agent of the CIA—was to see to it that Dr. Grey made it to a facility that could support her research. She had to continue to draw their attention and buy time.

Veronica eyed a stand of trees that was particularly dense—just what she needed for cover—and ran into them. She weaved her way through the pine trunks, listening to the incensed shouts of the army organizing to go after her. Confused, disoriented after the whirlwind action and firefight, she wasn't sure which way she should run. She passed a tree with a fern growing about six feet high out the side of the trunk and could swear she'd already passed it. She didn't really know but looking around she saw only this one. *I must have passed by it already and I'm running around in circles.*

And then, while deciding which way to go, she heard a rustling of foliage. Not caused by the wind, but definitely something moving. She didn't think the soldiers or zombies could have gotten this far so stealthily...*unless one or more were already positioned here?* Hopefully they weren't already stationed on Arcadia's side of the woods, too.

Veronica hunkered down between two trunks and waited. This time she heard more rustling, and from a different direction. Whatever it was, there was more than one of them. Forest animals, she hoped, like squirrels or raccoons? *Yeah right. Maybe it's freaking Bambi. Keep dreaming.*

She raised her pistol to the ready position, slowly swinging it from where she had heard the first sound to the second, and back. Then she heard a substantial impact, a smacking sound as something large hit the leaf-littered ground behind her. *That was no squirrel.* She spun with her pistol pointed from her kneeling position, then almost dropped the gun when her eyes registered the sight in front of her.

Not ten feet away, an adult raptor stood on its two hind legs, perhaps six feet tall. It whipped its head up and down while emitting a clicking sound that seemed to emanate from deep within its throat. But that wasn't what really floored her about the ungodly lizard. The unusual thing about it was the zombie rider sitting atop a saddle on the raptor's back. The one with the helmet, the one with his armor decimated with their bullet holes and still unfazed. He had obviously found a more suitable mount after they commandeered his ATV, and had been riding the prehistoric beast like an upright horse, or maybe an ostrich.

And then it spoke, in that horrible voice that grated through Veronica's skull. "Drop your weapon if you want to live."

Veronica was under no illusions that the raptor alone could easily kill her before she could take it down with her pistol. And with this gun-toting rider to boot? She was finished. Seeing no other option than to comply with the order, she tossed her gun onto the ground halfway between her and the raptor rider in front of her, then put her hands in the air.

She heard the smacking of boots on dry pine needles as the rider dismounted. "Veronica Winters, at last we meet."

Veronica briefly considered denying her identity, but decided against it, figuring that she would be killed if she were not someone wanted directly by President DeKirk. "Who the hell are you?"

The helmet lifted, and revealed an unfamiliar face—scarred and scaled, hideous yellow eyes and a bald head. But the voice...now without the helmet, it took on an arrogance she was all too familiar with.

"I'm sorry I couldn't find you directly, but my elite servant here will soon remedy that."

"What are you talking about?" *DeKirk? It had to be him...* Veronica felt the frustration welling up within her as the undead general put cuffs on her wrists and cinched them down tight.

Those eyes bore into hers, until the helmet went back on, and now she saw a lens directly in the middle—a camera.

"Where is Dr. Grey?"

Veronica shrugged. "Probably killed back at the Mountain."

"We know that isn't true."

She shrugged again. "Then you got me, we lost her a ways back. Good luck, asshole."

The zombie made a forced and ugly smile. "She will be found, but first things first. Come, we have a long flight ahead of us." He yanked her to her feet and spun her around until she faced the road, some distance out of sight through the forest, toward an awaiting ATV. Then he secured a rope through her cuffs, holding fast to the other end.

The general mounted his steed, which screeched and hissed, then took off, dragging Veronica behind it.

12.

Alex struggled against the bonds at his wrists. He wished he had the strength to tear through these plastic clamps, leap across the table and smash the monitor. If only symbolic, at least it would make him feel better—and deny that bastard DeKirk the satisfaction of seeing him struggle. Struggle, and most likely die.

He glared at the screen, at that face from his nightmares. That face that had haunted his days and nights for these past three months. How many times had that same man appeared on national television, on the one station left, broadcast to whatever receivers could still pick up the signal? Dressed in a sharp blue suit, red tie and enough makeup to hide his pallid appearance, DeKirk had gone through the presidential motions and made constant reassurances that humanity was winning, that armed forces were regaining ground and that vaccines were working.

"Everyone sit tight," DeKirk had coined as his catch phrase, repeating it over and over with a gleam in his eye as if to say *we're coming for you, and a sedentary target will make things a lot easier.*

Alex fumed. "Where are you, you son of a bitch?"

The others were hanging back, standing in the shadows. The vice president, Jules Norris, at the head of the conference table, her face clouded, her hands gripping the seat back tight. Charles Wilford, the treasurer, wringing his hands together, head down, stood behind General Neville Hughes, who alone seemed confident and not in awe (or fear) of their leader.

"Not far," DeKirk responded, still with that gleam in his eye, but seeming far less pale.

"Tropical?" Alex inquired. "Looks like a little tan you got there."

DeKirk grinned and wiped the side of his lip. "Just fed. A hearty meal tends to flush the cheeks."

"How nice for you. So, you've got me. Are you going to watch me die, like you did my father? You going to infect me and then use me for target practice?"

"Quite the imagination! And all good suggestions, my dear boy, but no. None of those things, at least not until I have General Hughes here let his undead soldiers have some sport with you. After you talk, of course."

"I don't know shit."

"I doubt that, and if that's true I'm really sorry because it will take a lot of agony and torture to convince us that is the case. In the meantime, is there anything you'd like to share about what your little friends have been up to? What are they hoping to accomplish with the CDC scientist in Colorado?"

Ah, so he doesn't know. Good. Alex forced a smile. Took a breath and leaned back, relaxing against the restraints. "We don't speak like we used to, but if they're still avoiding you, then that must really be driving you crazy. Good for them. Worried?"

DeKirk's eyes flashed pure hatred, then cleared. He leaned forward, filling the screen with his face. The lines that had been there when this all started and Alex had been in his father's office in the Antarctic station were all but gone now. Replaced with youthful vigor and alien-reptilian infused strength.

"I dislike loose ends. And I would dearly wish for you to be reunited with the lovely Ms. Winters. Perhaps that shall yet happen, except in your case you won't be in any frame of mind to enjoy anything about her, except your pure zombie lust, which I'll gladly let you satisfy, tearing your lover's flesh from her bones as she screams for you to stop."

"You're sick," Alex whispered, then turned his attention to the other cabinet members. "This is the asshole you've chosen to follow? The man you're trusting to run the country, to restore the world?"

His eyes locked on Jules's and she met his with defiance, but then looked away.

Alex returned to the screen and for a moment before DeKirk pulled back, he thought he saw something—a flash of a physical reflection in DeKirk's eyes. Something in his vicinity? A glimpse of what looked like a circular turbine. *A plane? A wheel?*

Then it was gone and DeKirk was leaning back, reaching for something on the keyboard. "I'll take my leave now. Much to do on this end. Ms. Norris, I assume you can direct events there now, continue with the plans we have in place. Leave Alex in the capable hands of General Hughes." He shut off the screen with a last nod to Alex. "Hope to see you soon, after you're one of us. If not, say hello to dear old Dad…"

The screen went dark and Alex twisted hard again in the seat, wondering if he could manage to stand despite the bonds around his ankles, and maybe ram the general, head-butt the little old guy and then…What?

The guards were by the door, two silent brutes with M5s at the ready.

I need one of those guns. Just one and a few minutes with my hands free…

But there was no chance of that, of anything close to escape or vengeance. His dream died here.

I'm sorry, Veronica, it's over.

#

Back in the arena.

Alex at least had his legs free, and they'd let him take a change of clothes so that horrid stench was gone, but his wrists were again bound—this time behind a lone post they had brought out and drilled into a slot in the center of the arena, and now he stood like a virgin sacrifice and awaited his fate.

"They sure clean up nice in here," he said to the pair of soldiers at the main entrance, men who were as dull and business-like as stormtroopers for the Empire.

"No talking."

General Neville Hughes arrived and slammed the door behind him. Alex sized him up and didn't like what he saw. This wasn't going to be fun. He steeled himself as the general came closer, dragging with him the cart that the previously-disemboweled nurse had left behind. Great, he would experience those surgical tools now after all.

"Listen," Alex tried, struggling against the bonds, his shoulders already in agony. "I don't know anything of use to you. Just get it over with."

"Quiet." Hughes, looked over the instruments. "I'll let you know when you can talk."

"Don't you have better things to do? Like firebomb some hapless civilians or kiss your master's infected ass?"

Hughes looked up and reached out fast, squeezing Alex's chin as he brought around a scalpel. "I don't like this bullshit either, but I need answers." He lowered his voice and the scalpel reflected a bright stabbing light into Alex's eyes. "Now tell me, *do you have a chance?*"

Alex squirmed and tried to pull away. "What?"

The scalpel touched his cheek, just under his left eye, as a big hand closed on his neck. "Can you do it…?"

"I don't know what you're talking about."

"The cure. A vaccine, something? Why go to the CDC, what did the former president have you rush to Atlanta for, and why is your partner escorting the scientist to NORAD?"

Alex closed his eyes. "I have no answers."

"Come on, kid…"

He opened his eyes and narrowed them at the general. "What's in this for you? Don't you realize once he's got complete control, there will be no need for armies or generals?"

"Stop talking."

"You know it's true. What kind of commander are you, when you have to know you'll be the last threat he'll remove. He'll infect the soldiers, converting them all, including you at the end so there definitely won't be any challenge left."

"Stop it."

"He needs you now, but as soon as the resistance is crushed, you're done."

"I'm telling you one more time…"

"Or did he promise to let you in on the secret?"

The general blinked.

"Let you partake of the great undead communion, eat the host, drink the wine, become like him?" Alex sneered. "Is that it? Selling your soul to the devil for immortality? Well think again, if you want to spend eternity like one of *them…*"

The scalpel pressed harder, drawing blood. "Do you have a fucking cure or not?"

"General!"

The pressure released and the blade pulled away, the brightness vanishing, replaced by sunspots and glare. He couldn't see. A woman's voice, someone else...

"You men can leave."

The VP? What was she doing here?

General Hughes echoed the thought. "Jules? DeKirk wants me handling this. Why are you here?"

Footsteps, high heels clanking on the stairs. "Our president also isn't too sure you're up to the task."

"What? So he sent you?"

"This is top priority, General. What this kid knows might be vital intelligence and the only thing we have to fear."

"I'm not a damned kid." Alex blinked again, clearing his vision. Guards were gone, door closing again, and Jules was approaching General Hughes.

"Whatever," she said to him. "You'll talk, and soon. We don't have time to waste on you, we need results."

"And I'll get them," Hughes spat back, blocking her path. "Let me work."

Jules slid around him, giving him a dark glare. "Sit and watch, but get out of my way."

"This is unacceptable. You have no clue what you're doing. I'd wager you haven't even been in a bar fight much less killed a man."

"How hard can it be? He's tied up."

"I'll speak with DeKirk, and be back."

"Be my guest." She turned and motioned to the door, and Hughes stomped away, glancing back only once, at the door, where he hesitated.

Then Jules was in Alex's path of sight, her face leaning in close, and in her hand—a wide bone saw that she moved to the center of his lips.

"Now listen," she said in a whisper. "We don't have much time, and we've got to make this look good."

#

Hope rose in his chest. *Knew it!* He had hoped there was someone among this crew, someone with a conscience. It was his only chance. For it to be the VP herself, second in command?

Even better, the best possible outcome! Finally, a little piece of luck thrown in his path.

He met her look, searching her eyes, maybe out of desperation. "How...?"

"Just tell me quick, what do you know? I need something to go on if I'm going to take a chance like this. He could be watching, ears and eyes everywhere."

Alex nodded, glancing past her, up to the ceiling, then to the vents. He had to trust her, there was no other chance. Otherwise the general might be back and pick up where he left off. "Can you get me out?"

"We'll both get out," she said, the lines around her eyes tightening. She'd been through a lot too, Alex understood. Maybe all this time with all that power, and yet helpless to save the ones she loved, the ones on the outside who probably didn't even know where she was, where she had been all this time.

Alex nodded. "Yes, cut me free, get me out of here. I can help, we'll turn this around. But we have to get DeKirk first. If we don't stop him..."

"The cure?" Jules made no move to set him free yet, just focused on his eyes, moving in and tightening her grip on his shoulder. "What is it? What do you have?"

"Something..." Alex started. How much to tell her? If he mentioned Xander Dyson's name would it convince her they did indeed have something? He would have to risk it. A muted warning bell was ringing in his head, but with everything that had happened, with all the pressure and near-death misses, with the pain of having to see his father change, and sacrifice for him; seeing his mother used by DeKirk in a nightmarish way, the very vessel of infection—and again he had to face her and put her down. Of course he was rattled, he didn't expect anything less. Now, though, he needed to trust someone. It had been too long.

"We have a chance."

The fingers squeezed. "What is it?"

"I've seen it, we—"

Something warm splattered over Alex's cheek the moment he heard the pop echo in the arena.

The pressure left his neck as Jules made a grunting sound; she spun clockwise and down, rolling and twitching at his feet, the left side of her head spurting blood through a neat little hole at her temple.

Alex blinked and shook away some of her blood and looked back toward the door—to see General Hughes rushing in, pistol drawn. Two soldiers were behind him, M5s drawn. They held the door and stood guard as the commander came closer, holstering his weapon—and reaching for the blade Jules had dropped.

"What the hell?" Alex squirmed and gave an attempt to jump and kick the general, but had his legs slapped aside. He was turned around and felt the knife at his wrists.

"We don't have much time," Hughes said in a whisper. "You forced my hand early by coming here, and now I have no choice."

Alex, freed, stepped back, then away from the corpse at his feet. Only now did he see something else—in her hand, a syringe still clenched tight.

"Was that—?"

"Yeah, meant for you after you finished blabbing what you were about to tell her."

"And now I'm supposed to tell you?" Alex sized him up, then glanced to the guards at the door. "How do I know this isn't all another scheme, another way to get me to trust you, and…"

"Just shut up, kid. Trust me or not, I'm going to trust you. Trust that you have something that will make this all worth it, because right now—we have a fight ahead of us. Right now DeKirk must be alerted to what I've done. He's going to unleash hell on us, and I don't have enough loyalists among the troops to overcome everything in this facility if it all goes FUBAR."

Alex blinked at him, still rubbing his wrists, still trying to process this turn of events.

"Don't just stand there," General Hughes said, "we have an escape to plan and a world to save."

13.

Nome, Alaska

Major Remington refused yet another offer of a cocktail from one of DeKirk's attractive female flight attendants. DeKirk's way of trying to loosen his tongue, he was sure. Then the General— aptly named Baal—plied him with questions the entire flight from Kansas City. Relentlessly, in that awful voice, everything he could ask about the Resistance movement. Most of them were the same, but phrased in different ways. Remington stood his ground, repeatedly insisting that, like he said back at the farmhouse, he wouldn't be divulging any information without first laying eyes on his wife and daughter.

Although the personal jet itself was impeccable in terms of the luxuries it offered, it had been a long and wholly unenjoyable flight—almost nine hours of sitting across from the monstrosity that did not nap, barely blinked, and just stared the entire time at Remington while trying to convince him to spill the beans before they landed. He seemed infused with energy, not fatigued in the least.

Remington was starved and had to eat in order to maintain his stamina in the face of the unknown, to give himself strength for the ordeal that no doubt waited for him in Alaska, so he had taken the proffered leather-bound menu from the blonde flight attendant and perused its thick pages for thirty seconds before ordering lamb chops and rice with a mineral water ("unopened bottle, please").

When his food arrived, Baal had excused himself and retreated to the rear of the cabin, behind a closed partition, where presumably he had dined alone. Whatever the case, the blonde never returned, and Remington had little doubt as to her fate.

Remington was grateful to be left alone for twenty minutes while he ate without being scrutinized and peppered with questions.

The major mulled over the possibility of attacking this undead freak of nature but no, he couldn't risk his family's life by attacking this maniac right here and now. He would have to wait, think things through.

Presently, the pilot's voice came over the intercom, starkly banal despite the state of the apocalypse. "Prepare for descent to Nome. Current temperature, thirty-eight degrees Fahrenheit."

Remington lifted the window shade and gazed outside, happy to have any reason to look away from Baal's yellow-tinged eyes, which seemed even brighter following his meal. Snowcapped mountains rushed by, with the Pacific Ocean a shimmering silver blanket unrolled below. Between a crescent of mountains and the sea lay a flat expanse of land covered with buildings—a small city in the midst of unbridled nature. A string of islands were scattered about in the ocean off the coast. The major reflected for a moment that despite his extensive travel in the service of the military, he had never been to The Last Frontier.

Now, he contemplated grimly, with a camp of humans confined to this frozen north, it truly was the last frontier for humanity. For as worried as DeKirk seemed to be about the Resistance movement, willing to fly him all the way to Alaska instead of simply killing him for refusing to cooperate, the truth was that the Resistance was never all that strong, and right now was in a very loose state of organization. It wasn't nearly as capable as DeKirk seemed to think it was. One, maybe two cohesive factions remained that could really be counted on to get anything done, in particular South Wolf, the first group which he had started and trained himself. The rest of them were in dire shape due to the stress induced by prolonged interruptions of power, food and in some cases, water. So, Remington racked his brain as he stared out the window while the ground drew nearer with each passing second... *Will you give them up? Their locations, number of soldiers, equipment, capabilities, plans—any or all of it?*

The major flashed on the faces of the men and women he'd met personally in those groups. A few of them had even served alongside him in the military at some point in their careers, whether in battle or in the office in a support role. They were good people, now fighting with their last breaths to save what precious little remained of our once great nation.

But even so, as Remington leaned his face even farther into the airplane window, mashing his nose into the outer Plexiglas shield that guarded the actual glass window, he knew deep down that if he were to actually see his wife and daughter alive—make that his wife *or* his daughter—alive, that he would have to give up at least something. He might be able to pretend he only had limited information, but would that even work? Maybe give up a couple of the remnants, rag-tag pseudo-militias that had been whittled down to nearly disorganized states by death and abandonment. That might be enough to satisfy DeKirk, to keep him from...

"Major?" Baal leaned on the edge of his seat, eyeing Remington intensely, and DeKirk's voice came rumbling out of his throat. "I know the view is spectacular, and right now you're admiring the very last vestige of safety for your species, but you really should be thinking about your family and what you might provide to save them."

Remington said nothing but pulled back from the window and fastened his seatbelt.

#

When they deplaned, Major Remington was escorted to a waiting military jeep. Baal sat in the passenger seat, turning to stare at Remington, who got in the back. Behind the wheel was a human attendant in a crew-cut and camo fatigues; he nodded to Remington.

"Welcome, sir. I'm Corporal McGee. Assigned to escort you around the premises and then, to your family."

Remington ignored the human traitor, and continued just to eye the general, who had a string of drool trailing from his mouth. "Looks like you've got some loyal lapdogs up here too, *Mr. President.*" He couldn't resist the barb, placing sarcastic emphasis on the title, but inwardly Remington cautioned himself. *Easy, tiger. You're almost there. Don't piss him off now.*

Baal merely held a hand out and pointed, directing McGee to get on with it.

"Talk to you soon, Major," DeKirk's general spoke. "I'm going to attend to other matters for a time. You are in capable hands, and I fully await your cooperation, very soon."

Remington resigned himself to the fact that he was going to have to see DeKirk's human zoo while being driven around by a loyalist and a zombie tour guide. He noticed two cameras mounted on the hood of the jeep, one aimed at the view ahead, which right now consisted of the tarmac with a complex of buildings perhaps a quarter-mile distant, while the other was pointed back at them.

"So Corporal," Remington said, pretending for a moment that he was being driven by a normal human under normal circumstances, simply being taken from the airport to his hotel, "Busy lately? Lots of visitors?" He wasn't expecting an answer, which made it all the more surprising when McGee responded.

"Ahead is a checkpoint to enter the HABITAT-- Human Area for Breeding and InTensive Anthropological Teaching. Remain seated, please." The jeep slowed as they neared a walled and guarded perimeter. He pointed to a sign spelling out the acronym for HABITAT, which Remington stared at and processed with a potent mixture of disgust and disbelief. *My wife and daughter are in there.*

"You've put them in a zoo, haven't you? It's a fucking zoo."

"Human subjects are free to go about their lives as they normally would."

"Human? Like you?"

McGee's eyes flashed to him in the rearview mirror, then on Baal, then back to the road. Remington blinked at the General and gave him a smirk. What else could he do? The damn thing was still staring at him, like a statue, but full of hunger. McGee eased the jeep up to a manned and gated entrance with a large flashing sign reading ALL VEHICLES HALT. Remington noted with extreme unease that a herd of six or so velociraptors hopped back and forth along the perimeter wall.

A yellow-eyed soldier, a zombie-human with scaly hands, stepped up to the driver side of the vehicle while another remained sitting atop a guard post, an automatic weapon trained on Remington. The standing guard said nothing while eyeing both the general and Remington carefully. Then a male human voice issued from a speaker inside the jeep.

"This vehicle is pursuant to Directive #7B, Lieutenant. Permission to enter HABITAT granted, conditional upon passenger being guided and accompanied by General Baal at all times."

The lieutenant smartly saluted Baal, who made an offensively mechanical return of the gesture. They heard a humming noise and then a rattling as the wire mesh gate slid open. Baal put the jeep into gear and rolled into the enclosed area, the gate sliding shut again after they passed.

The general guided the jeep onto a paved road with a street sign proclaiming Main Street. Buildings, one or two-story wooden affairs, lined both sides of the street, and Remington realized with a start that they were shops, stores. Daggart's Deli, a Yogurt Shoppe, a barber... A few people walked down the sidewalk, dressed in civilian clothing, seemingly going about normal business. Remington wanted to shout at them, *Do you know what's happening out there?* He looked at each one to see if he could see Olivia anywhere, maybe someone pushing a stroller, but couldn't recognize her. He tried but was unable to establish eye contact with anybody walking by on the sidewalks.

McGee stopped the jeep at a light, where 1st Street intersected with Main, then made a right turn onto 1st, where a sign proclaimed the speed limit to be 35. Remington wondered if there was a human police force in this "town" but figured that even if there was, the military were no doubt the actual police.

He leaned toward the front seat, keeping as far from Baal as he could, and addressed the corporal. "So, how many people—real humans—live in this facility?"

McGee answered in a creaking voice, almost by rote. "About two thousand."

Remington raised his eyebrows in genuine surprise. Looking around at the streets, it didn't look like the town supported nearly that many. Although, the buildings on 1st appeared to be mostly offices, and he supposed there could be lots of people inside. He wondered if they conspired with one another to escape, or even if there were members of any of his Resistance movement here. Why wouldn't they try, though? It wasn't as if they had any actual work to do. *Hey, Jim, you have those TPS reports ready?* Remington found himself about to laugh out loud and disguised it as a cough.

Talk about being in the belly of the beast. But before he could help anyone else, he had to help his family.

"Up here on the left is the town newspaper, the *Daily*—"

"*The Daily Bullshit*. Enough already. Could you just let me see my wife and daughter, please?" Now he addressed Baal, staring right into those eyes. "You want something, I want something. Let's make a deal and get on with it."

McGee coughed. "Don't you want to see where they live?"

"Is that where they are?"

"In due time. I meant the general town where they—we—have been lucky enough to have been chosen to live out our natural lives." The corporal waved an arm outside of the jeep to indicate the town as a whole. Remington eyeballed the gun on the right side of McGee's waist. He wondered if he could snatch it out of the holster and then conceal it beneath his clothing without the general noticing. But then he looked at the camera not three feet in front of him, aimed into the jeep. *Don't*.

"What have they been doing since they were taken here? How have they been treated?"

Remington had already asked these questions to Baal/DeKirk directly, on the plane, but the president had refused to answer, responding, in fact, with "In due time."

In due time I'm going to kill you, DeKirk.

Remington decided to do something of possible tactical benefit instead of merely listening to the drivel spewing from the Kool-Aid drinking asshole inside the jeep, and so he began counting the blocks as he drove in an attempt to estimate the size of the town. The main square of shops, and it was truly a square, was only about two blocks to a side. Beyond that was some open space— pruned trees, a grassy park where a lone figure walked with a dog, and past that lay a long, low building made of concrete. To Remington's right, he could see the HABITAT containment wall. He heard a distant screeching and looked up in time to see a squadron of four pterodactyls fly by overhead, patrolling the airspace over the human containment area. He watched them until they abruptly turned upon reaching the perimeter wall, no doubt following a prescribed pattern. The corporal turned the jeep toward the low building.

"What's that?" Remington asked, pointing at the concrete structure.

"Housing units."

The major waited for him to elaborate but McGee remained silent, stopping at an intersection even though no one was there, before continuing on toward the building.

"Some utopia. The people don't live in houses, they live in *housing units?*"

The driver had no reply.

"I asked you a question."

"The HABITAT project is still in its early stages. For now, they live in the Central Housing Units. Once they are paired off with mates to become nuclear families, they will be placed in single family houses, such as those you see over there..." He pointed to the left side of the road where a row of modest clapboard houses squatted behind postage stamp lawns and white picket fences. Remington looked but detected no signs of life—no mailboxes, for one thing, no trash cans, no people, pets or toys in any of the yards.

"What the hell do you mean, 'paired off'?"

"This is not the proper time to discuss details of the human breeding program, but I have a feeling you know exactly what it means."

At this, Remington whipped his head sideways to look at this vile creature driving him around, and he wasn't sure which of the two individuals sitting in the front was the bigger monster. A ropy string of pinkish drool swayed from Baal's chin with the motion of the vehicle. The major wanted nothing more than to slaughter the crap out of this heinously twisted organism, and to rifle-butt the sympathizer-driver, but with his family now within reach, he willed himself to exercise restraint.

He rode in silence until they reached the Central Housing Unit. The place reminded Remington of a minimum security prison contained within the walled perimeter of the town. Coils of razor wire topped a twelve-foot high chain link fence that surrounded the facility within a facility. The jeep pulled up to another manned checkpoint, and this time both guards really did appear to be actual human men, Remington ascertained. Or at least hybrids. Once again an audio directive issued from the jeep sound system—the only part of it that meant anything to Remington was "Pod 6"— and then the guards let them pass into the compound.

They drove to a parking spot close to the housing unit and pulled into a lined space apart from the others with a sign proclaiming, RESERVED.

"You must be an important guy here, McGee," Remington quipped as he exited the jeep, alongside of General Baal.

The chuffing and wheezing that emanated from the dead thing's oral cavity was positively revolting to Remington. He wondered for a fleeting moment who this guy, this... Baal was before he became a zombie in the service of President DeKirk's twisted army. Then he reminded himself that he needed to focus if he wanted to escape from this hellhole with his wife and child.

"This way, Major." The corporal walked up to an automatic door that did not open until he pressed one of his eyes up against a retinal scanner. Remington, followed now by Baal, walked inside through a narrow vestibule area that opened into a long hallway in either direction. He could hear people in here, mostly yelling, like the sounds of a prison. He looked through the small windows set into the closed doors they passed and saw hellish rooms of squalor—fifty people crammed in a space meant for perhaps ten. Laying on the floor because there was no furniture. He saw no fixtures of any kind, no sinks, bathrooms, kitchens, nothing. Just bare cells. He smelled urine as he passed one of the rooms.

He was about to say something when the corporal opened a door set into the right side of the hallway. To Remington's surprise, it contained a stairwell leading only down. As they stepped into the landing, his tour guide pressed a button on an intercom mounted on the wall and spoke into it. "Prepare Pod 6 for visitor."

Remington felt his blood pressure rise as he descended the stairs, the zombie behind him no doubt a deliberate strategic choice. *Was DeKirk still watching, waiting to see his reaction through the little camera lens?*

This was it. Pod 6. He steeled himself for how he should react if he was to see them crammed into a room like the ones he'd seen above. He wasn't sure if he could handle that, but as each concrete step echoed with his heavy footfalls, he knew he had no choice.

"Keep going." Remington followed as Baal gave him a shove. They passed the door on a landing, continuing down the steps. They descended two more flights and then his guide ordered him to stop.

"Step aside." Remington complied and McGee stepped aside as well. "Higher security here." He motioned to Baal, who moved ahead. The zombie pressed his pus-and-scaled eye to a scanner. The door slid open.

"Guess you know your place," Remington said to McGee as they stepped inside to a blindingly white tiled floor, waxed and lit from above by high wattage fluorescent tube lights. Remington's heart skipped as he saw POD 2 stenciled onto a door to his right. The door had no window so he couldn't get a clue as to what kind of spaces these were.

But he wouldn't have long to wonder. At the end of the white tiled hallway, the zombie guide stopped at a door on the left marked POD 6. He turned to Major Remington and extended his armored hand, pointing.

McGee cleared his throat but moved no further. Just lowered his head. "They're in here. Ready?"

Remington nodded.

"Sure you don't want to use the restroom first, wash up? You look like you've been roaming the country fighting off roving bands of monsters."

Remington glared at the corporal. "Just open the goddamn door."

"Very well." McGee pressed buttons on a keypad fixed in main terminal next to him and a hissing sound echoed from down the hall. Remington was already moving, even as the zombie stepped back and opened the door for the major, who promptly entered the space. To his dismay, it was set up like a prison or jailhouse visiting room, with steel chairs and tables bolted to the floor in front of a long window with partitioned cubicles behind it. It took every iota of his willpower to scan the walls and ceiling for cameras rather than look directly at his imprisoned family. He had to remain vigilant and not let himself get complacent now that he was so close to his goal.

But there they were! The only two people behind the glass, the only two people in the room at all—his wife and daughter, his baby…in a basinet. Olivia jumped to her feet from where she had been sitting on the floor. Ran to the glass, pressed her hands against it.

Remington ran to the glass and did the same, then waited until she rushed behind her, lifted the child and brought her forward, displaying his daughter for the first time to him. He dimly registered a speaker set into the window. He pressed a button and said, "She's absolutely precious!"

"Meet Hayden," Olivia said, her voice choking up.

"I'm so glad you're safe."

"And I knew…knew you'd be alive. Are you…?" His wife's eyes looked behind him, and registered fright, seeing the general zombie. Then she mouthed something in a low whisper: giving him the real message. *We are in absolute hell. Get us out, Anyway. Anyhow.*

He opened his mouth to say something else when DeKirk's remote-controlled zombie slapped its cracked hand over the speaker button.

"Enough!" The voice was back. "Lead the Pod 6 residents back to their unit, now."

Remington heard a clicking sound and then a door in the glassed-in room opened and a hefty bear of a zombie man stomped into the space and grunted at Olivia, pointing toward the open door from which he had come.

It frightened Remington to no end that she seemed resolved to the fact of this obtrusive action and did not try to linger for even an extra second, but scooted to obey at once. With just one last fleeting glance for help, as if so afraid of what would happen she didn't comply instantly with the slightest order. The door slammed and then he was alone again with the remotely operated zombie, and the corporal with his head down, almost finally out of shame perhaps.

"Where are they being taken?" Remington asked Baal, but directed his fury at McGee.

"That is up to you, Major. Are you ready to tell us what we want to know? If so, then they're being taken upstairs to be released to you. If not..." The zombie made a clucking sound while shaking its head, swinging saliva onto the floor. "...they will spend their time in one of the rooms you saw upstairs. Your daughter...well, infants really aren't much use to us for years, so... But your wife, she is obviously of good breeding stock, and her potential won't be wasted."

Images of Remington's cohorts in the Resistance movement flashed across his mind, their faces frozen in time, to some pivotal moment for each of them, where they had just risked their lives for a milestone in the war to save humanity. But it was no contest. He had to do anything to get his family out of here. He would give his own life at this point if he could, and so giving up one of the remaining factions was something he regretted but saw no way to avoid.

"I'm ready to talk."

The zombie tilted its head, as if not expecting the response. "Excellent, Major. Tell me, where can I find the leadership of the faction known as Southern Wolves?"

Remington stared at the zombie, stared as if he could see DeKirk right though its lifeless eyeballs. This request came as no surprise, although Remington had hoped the name would have escaped DeKirk so far. South Wolf was the crown jewel of his remaining factions, the strongest by far. Remington was about to speak and then hesitated. What could he do if he gave up the information and DeKirk didn't let his family out? He could keep demanding more, another piece of info, just one more piece, and then of course the risk—that they would never be freed, and instead suffer a fate worse than death here.

He had to buy a little more time to formulate a plan. He had a lot of mentally stored intel he'd gathered so far by carefully observing things as he moved through the facilities, by maintaining peak situational awareness. He just needed a few minutes to think through it all, to analyze it and come up with some sort of strategy for what to do if DeKirk didn't play ball.

"Major Remington? You said you were ready?"

One stalling tactic perhaps.

"I'm ready, but I will only divulge the information directly to President DeKirk himself. Not this undead husk. You, DeKirk. In person."

14.

As far as labs went, this back room of the local Colorado Springs CVS Pharmacy on 6th Avenue was a little light on the high-tech equipment and the resources Arcadia had been used to in her state-of-the-art lab back in Atlanta, but it would have to do for now. She had doubled back after Veronica's gambit-sacrifice had given her time and bought her freedom. But Arcadia hadn't survived this long, and at the experienced agent's side, without learning a few tricks. She knew DeKirk had eyes everywhere, that she wouldn't get far on the main road, wouldn't make it another day in fact if she just continued being predictable.

At the first chance, she had done a U-turn, found a burnt-out, deserted section of whatever town this had been, then found a vehicle with the keys still inside. After waiting for dusk, and ensuring the coast was clear, she turned around and doubled back to find a southward-heading road, hopefully parallel to the main highway. In short time, she saw the mountains and the relic of Colorado Springs nestled in the valley, and then waited until nightfall. She coasted the rest of the way, carefully avoiding pockets of roaming zombies, and of course the few zones of lights—soldier camps where the humans were doing anything except protecting the citizens. More like rounding up survivors or eliminating threats to the new world order.

She had seen enough of that on her cross country trek. Certainly there had been bright spots—ordinary humans elevated into roles of surprising heroism and courage. Sometimes all for naught, and too often Arcadia and Veronica had to wish them the best and hope they could hold out and stay out of sight, but knowing that unless she could succeed, the world would be littered with the corpses of such heroes.

All the more reason she had to do this, had to find the solution, at all costs. The car ditched several blocks away, she had stealthily moved through the shadows, and found her way by starlight as the black behemoths of the Rockies shrouded her western flank and the desolate buildings of downtown stood in mute appreciation of her efforts to the east.

This drugstore was perfect. One entrance, which she barred upon entry, shelves still stocked with over-the-counter drugs, first aid, and of course...junk food. After binging on Cheez-Its and Gatorade, she almost paid the ultimate price. In her haste, she hadn't checked behind the counter at the pharmacy. Given her previous job, that area should have been her first stop, but she had let two days of hunger rule over her brain, and the undead female pharmacist laid dormant back there until Arcadia's crunching and swallowing sounds had woken the ravenous monster.

She cringed, still counting her blessings that she had just used her knife to cut open the bag of Cheez-Its to save time, and it was right there in reach, to snatch up and jab the rushing zombie in the jawbone before those jagged fangs could lock on her flesh.

The better news was that her stroke hadn't killed the thing, only dazed it. Thinking fast, realizing this was a gift, another test subject delivered right into her hands; it could save her the dangerous effort of going back out there to rope one in. She quickly rolled around, got behind the lurching thing and before the previous pharmacist could get up, Arcadia slashed and severed both of her Achilles tendons, nearly separating the feet altogether.

Now the thing could crawl, but it wasn't very effectively chasing her. She went to the next aisle and gathered supplies—duct tape, gauze and an extension cord. Now the zombie pharmacist was tied to the chair in the back, gauze and duct tape secure in its mouth (so it wouldn't be phoning friends for help), and her wrists were bound behind her back.

Arcadia looked at the muzzled zombie and admired her work, the thing that had until recently been a soccer mom maybe, or an upstanding member of the local PTA. She was lean, fit, probably a jogger or Pilates fan, maybe yoga three times a week with the other suburban moms. Now, this creature before her was a different species altogether: a monstrous killing machine, part ancient lizard DNA, part modern horror story.

And she was going to either cure it or find a faster way of dispatching it.

One way or another, and nothing else mattered. Nothing. She had to face it now, she was changed. These three months...the last time she looked in the mirror she had no idea who was looking back at her. At first she thought she saw a reflection of her old boyfriend, Xander Dyson. His calculating genius, his ruthless cruelty, his win-at-all-costs mentality. Maybe it had always been there.

The zombie attempted to snap at her, missing by a foot, and Arcadia barely noticed. Scalpel in one hand, syringe in the other, she was somewhere else, lost in the past...

A filthy, dust-bowl of a village in Uganda. Armed soldiers everywhere, a perimeter blocked by jeeps. A helicopter circling overhead. Arcadia looking out from the medical tent, sweating like she never imagined, boiling in her own private hell inside the CDC-issued bio-hazard suit. So tired, and surrounded by beds...all of them occupied by villagers in various stages of Ebola.

"No one gets out," she says again to no one in particular, to everyone, to the guards. She sees their eyes, all of them on her, all day; all night. Even the kids, they're the worst. The elderly—they understand, they know their fate, but the young ones? How do you explain this is all for the greater good? No, they can't slip out and go run over that hill back to their homes and see their brothers and sisters, their moms and dads. No, kids, you just have to lay there and die, suffering because some asshole warlord intercepted our last shipment of medical supplies and we can't even make you comfortable in your final hours.

No, you will die here, you will all perish, then we'll burn your bodies, incinerate your clothes and toys, and then pack up and go home. Quarantine served its purpose and this damn disease contained—at the expense of just you hapless lot.

A rattling sound and a crash as the zombie-mom lurched against her bonds in one more vain attempt at freedom, only serving to pull Arcadia back to the moment. She shook her head, trying to free herself from the phantoms of the past. From Uganda, where she did what she had to do and had no regrets, only nightmares. She had been rewarded for her dedication, and for her methods—traits and strength of will that led her to the position as head of the CDC, where almost immediately the worst-case-scenario had fallen into her lap. Maybe it was punishment for her affiliation with Dyson, maybe karma had come back to bite her hard, but she wasn't about to change.

"I had no choice," she told soccer-mom-pharmacist, who only growled and wheezed and thrashed in a rebuttal.

"Had to do it, everything... That kid... Zephyr." Arcadia held the syringe up, staring at the liquid—and her reflection—inside. "He was slowing us down." Arcadia focused back on the pharmacist. "Don't look at me like that, you would have done the same thing. Veronica would have done everything to save him, that's just how she is. She would have, and the whole mission could have been screwed. Had to be done."

She shook her head. "Same difference, same result. Only move if we wanted to live."

Sighing, she turned her eyes away from the accusatory glare of the mindless creature, her test subject. "Don't...you'll never understand what it's been like. What I've had to do. What I...could have done. Xander was my fault."

She looked up now and with her free hand grabbed the bloody mass of once-fine auburn hair and yanked the pharmacist's head backward, exposing the neck right under the crimson gouge she had formed in the woman's face.

"I could have stopped him. Too lost back then, too naïve, too trusting. I'll never, *ever* make that mistake again."

She plunged the needle in deep and pressed the stopper down.

"I can't let everyone—whoever's left—down again."

She released the hair and stepped back as the creature thrashed and thrashed and shook like it was about to explode from every pore and every cell...subsiding finally under Arcadia's muted observation, after a few minutes, then snarling and snapping again as if nothing had happened.

Arcadia prepared another dose after fussing with the chemicals, calibrating and re-measuring, before offering a weak smile to her patient. "Ready for Round 2?"

15.

Springfield

Alex felt like a VIP, or head of state, in the middle of four soldiers and the general, guns trained in all directions as they hustled through the compound. Gunfire from right next to his ear, and he spun around in time to see two zombies (at least he hoped they were zombies) with their brains scattered on the wall behind them just as they had started to give chase.

Nice shooting, Alex thought.

"Keep moving!" General Hughes fired off two more pops. Alex looked, but in the jumble of camouflaged bodies ahead, along with the flickering lights down here, he could only make out shambling figures up ahead. One more lurching fast into view only to be cut down just as fast.

"Where the hell are we going?" Alex hoped the answer was, 'into an awaiting Apache chopper,' but instead all got was more gunfire and the men behind him shoving him forward. They rounded a corner and Hughes made a fist, bringing everyone to a halt.

What now? Alex stood on his toes to look over the bulky shoulders of the three men ahead, and wished he didn't.

"Raptors are free," Hughes said in a nonchalant voice as he put away his pistol and withdrew a larger revolver. "Switch to high-impact, armor-piercing ammo."

The men removed magazines and snapped new ones into place, just as the raptors feigned an approach, then dropped back, and a flood of zombies burst around them and charged. Men, women, ragged clothes, business suits, all manner of physiques, all with one thing in common: bloodlust and very sharp teeth…

\#

Alex cursed again that he hadn't been trusted to hold a gun. Just as the onslaught came at them and both guards at his back had turned to lend their support, Alex tried to scream over the blaring retorts: *this is their ploy, the true threat isn't the frontal assault, but they're coming from…*

Behind.

A door burst open and two more raptors came out as fast as they could wriggle through, fighting over each other, one with a badly decomposed left arm and chunks missing from its knee, the other with its skull plate visible beside a mostly-chewed off face. Light glinted off its cranial plate, but its teeth matched those of its mate as it opened wide and rushed them from behind.

We're done.

Two possible scenarios of survival came to his mind. One involved ripping a weapon away from the closest marine, the other involved dropping and playing dead. Neither had much hope of success, but he was out of options.

Until—a door he hadn't noticed just to his right opened up, a snarling face appeared, freed to join the fray.

Better than forward or back, Alex thought. He charged the zombie, going in low and using the thing's momentum to flip it over his back—into the path and jaws of an onrushing raptor. He heard a monstrous sound of flesh and bone rending, then more gunshots and screams, hissing and growls, then he was through the door and into what he gratefully found to be another enormous space.

A silo? Massive containers here and there, propped against the walls, a huge cylindrical storage unit in the center, and again everything flanked by large pillars. A forklift was nearby, along with flatbed trucks and golf carts parked carefully in spots, as if decorum and procedure were still vital in keeping up this place, here at the End of Days.

Minimal lighting, but enough to see he wasn't alone. A makeshift prison had been constructed out of metal fencing and posts, and secured what looked to be about a dozen former employees inside. Ragged, hopeless. Had it been months they'd been locked up? Questions swirled, and Alex didn't have time to ponder them, much less make sense of the captives' condition: one glimpse was enough. They were starved, and the smell…masked partly by the dead down here, but certainly these were people saved for experiments or for bargaining chips. He thought briefly of the arena and the mad doctor, and shuddered.

He'd do something about freeing them soon, but first…

The door—

The raptor had made short work of its prey, not realizing or caring it wasn't the original target. Once its hunger activated, there was no stopping it. Rearing its head, blood and gristle flowing from its jaws, those dead eyes locked on Alex.

No chance to shut that door, no chance but to run...

Bullets riddled the monster's throat and lanced off its jaw and sent it thrashing to the side, perhaps saved from a brain-shot. Another human zombie was kicked back and another toppled as bits of its head landed beside its body.

General Hughes shouldered into a snapping raptor, kicked another human zombie, and then backed into the room. He emptied the M5 clip as others came charging into view.

Alex could only assume the worst for the other soldiers; caught in the gauntlet, they were likely shredded mincemeat, but the general had made it through...and he needed help. Alex looked around and started running before he even had a plan. Or maybe the plan was there already the moment he saw the forklift.

\#

What seemed like a minute later, but really much less, after he got the motor going and recalled how easy one of these things was to drive, Alex was rumbling toward the door, where Hughes had dropped the spent M5 and had dropped to one knee, firing with two .45s, slapping down zombie after zombie in precise headshots, while taking a few potshots at the raptors, who were cautiously darting back and forth into view, content to let their human shields take the brunt of the assault while they waited for the perfect time to burst through.

Alex wasn't about to give them that chance. There was another door in here, out the back, but fortunately these things didn't have the coordination to figure that out, or there wasn't time. The assault was here, and if Alex and Hughes were going to make it, in order to release these captives and have a chance down here, they had to do this.

"Move it, General!"

Hughes glanced back, took it in with a look of bemused surprise, then fired off three rounds into a raptor's cranium, ducking to the side as Alex rumbled through. He raised the forklift arms and accelerated toward the gruesome pile of corpses. The two forks punched through ribcages, skulls and organs; he moved the pile a few yards until the width of the forklift rammed into the reinforced doorframe and jammed hard.

The bullet-ridden raptor popped up and snapped its jaws between the bars, reaching into the cockpit. Alex ducked and the teeth snapped at empty air. Three sets of hands reached out past the leathery body and another hungry raptor tried to climb it. Soon, the bottleneck was massive and unbreakable, a huge pile of human and raptor flesh and bone and snapping teeth, but nothing could wriggle past the initial dinosaur with its body caught in the forklift aperture and wedged within the doorframe.

Alex pulled away from the stare of death he found himself locked in with the raptor. Those hideous eyes, devoid of even animal cruelty and instinct, entirely vacant and haunted, bristling with nothing but alien hunger. He dropped and slid out of the seat, hit the floor and rolled back to the general who stood there, admiring his work. Hughes reached into his pack, pulled out a couple clips of ammo and hammered them home before tossing Alex a .45.

"Wow, guess I've finally earned a seat at the big boy table?"

"Don't get cocky. This ain't over yet."

#

"What the hell is this place?" Alex asked as they backed away from the door and toward the pens where a few captives stirred, some hope showing in their eyes.

"Use your imagination," Hughes said. "And then imagine a lot worse."

"Got to get them out."

"Be my guest, but they're safe now. I'd vote for after you take care of the bigger problem."

"We could arm them—every body is a help."

"They can't fight, can barely stand."

Alex eyed the occupants of the cage, and shuddered but had to agree. "We'll come back for you," he said as his heart cracked and he couldn't bear to make eye contact. A young woman looked up at him through grimy hair, and before she could talk, General Hughes pulled him aside.

"We have to move, now. I just lost six men, and alarms are all going crazy and you and I are public enemies number one and two. Come on, there's another way out. I think I can take us the back way through the delivery tunnels to get to the lab."

"Lab?" Alex followed as quickly as he could, briefly glancing back at the captives and wishing he hadn't. "Don't we want the control room?" He imagined them overriding security measures, opening the exterior doors or flooding the vents with zombie killing dust.

"No, too late for that, and we wouldn't stand a chance. DeKirk has a small army inside here, all programmed to his whims."

"So...? What's our play?"

Hughes stopped at the back door. "Let me ask you first, what was your play coming here?"

"Killing DeKirk," he said flatly. "One way or another, I know we have to cut off the head if this damn scourge is going to end."

Hughes stared him down. "Let me ask you again, do you have a chance, after that, of curing this thing? Or is it all just a mad effort to punch a giant wall and make yourself feel better?"

Alex thought hard, then nodded. "The truth? Yes, we have a shot. A long one, but we have the head of the CDC, who believes with the right resources she can either fix this thing, or at least prevent it from spreading."

Hughes searched his eyes. "Good enough for me."

He pushed through the door and into a hallway, first checking it, then waving Alex forward.

"Hold on," Alex said, "you didn't answer me. Why the lab?"

"Because we have to counter DeKirk's influence, and that means...well, I'm not sure what it means but the answer is in there. I'm just not sure we would like the question that needs to be asked."

Alex followed, more confused, and went through another door, ducking inside just as he heard a hissing and scrambling sound from around the next corner. This room—some sort of kitchen and food prep area—wasn't quite empty, but if the young raptor gnawing at a fresh kill in the corner was supposed to be a surprise attacker, it failed in its role. Alex and Hughes both fired at once, cleanly punching huge holes in the thing's head, just above the right eye.

Armor-piercing rounds, nice. Alex wanted to gloat over the carcass of the thing whose ilk had caused him such horror and pain recently, but Hughes kept him moving. Out a service exit and through a series of bewildering moves, door after door, fighting a few more times, engaging when necessary.

"In here," Hughes said, reloading as he reached the end of a long hall with a series of flickering lights. The general seemed to be faltering, Alex noted over the long minute they traversed the corridor. More than he would have expected for a man of his size and physique. They had passed a state-of-the-art fitness center, and Alex imagined the general and his men had put in quite a few hours in there over the years. But something was clearly wrong with the man now. Exhaustion possibly, but...

"Hold on," Hughes said in a hushed voice, with his fist up. "I'm surprised this isn't more heavily defended, so be ready."

"Maybe you were right," Alex hoped. "They think we're going for the control room and have everyone guarding it."

"Let's hope." Gun trained on the door, Hughes got his keycard ready to swipe, but first...

"What's wrong?"

Hughes sagged against the door. "Kid, I ain't been entirely honest with you."

Alex shifted his aim, lining the general's face up in his sights. "Talk."

Closing his eyes, Hughes took a deep breath and shifted slightly, then lifted his left arm.

"Oh shit." Alex lowered the gun, slightly. "Is that—?"

"I wish I could say it was a bullet wound, friendly fire or just a knick from a stray knife thrust, but no."

That side of the camouflage jacket was a bloody mess, and Alex could make out at least two puncture sites. "Raptor bite?"

Hughes nodded wearily. "Not going to make it much longer, kid. So what we have to do in there is going to be a little...unorthodox."

"What are you talking about?"

"I swore an oath to this country and to its people. Screw the current 'Commander in Chief.' I can't do nothin' about him right now, but I can see to it that you can."

"That's all I want," Alex said, lowering the gun the rest of the way. "But how? He's not even here, and from what I can tell he's still got a near monopoly on controlling these monsters."

Hughes coughed, then let out a wheezing sound that made Alex cringe. *How much time did he have?* It varied by person, and maybe some other factors of transmission and host resistance, but Alex couldn't take many chances. They had to move this along, as bad as he felt for the man. Still, he admired the dedication, and the sacrifice he knew was coming.

Motioning to the door with his keycard, Hughes coughed. "In there, the doc and DeKirk...they perfected what he is now. Played with the sequencing of the prion, altered its chemistry, some sort of molecular genetic bullshit." Coughed again, and now black veins were bulging on his neck, spreading to his temples.

Alex glanced back, probing the flickering shadows in the corridor, afraid any moment a surge of undead would come loping their way.

"So how does that help us?" Even as he asked it, Alex thought he might have the answer.

"I was going to do it myself," Hughes said, "assuming I could figure it out and I was a proper host. But now...it's too late. Once infected, it won't work. I remember hearing the basics, and the only way DeKirk managed it was to infect himself with the prion-along with the controlling agent—*together*. Wouldn't work after the fact."

"So..."

"So kid, you're not infected."

"No, and I'm not about to be."

"Think about it." Coughing again, the veins spreading—and with them the skin toughening, turning sickly yellow. Wouldn't be long now.

"Sometimes, like right the hell now, the only way to stop a monster is..."

"*...to become one?*" Alex shook his head. "No way, I..."

"May have no other choice. Listen, I was going to do it. It would have been perfect—I already had the control over my soldiers. They would still follow me, and if I could then also control these dinosaur fuckers and all those other rabid zombie bastards out there, pull them away from DeKirk's control—"

"How do you do that? How exactly would this work?"

"I honestly don't know. It was a long shot, but short of wresting the nuke controls back and finding a way to herd all the zombies into one city and mushroom cloud 'em all to hell, along with our asshole president, this was all I got. I kind of hoped I'd just figure it out."

"Was anyone else on board? Obviously not Jules."

"No, but Wilford could be. He'll follow whichever way the stronger wind blows. And you better get him on board, priority one after...you do this..."

He sagged again, then shook his head, wheezing. "Got to happen now. Going in, clearing the room, and then—it's your show, kid."

"Wait—!"

The general swiped the card, and with his dwindling strength of humanity, kicked open the door, barged in and started firing.

#

The room was cleared and the door shut and locked before Alex could even find a target. Efficient to the end, General Hughes lowered his gun, stumbled to the center lab station—a great stainless steel table set in the middle of various counters, track lighting, overhead flat screens, and a large centrifuge beside microscopes and other high-tech biological equipment. He gave a last view to the three bodies in here he had just put down: two loyalist scientists (Alex presumed they were loyal, anyway), and a muscle-bound zombie sentinel, one that had failed in its task.

"You're up," General Hughes spoke, the words coming out as a rasping drone. He pointed with the gun to the centrifuge. "Doc Nietzman kept a sample, the one thing he hid from DeKirk, as a little insurance. I knew about it, and said nothing since...well, we needed an insurance policy. I had it protected, guarded. Not sure if what it does would be a permanent thing, and I think we were both waiting to see what happens with our leader, but it seems to be having the intended effect."

"Nastiness, immortality. Megalomania?"

"Maybe your CDC doc can help you in your…conversion and maybe if you're successful in taking DeKirk down, I don't know…"

"Maybe she can reverse it?"

Hughes nodded, hacking now. He looked up, then toward Alex's location with eyes that were completely reptilian now, set below a protruding brow lined with veins spreading the prion, killing the host in order to quickly regenerate it.

"Good luck, kid."

Alex tried to move, thought he should say something at least, maybe confine him and hope to get a cure, maybe…

Hughes brought the gun to his mouth and squeezed the trigger.

And Alex stepped over the body, approaching the centrifuge.

Before he could even contemplate what to do next, movement on one of the screens caught his eye.

It took only a moment to register. The scene was from outside the door. The long corridor. The gunfire must have alerted the guards to where they were, that this was the destination and not the control room.

Raptors led the way, followed by a jam-packed hallway full of thrashing undead,

He was out of time.

#

Grabbed the syringe, prepped it.

Shit, here goes…

Jammed it into his arm—just as the TV screen above flickered and the face of his enemy appeared.

"Ah, there you are!"

With a shift in DeKirk's eyes toward the herd rushing with ravenous hunger toward the helpless prey, the raptors stopped short, feet away from Alex, who turned slightly, finished the injection and then let the syringe drop, out of DeKirk's sight. *Can't let him know. And then just…*

He nearly crumpled in agony, a feeling like someone just twisted a barbed plumbing snake into his veins and shoved hard.

All he could do was drop to a fetal position, feigning fear and imminent death—which wasn't at all a deception—while he endured the agony, lest DeKirk sense anything.

"Sorry I couldn't witness your devouring in person, my dear boy, but I had to get out of that stuffy hellhole and enjoy a little cruise while your world dies."

The raptors wheezed slowly, their heavy heads bobbing up and down with impatient malice, their fangs dripping saliva and blood from Hughes' men.

"But this is just as good. A ringside seat, something I'll record and savor. Oh, and I'll be sure to let your spy girlfriend watch it over and over while I consume her flesh inch by inch."

Alex's head turned sharply, his eyes glaring, hands in fist. "No..."

"Oh yes, she's been captured and on her way to see me as we speak. It'll be such a pleasant reunion, I can hardly wait. Starving as I am."

Fury bubbled over in every cell of his body, mixing and streaming with the new reagent, amplifying, accelerating the effect and dulling the pain. Alex didn't even think about what it was doing to him, didn't think that he had just hastened his death sentence. All he cared about was loosing his fury on DeKirk, imagining no separation, no distance. The monster was right before him, and in animalistic bloodlust, Alex launched himself at the monitor, leaping onto the table and then crashing arms and headfirst into the shocked visage of DeKirk, just as it shattered. The screen exploded in burst of sparks, transistors, plastic and glass.

Alex roared through it, landed beside Hughes' body, then turned and sprang to his feet, ready to meet the rush of the raptors and four more raging zombie soldiers.

Fists raised, he felt the change rush over him.

Felt the fury abate just as suddenly as it had come, felt it replaced by something else: an awareness, a fullness of space and a connection to parts of himself that were alien, distant and yet close. An affinity and a bond at once formed through conscious thought, through spreading pheromones and a pulsing biological communication pattern that lit up in his brain, now energized and changed.

The first raptor hit him hard and low and knocked him onto his back, then leapt on his chest and lowered its jaws.

Alex calmly locked onto its eyes and lifted his head...lifted, straining his neck until he was eye to eye, until his nose was up against its snout, until the blood dripped from those huge fangs onto Alex's lips—and he greedily licked up each drop as he reached up with his right hand and grasped the raptor's throat. With his left hand he splayed his fingers and held them up, and the motion stopped the other raptor in its tracks and halted the rest of the zombie assault.

Sliding out from under the tamed raptor, Alex gently tugged on its neck, then turned its head, allowing the body to follow suit. Never losing eye contact, Alex stared it down until he reached past the alien darkness, past the rage and the pain of millions of years of unfulfilled hunger, and he whispered (or thought) assurances of satiation, of connection, of trust and finally...of guidance.

There was another force in there, another loyalty, but it was weak. As if once met and established, then departed with but a contingent element left behind as a slight means of control. Alex found it, left it in place but took over other aspects, offering immediacy and issuing his own order:

"Follow me, and let no harm come to me."

Holy shit, a resurging part of Alex thought. *It's working. I don't know how, but it's working!*

Petting the raptor on its rotting, wounded neck, gently caressing the recent bullet holes, Alex let the beast meet up with its mate, and then the three of them walked calmly through the crowd of zombie humans. Their eyes followed Alex. Their chests eerily still, with no breath, no motion. He could feel their confusion in this turn of events: their hunger denied, a feeding cancelled. That would have to be rectified if he were to retain this tenuous hold, but for now...

I'm safe. I'm one of them. Sort of...I think.

He had to figure out exactly what he was now, had to fulfill whatever General Hughes believed he could do with this power. Had to challenge DeKirk and end this, but... He had to get the hell out of here and rescue Veronica. There wasn't much time. DeKirk surely thought he was dead, and Veronica was going to meet a gruesome fate if he couldn't get to her first.

Yet there was still an opportunity here. He was still in the heart of the seat of power, the shadow government running what was left of the United States. Surely that meant something.

He picked up the pace.

Time to meet the next in line…

16.

On the Mississippi, nearing New Orleans

Veronica had lost track of the time. She worried about a concussion, drifting in and out of consciousness, and upon the brief moments of waking, made sure to check herself for bites, or infection. Dimly she'd been aware of the slight motion of a plane, of pressure drops, of that monstrous general, still wearing that Viking-like helmet and glaring unblinking at her with hideous eyes in a misshapen face. It was nighttime, so likely they were flying back into it, back to the Midwest or East Coast, wherever DeKirk was, and the only thing Veronica grasped to keep a glimmering touch of hope was the thought that at least she was heading back toward Alex.

Landing…

She tried to rise out of the chair, tried to move but found her ankles bound. The general leaned forward and his eyes blinked finally, and focused, and the dried, blood-caked lips parted—but it was DeKirk's voice, tainted and echoing for sure, but unmistakably his—that issued out. "Won't be long now, my dear. You'll get your wish. We'll meet in person."

"What's left of you," she said.

"Oh, you'll find I'm much, much more."

"Lucky me."

The general grinned, and those extra rows of shark-fin-shaped teeth inched ever closer to her lips. "Indeed. And lucky me, I haven't had a human visitor in far too long. At least, one that didn't last through dinner. I hope to take my time with you."

Veronica shuddered. The cockpit door opened and the lights came on. Still, she had to keep up her strength and resolve, no matter how dire her future was now. Had to keep believing her gambit would pay off, that Arcadia would find a cure, that Alex and Remington would somehow find a way to fight back and end this apocalypse before it ended them.

"So can I ask what's on the menu, and the topic of dinner conversation?" She tried to match the general's grin. "I'm famished and could really use a nice eggplant parm, maybe some crab cake appetizer. Where are we, by the way?"

The general pulled back, grabbed her by the wrist and hauled her up, then over his shoulder like a limp doll. "No more talk. You'll find out soon enough."

He stomped toward the exit of the small executive jet, jarring Veronica's head with every step. "But yes," came the cackling voice, "there will be crab cakes."

#

A sternwheeler riverboat? Veronica wasn't sure she hadn't hit her head harder than she remembered. Her ankles finally freed, now her wrists were bound behind her back. As the general dragged her out of the jeep, she stepped into the thick humidity and onto a boardwalk dock flanked by two thick sycamores.

Except they weren't sycamores.

Her primal senses triggered, and she almost collapsed in fear.

Cryolophosaurs. Two of them. Silent, tense, but unmoving as if they were trained dogs awaiting their master's command.

Show of force, she thought, duly impressed and yet unable to shake the fear. She knew it wasn't going to end now, not when DeKirk had other plans for her, but this was what it was—pure and simple.

She turned her head to the general. "Color me impressed, and put in my place." She nodded toward the waiting boat where now she could make out the figure standing at the end of the boarding plank, arms crossed, draped in shadow. A host of cicadas struck up a song, full of trepidation and menace, likely sensing the presence of something primordial and out of place, the intrusion of a nightmare into their realm.

Under her breath, as she was pushed ahead and shuffled along the plank, feeling the hungry eyes of the cryos on her with every step, she muttered, "I'm still going to kill you."

"Welcome to my mobile command center," DeKirk called out in a voice resonating with power and lordship, dominating the landscape, silencing the cicadas and stilling the breeze. "My home away from home, my throwback to the days of old, to the sweeping advance of civilization that once was, and to the return of the good old days." He made a mock bow as she approached. "Be it ever so humble."

Veronica paused, sensing something moving behind the great wheel. The waters stirred, and in the gloom punctuated by lights stirred something immense—a glimpse of an aquatic monstrosity that shouldn't be.

Pets on land, pets below the waves. She wanted to take in everything, the defenses, the armaments, and the location. Not that it likely mattered, but she was going to cling to a hope that she could survive this. She had to, she would see Alex again, and she would stand over DeKirk's corpse, watch it burn, and then spread the ashes over the rebirth of this civilization he had tried to annihilate.

For now, though, she continued walking, head high until she stood before him.

"At last," he said, bowing again. "You got your wish. How long had you been searching for me?"

"Too goddamn long." She tried to smile. "I imagined it differently."

"No doubt with an army of Kevlar-wearing agents backing you up, with automatic weapons trained on my head."

"Would have been nice."

"Sorry to disappoint. Bet you didn't imagine undead dinosaurs—and at my command."

Her eyes flashed again to the waters behind the wheel, and the circular current caused by the creature beneath the surface. "Nope. And definitely not here in…where the hell are we? Louisiana?"

"The Big Easy! Not far in fact. Always wanted to stroll down Bourbon Street, a little early for Mardi Gras, but the Day of the Dead…well, it's pretty much every day these days, wouldn't you agree?"

Veronica stared at him until the scaly flesh and the haunting yellow eyes and his throbbing veins across his forehead made her glance away. "Well, let's get on with this, unless you're going to show a girl a good time and break out the wine and crab appetizers and stroll the deck during a leisurely night cruise?"

"Maybe later," DeKirk said, motioning her aboard. "We have much to discuss, and I'm sure you're exhausted from all that traveling, hiding and killing you've been doing."

"No thanks to you."

"How's that been going for you?" he asked, still grinning as she boarded and paused at the threshold.

Screw this. Only getting one chance, and who knows what's down there in his cabin. Better to go out fighting.

She tensed her fists, letting her wrists relax against their bonds. She didn't need them free for this, and the likelihood of victory was near nil, but...all the pain this man had caused. He had given the order for her fiancée's murder, he had hunted her and Alex relentlessly for months, killed Alex's father and mother and unleashed this unimaginable hell upon humanity...all while safely locked away in a bunker, biding his time until his bid to assume the mantle of leadership. Running the very country he had brought down.

Someone had to strike back, and no one wanted it more. Maybe that would count for something.

Stepping in on her left foot, she bent slightly and tried to see everything as if in slow motion, planning her next moves in case this worked. The general was four steps behind her, moving slowly, and behind him, the two dinosaurs, heads bowed, snorted to themselves and restlessly stayed put. Then there was the thing in the water, and the sense of more movement ahead, along the deck, and below, where surely other zombies waited, a security contingent at least.

But this was the best shot she might ever have.

She launched into the air, angling toward DeKirk, tucked her legs then brought them straight down on his left kneecap. All her weight and both feet catching him right in the meniscus at an angle. She heard a snap and a surprised grunt and DeKirk crumpled.

Didn't see that coming, did you?

On his way down Veronica funneled all her rage, called up a vision of her fiancée (merged with Alex), and realized she was doing this for him now, because he was her future, her present, and everything this monster in front of her had all but destroyed. Arms back, fists clenched together, she twisted and then struck upwards in a great blow with all her strength. It connected with the side of DeKirk's jaw and she followed through like a major league batter. DeKirk spun with the impact and his head thunked against the railing post.

Her elation was short lived, and even as she prepared once more, hoping to duck low, then lift him up—and over the side, maybe enraging the thing down there to involuntarily consume whatever was tossed in its direction—a huge hand caught her shoulder. Undead fingers dug into her muscle, a deathly vile breath wafted over her face and suddenly she was slammed against the cabin door, the general bending his teeth to her neck.

Suddenly the weight was off and DeKirk was there, twice as menacing, somehow fine again on his shattered knee (or was it healed)? With a casual one-handed toss, he sent the general somersaulting back down the boarding plank, where he landed at the feet of the snarling, snapping cryos. Veronica's scream was cut off as an enraged DeKirk lifted her by the throat—up over his head, above the very railing over which she had hoped to flip him.

He hung her there, gripping her under the chin in a vise-hold while he whispered something ancient and melodic that she could barely make out over her gasping. Her legs kicked out frantically twenty feet over the black water—where a surging of bubbles announced the rise of something out of Dante's nightmares.

A leviathan of pure undead terror. Teeth and red eyes, rotting, stringy flesh and a gaping maw full of bony protrusions, bubbling, bloody froth, half-digested human remains clinging to jagged, broken teeth.

It was hungry, and it wanted this offering.

"Bitch," DeKirk hissed. "I should feed it your legs first, then your thighs and hips, leave you half a woman then bring you back to my cabin so I can devour the rest while you watch."

"Aghh," she tried to say, and her courage was gone as she felt herself lifted just in time and heard the snapping of undead jaws below, and a wicked splash that drenched her and DeKirk and half the boat.

He hauled her back over, then pulled her close to his face. "I've already healed your attempted assault. Bones back in original form, and nothing bruised but my ego." He took a deep breath, then relaxed his hold on her neck. "Won't make the mistake again of letting you move, but tell me, do you feel better now? Got your shot in?"

"M…much," she said.

"I'm glad that's out of the way. Now," he spun her around and shoved her toward the mahogany stairs leading down to his cabin.

"Let's begin the true festivities. I hope your throat isn't too sore, you'll be talking plenty soon enough."

17.

Nome, Alaska

Corporal McGee and the zombie called General Baal followed Major Remington out of Pod 6 and up into the same stairwell. Remington had bought a few precious minutes by requesting to speak with DeKirk in person, but what to do with them? As they passed one door and turned up another flight of steps, the major found it harder and harder to contain his growing sense of panic.

What had he been thinking? DeKirk wasn't going to simply release his wife and daughter to him and then let all three of them ride off happily into the sunset anymore than a *T. rex* was likely to drop him unharmed out of its jaws. At best, the very best, the three of them would be allowed to live together imprisoned in this thinly disguised work camp. He felt a sense of duty to the rest of society, too—what remained of it. To surrender himself to DeKirk would be a major blow to the freedom movement.

Then it dawned on him. This trip was never about the Resistance movement, was it? Sure, eliminating it would be the icing on the cake for DeKirk, but Major Remington—he *was* the cake, wasn't he? He was the highest-ranking surviving member of the former military, as well as the leader of the Resistance. Of course DeKirk wanted him either dead—*but he could have had the zombie do that back at the farmhouse in Missouri...*or even better, controlled.

So here he was, under the thumb of this remotely controlled zombie marching him up the stairs...*It's only going to get worse from here.* The zombie general's inhuman voice jarred Remington from his thoughts—

"Keep going, one more flight, take the next door."

—but not from his newfound direction. *It's up to you. You have to break out of here or it's game over for everybody.*

The major glanced ahead up the steps, where there was one more half-flight remaining until they reached a landing with the door through which they would exit. On that landing was a CCTV camera mounted high on the wall; there was one above each stairwell door, he had noticed, but not anywhere on the flights between floors. So this was his chance to act unobserved, and while it was still one-on-one. *Okay, two if you counted the pasty-faced punk sympathizer.* Now was as good as it was going to get if he was going to try anything. He decided to distract the zombie by asking an out-of-the-blue silly question so that they would be already distracted and confused when he made his move.

"So after our deal, will my family and I be in one of those nice high-rises, and have access to old Netflix streaming services? I need to finish binging on *Breaking Bad.*"

The general turned and frowned as he climbed the steps behind Remington. "I told you already, you will be able to—"

Remington whirled around and leapt, launching himself fast and hard against Corporal McGee. Against normal tactics, he was taking out the weaker opponent first; but not only that, he had observed how McGee wore his sidearm. Remington kept his focus unwavering on the pistol as he collided with the corporal. He knew Baal had only to bite him deeply but once in order to zombify him, so he wasn't going to risk anything in close range of that asshole. Instead, he pinned McGee back to the wall with his left arm, then relied on his muscle memory when it came to unsnapping a holster safety catch with one hand and slipping the gun free in a single smooth motion.

McGee was too surprised to do anything but gag and whimper—and close his eyes in terror as General Baal, his face a mask of frenzied bloodlust, roared toward them in the blink of an eye. The zombie was leaping now, in a complete disregard for its own safety, if it even held the concept of safety any longer, while it outstretched its arms and opened its jaws.

Remington slipped the gun into firing position with practiced ease even as Baal's fingertips brushed against his jacket sleeve. Jammed the barrel of the gun hard underneath the general's chin, under the helmet, ducked and released McGee, then pulled the trigger, instinctively turning his head away from the resulting spray of blood and gore. General Baal continued his motion, colliding with McGee and taking the corporal back down the stairs in a violent, somersaulting tumble, finally slamming McGee hard on the landing. The corporal's head cracked open and his stunned eyes clouded over, looking up at the general lying prone—and now absolutely dead—on top of him.

Composing himself, Remington got up from his crouch and quickly went down to drag the body back up the steps until he was sure it was outside the camera's field of view. He listened for reinforcements drawn by the single gunshot, but so far didn't hear anything. Bending down, trying not to look at McGee's eyes, he stripped the corporal of his utility belt. A quick examination showed he had just acquired, in addition to McGee's gun, a small fixed blade knife, a baton, a pair of handcuffs, and a two-way radio.

He hadn't acquired more time, though. That was slipping away fast. Remington jumped over the dead zombie-human pair and bolted back up the stairs to the door he had been about to enter with the general. He wanted to pause and listen at the door to see if he could hear anybody on the other side, but he was aware of the camera directly overhead. He tried to act like anyone moving with purpose to get up some stairs and onto the floor they needed without drawing attention.

Remington pulled on the door and his heart stopped when it refused to open. He glanced at the stenciled number again, confirming that it was the proper floor. Then he saw the retinal scanner set into the wall. He moved back down to the landing, suddenly enraged at being trapped in here, at the enormous scope of DeKirk's world takeover. He was getting out of here and taking his family with him. He still didn't know exactly how, but he was going to do it.

Back in the stairwell he grabbed the dead zombie and rolled him over, then knelt by Corporal McGee's body. "Sorry, asshole. I know you were probably just doing what you had to in order to survive, but...well, now so am I." He lifted the young man's head by the hair and tilted it forward. From the utility belt he pulled out the knife and—with revolting distaste—used it to scoop the right eyeball from the face. He tried to avoid getting too much blood on it, lest the machine not be able to read the iris pattern. Then he climbed the stairs, slapped the eyeball in front of the retinal scanner, and waited for what seemed like an eternity but in actuality was only three seconds before a light turned green and he heard a click.

#

Instead of turning left to go outside, Remington made his way to the right and deeper into the human housing complex on this level. On the inside of the security gate entrance, he'd noticed an electrical panel with labeling indicating it might be used to control the dinosaurs. Some kind of antenna installation mounted above it likely transmitted the signals, but the major knew there must be a master control station somewhere; the simple panel of buttons at the security gate was only to allow the guards to control the beasts. He had to find the master unit and destroy it. Neutralizing the threat of the raptor sentries and ptero air patrols would greatly enhance his chance of escape.

Thankfully, other than established checkpoints and isolated hubs of activity, the place was mostly deserted, even understaffed. Maybe Remington would be able to move about long enough to make something happen. He fast-walked through a semi-enclosed area consisting of a wall on his right side and open air on the left, with an overhang for a roof. Up ahead he could see that the walkway led back into the building, but on the right only a few feet away he saw a break in the wall. He ran to it.

A series of cages was set into the wall, an adult velociraptor in each one. They stamped their feet and hissed as Remington approached, but seemed to recognize there was nothing they could do, as they stopped short of flinging themselves at the bars. Examining the cages he could see that the entire front was set on a rolling track. He couldn't see a control for opening it, not that he'd want to in such close proximity to the zombified animals.

He continued down the walkway. He didn't know for sure, but his wife and daughter must have been taken up here somewhere. If, that is, DeKirk had any intention of even playing along like he would release them. Remington harbored no illusions that he'd be able to simply find them and slip out of here undetected, but at the same time, he'd feel mentally better once he was with them. Not only that, but Olivia might be able to furnish him with additional Intel, no doubt being more familiar with the layout than he was.

He pushed on toward a set of closed double doors that led into the building.

Immediately, a zombie-human guard turned around to see who was coming in. Fortunately, he was the only individual in the hallway. He appeared confused, clearly not recognizing Remington, but his eyes lingered on the radio on his belt which made him look like staff. Remington closed the gap fast and dispatched him almost silently with a blow to the back of the head, hopefully just knocking him out. They might need him later. He opened the nearest door, saw that it led into a small room with electrical and HVAC equipment, and dragged the guard inside.

Moving on down the hall, he spotted a sign over a door on the left marked CONTROL ROOM. This door had no handle and he spotted the retinal scanner mounted in the wall. He reached into his pocket, fished out the corporal's trophy and pressed it up against the scanner. A light flashed green and he pulled the door open softly.

A lab coat-wearing man sat in a wheeled swivel chair on a white tiled floor in front of a bank of computers and other electronic equipment. He was leaned over a monitor, apparently studying its screen intently. Remington grasped his knife (silence was his watchword whenever he could afford it, not to mention he had a limited number of rounds for the gun) and rushed toward the equipment operator. His target spun in his chair upon hearing the heavy footfalls of the major's approach, and drew a gun.

Damn, was everyone armed around here?

Remington had to change tactics. No knocking this one out. He moved faster than the tech's arm could bring up the gun, and slashed his knife sideways across the tech's jugular in one smooth motion. He even managed to stop him from falling over onto the floor, making less noise and making it easier to search him. A quick stab to the brain for good measure, then he relieved the man of his service pistol, glad to now have a backup. Nothing else the former human possessed interested him, except, that is, for his workstation.

Remington eyed the screen the technician had been staring at. A CCTV feed split into four panels, each showing a different sector of the HABITAT compound. Two offered views of indoor locations he didn't recognize with no one there, while the third had the main security gate he'd gone through earlier. The same two guards were there, and they didn't appear to be alerted to anything special. Yet. Remington knew it couldn't be long. The fourth was focused on the row of raptor cages he'd passed earlier. If this dead guy had seen him, he hadn't put out an alert. *Or had he?* Silent alarm?

He continued down the row of machines. A few feet further down the console, he found one of the things he was looking for. A row of controls labeled OPEN and CLOSE. He was guessing, but they probably opened the raptor cages. He flipped one of them OPEN and then moved to the video monitor to see if anything had changed.

One of the cages was now open, the raptor inside already more alert and hopping to the edge of its enclosure. Remington moved back to the joysticks and flipped all of them to OPEN. He needed a diversion.

Time to wreak some havoc in this place.

Another look at the machines in front of him and he was tempted to simply destroy them all, to indiscriminately rip out the wiring, smash the screens, shoot holes in all of it, but a cloud of reasoning floated through his panicked brain and he realized he could make things harder for himself by doing that. Lockdown all the doors, for example, sealing his family inside. No, he had to be careful with his actions. Next to the raptor controls was another set of controls consisting of a series of round black buttons. A label reading PATTERN INTERRUPT was taped above them.

Probably some kind of control pulse for the zombies. Or the dinosaurs. Remington hit all of the buttons. Whatever patterns were in place here, he needed to change them.

Unknown to him, outside the flock of ptero's ceased to turn when they reached the HABITAT wall and instead continued flying beyond the perimeter of the compound, temporarily under no control other than that afforded by their tiny prehistoric zombie brains.

The major was about to leave the room when one more section of controls caught his eye. Labeled MICROCHIPS, there were toggle switches numbered 1-24. All were all flipped up except for two of them. He flipped all of them to the down position and checked the CCTV for the main security gate again. One of the guards was now slumped in the booth against the wall while the other stood lifelessly nearby, shaking its head and apparently sniffing the air.

Good. Go, eat...

As he watched, a new form appeared on the screen. A raptor, moving fast. It wrapped its jaws around the standing guard's neck and stamped its powerful hind legs at the same time, then it was gone from view and only the headless body remained. Another raptor ran by the camera's field of view, into the compound.

Remington couldn't resist a wisp of a smile as he turned and fled the room. Finally, he'd managed to strike back, if just a little bit. He had to make the most of the momentum and get to his family while the small contingent of actual human guards was preoccupied with correcting the pandemonium he had caused.

He turned right, down the empty hall, fixated on a closed door at the end with a lighted sign above it reading, SECURE ENTRY. The major ran to the door and noted the retinal scanner. He was pulling the eyeball from his pocket when the door swung inward in front of him. A human soldier, decked out in full riot gear and armed with an AK-47, was shouting something into a radio. When he looked up and saw Remington, he dropped the radio and tried to raise his weapon, but the major's blade, thrown expertly like a dart, found the man's Adam's apple first. Remington ran up, tore and twisted the blade free, then relieved the dying man of his automatic rifle.

He stepped into the new space before the door could close again. Stenciled on the wall in red paint was HOLDING AREAS 1-3 with an arrow, and then on the opposite wall, HOLDING AREAS 4-6 with another arrow. They both appeared to be accessed by doors at the end of this otherwise bare room, which featured only a single elevator and the two holding area doors. Remington forced himself to take a second to listen but couldn't hear any activity. He glanced at the elevator buttons to see if they offered any clues as to the layout, but there were only two buttons, up or down. He decided to forgo the elevator in favor of the holding areas, which sounded, ominously, like somewhere his family could be.

18.

The hunger was like nothing he'd ever imagined.

Alex finally had a moment of sympathy for all the zombies he'd killed, all the undead dinosaurs and ravenous monsters whose appetites were so insatiable that nothing else—even self-defense—mattered. Once, what seemed like several lifetimes ago, Alex had joined his fellow eco-nuts in going on a hunger strike, going two weeks without a nibble, while blogging and broadcasting from the forest. That was brutal.

This was hell.

He had to eat, and soon. His cells were starving, his skin felt like it was on fire, his stomach groaning with every step. General Hughes' body was right there, still warm...but for some reason that had even less appeal. He wanted, craved, something fresh, something still moving, something *other.*

The raptor at his side grumbled and a wheezing cry came from its gullet, sounding like a hungry bird.

"I hear you," Alex said, again petting its rotting neck. He surveyed the others in the lab—the room full of zombie humans, one more raptor and a dilophosaurus—and again he couldn't believe that first, they weren't madly attacking and trying to devour him, and second, that he had so quickly realized how to control them.

This thing...the modified serum that still stung his arm and felt like frozen death moving in his veins...it brought power with it, a power he savored. It was like his sphere of conscious control had expanded and now he could sense these others as if they were a part of his own body and mind. It was at once alien and familiar, terrifying and yet expected. He could sense something that was not quite telepathic but more like an animal instinctual reaction, like the same way predators could freeze their prey while not yet within attack range. Inherited traits maybe, recognition of an 'alpha' and overriding commands of obedience.

Whatever it was fueling these prions, and whatever DeKirk (and Xander Dyson, likely) had perfected here, Alex couldn't rightly complain at the moment. It worked. He wasn't dead. At least, he hoped not. Didn't feel like it. No, it had surely infected him, though. He felt the hardening of his skin, the scales forming and tightening even now. Felt the powerful surges carried along in his blood, and the power to control, to reach out and sense with his thoughts that these others were being steered along by a remote DeKirk. It was but a tenuous hold he had on these, like he had them tied with a long length of rope to a boat's rudder, and continued to lead them as he sailed on from a faraway location.

Now, it was an easy matter to intrude, to clip that tether and assert his dominance. Alex was here, DeKirk was not. Alex was the prime, the alpha, the controller. And they needed control. Listless, drifting, existing only to eat and spread the prion, to reproduce—it was their greatest imperative, Alex realized, but only in lieu of another commanding presence, something that could order them toward even greater accomplishments by organization and strategy.

Alex licked his lips. It would take a lot of getting used to, and a few times already he'd felt control slipping. His own hunger, meshed with theirs, was almost too much, and if he gave in and let it control him, he would lose the aspect of control, would fall to their level and then nothing would matter. Everyone would be out for themselves.

He stepped into their midst, ignoring for now the body of the general. He'd have to see to it the man got a hero's burial or service at least...but he wasn't sure when or how he would get to that when the clock was ticking and he had so much to do. Not the least of which was still to survive and escape this place.

Easier thought than done.

He had just entered the midst of the larger throng of zombies, being so close to their scaly skin and underlying stench of rot, feeling all those gazes on him—a mix of respect, fear and hunger—those hideous eyes so close... He fought the primal urge to run, to escape these ancient beasts and this curse where a single bite would kill so hideously...

He focused his thoughts, trying to shut out the ones urging him to eat, and for a moment his new heightened zombie senses kicked in with a vengeance and he felt out down the hall, around the corners, through another room and into the warehouse where the penned captives waited. He sensed their heartbeats, felt their lungs expanding and contracting, smelled their fear and tasted their hopelessness.

And then Alex reasserted control.

There will be no feeding.

Time to free them and regain this bunker.

#

Charles Wilford watched the procession of zombies marching on his location from the closed circuit live feed inside the War Room. Despite the two armed soldiers posted at the entrance, the mirror of two more standing outside the locked and steel-reinforced door, Wilford felt both alone and entirely vulnerable. For the past two years, give or take a week's vacation on the outside to see his family and assure them he was still among the living, just doing important work for his country, work he couldn't disclose at a location he couldn't reveal—Charles had prepared for this day. He had prepared for the worst, but never really expected to be in this position, and who could ever expect what had happened out there?

Behind him, monitors tracked various key metrics like infection propagation rates and vector transmission. A large world map displayed regions mostly in bright crimson with just a few slivers of white left: remote islands in the Pacific, Madagascar, the Amazon rain forest, Mount Everest, parts of the rural Midwest, Greenland and much of Alaska. Paradoxically, the most remote place of all, Antarctica, was solid red.

All that red. Wilford ran his fingers through his thinning grey curls and tried to focus on the incoming threat and not think about the past three months. Not think about William DeKirk, 'Bill,' the man he had befriended and spent two years with down here in this subterranean city. The man he had been taken in by, like the rest of them, believing in his leadership prowess, his mild-mannered outlook; and despite a ruthless drive when it came to billiards, DeKirk seemed like an ideal man for the job should the unthinkable happen and the chain of succession fall to those locked away in here, far from harm's way.

The Shadow Government. Wilford had his skills, twenty years in banking and public-private equity management. Municipal budgets and taxation, international finance. He was more than suited to step up and take over as treasurer, should the need arise, but so was DeKirk. The man was CEO of a vast empire, with subsidiaries all over the globe. His leadership was unquestionable, and Wilford learned, his methods were ruthless and callous; but perhaps that was exactly what was needed to rebuild the world.

But what kind of world would it be?

This infection…this catastrophic plague of death and violence, of swift destruction that annihilated and changed everything in its path… It was what they were down here for: the worst case scenario, but he had always imagined the usual culprits of apocalypse. Nuclear war. Asteroid impact. Terrorism. Biowarfare.

He shook his head. Not like this, nothing like this. The world had turned on itself, and our entire species was eating itself into something else.

The worst part? DeKirk appeared to be behind it all. He had to be. He was so prepared, and although he played it off as just being ready and having enough foresight for this very eventuality, there was no other explanation.

He had the means and the opportunity, with that business in Antarctica, but no one could question him once it began. Those things…down here with them. Opposition gone in seconds. Opposition that, Wilford learned later, DeKirk couldn't control. Men and women with nothing on the outside to live for, no one to protect.

He had moved fast to isolate Wilford's family—his two college-age daughters, his wife. They were safe in the Alaska compound along with Hughes' and Norris' families. *Just a little insurance in case any of us wanted to be heroes.*

Now, however, the would-be hero of the moment was coming toward him, down the long corridor to the War Room. Wilford had watched on his own surveillance circuit—the one safety measure he had managed to incorporate, with General Hughes' help, over the past week. After the massacre at the moment of succession, as they watched DeKirk—the *changed* DeKirk —issue a coup and slaughter his other coworkers at close range and in an obvious show of force, Wilford knew the true nature of the president. Knew that his ambition had no bounds and his depravity and madness—possibility a result of his transition—could not be trusted. He and Neville Hughes had met in secret and had no qualms about planning a counter-attack. This went beyond personal needs; this was about the survival of the entire human species. And up until this moment, up until this kid—this threat DeKirk had personally singled out—had done what he just did, up until now, Wilford wasn't sure there was any chance to stop the end of the world.

Now he leaned forward, and with another last thought to his friend Neville, whom he had hoped could lead the charge against DeKirk, could rally the armies and retake the country after destroying the zombie threat, he spoke into the little microphone beside the monitor.

"Alex Ramirez. Halt your approach. Listen to me."

#

The intrusion of a human voice over the intercom almost jolted Alex's concentration enough that he lost the connection to these things all around him. The zombies, the dinosaurs, the hissing raptors especially—ancient, malevolent, hungry. So hungry, he felt their power, one with their need, again like an extension of himself. They were all part of his thoughts, appendages he could manipulate.

It was a pure adrenaline rush, a powerful thrill ride. *No wonder DeKirk has gone off the rails.* He had to control it, had to stop the urge to send these things out to wreak havoc, let them off their leashes so to speak. They could tear through those two guards, then raptors could be ordered to bash the door in with their thick skulls, pounce inside and devour the remaining morsels waiting in there like defenseless lumps of seafood inside a clam shell.

The aggression and pure drive to conquer and expand was, Alex imagined, part of the prion's genetic sequencing, its instinctual makeup straight out of the primordial evolutionary gate. He wanted to direct half of these monstrous things the other direction, to tear open the pens and feast on those inside, saving one or two for himself, as he would need to regain his strength after devouring the remaining cabinet member and whoever else was in the War Room, but...

But he checked that drive, blocked it with a single thought:

Veronica.

She needed him. Forget the world, if there was anything even left out there worth saving. He had to get to her, fulfill his promise.

He fueled all that aggression and hunger, focused it on where it belonged, and shouted back to the disembodied voice:

"Where is DeKirk?"

At the name, the raptors hissed, and one of them, the closest, snapped its jaws in his direction.

"Leave your 'friends,'" came the voice, as the nervous guards by the door took aim. "I know you, Alex, and if your goal is what I believe it to be, we may have something to talk about."

"Where is he?" Alex spat back, licking his lips as his stomach rolled. He turned his attention up and to the left, to the camera focused on him. "Is he—?"

"I've disabled the remote feeds," Wilford's voice came back. "For now, but that won't work much longer, and it's putting the rest of us in terrible danger. I have to re-enable the feed very soon and then sell a convincing lie about a transmission glitch." A pause. "If there's something you plan on doing, it has to be swift. And it damn well has to work, because kid, we've only got one shot at this."

Alex smiled.

He held out his hands and made backwards motions with his fingers. The two raptors stepped back, pushing the crowd of hissing, snarling, grumbling zombies with them as Alex stepped ahead.

"I'm coming in." He kept his eyes on the camera and with his senses reached out and felt Wilford's quickening pulse, his accelerating emotions. "You're going to give me DeKirk's location, then a plan to get out of here, including what you're going to sell to DeKirk to make him believe I'm currently raptor food. Make him think the general's threat has been managed by you, his loyal servant."

"I..." came the voice from the speaker. "Okay, I think I can do that."

"Good, because I'll need you still. The world will need you, and everything that can be done from this, the new capital."

Alex cracked a grin as his senses reached out to other areas of the facility. "Oh, and I want that pterodactyl on level four fueled and ready for me."

19.

Remington heard the cacophony of humans shouting as soon as he entered the holding area. A zombie guard occupied the room, but it shuffled itself aimlessly into a wall, its control functions having been interrupted when the major threw the switch in the control room. It took five seconds for Remington to silently let the ghoul drop onto the concrete floor, a knife wound to the brain; no reason to leave it there waiting for the signal to come back on.

With the AK over his shoulder, knife in hand, the major took a look around the room, finding himself the only one standing, although he could hear many others in the rooms beyond. He warned himself not to get complacent. *If it seems too easy it probably is.* But his unchallenged movement through the compound was encouraging. He moved to a door at the end of the fluorescent lit room. This one was not fitted with a retinal scanner.

He pulled it open and held the door wide while he stared into the next area, a vestibule type space that led deeper into the so-called holding area. The voices of humans—at least he hoped they were humans—were loud here. Two more inactivated remote-controlled zombies shuffled about in here, where metal poles ran the length of the hall-like room, chains and irons dangling. Remington knifed them both without much struggle.

He got to a door with a retinal scanner and saw that it had a narrow vertical window reinforced with wire mesh embedded into the door. Looking through it he could see about a dozen people…

…including his wife and child. No one chained or tied up in any way; that was fortunate at least. He could see another door like this one on the other side but couldn't tell for sure what it led to. He tried the door handle but it was of course locked. Pulled the eye from his pocket and pressed it up against the scanner, but this time nothing happened. No green light. No click. *Damn, McGee. Didn't you have VIP access?* In frustration, he threw the eye against the far door he had come in through, and then his gaze lingered on the dead zombie he'd just killed.

He held up a finger to the glass, mouthing the words, *Be right back!* to his wife.

Olivia hugged Hayden close, and when she saw him her face beamed with hope. She nodded fast, mouthing back, *Hurry!*

Then he ran to the corpse, figuring the guard must have been granted access. He went to work with his knife, surgically removing the left eye from the orbital socket while positioning his body to shield the ghastly sight from his wife, who he knew was now probably watching him through the glass. He cupped the eyeball in his hand, then took it to the door scanner.

Green light. Door open. His wife and daughter in his arms, half a dozen other humans in the room with them, looking on while wondering if they should run out now while they had the chance, but scared of the unknown, of how Remington had breached the place, of what was happening out there.

"Baby, listen. We've got work to do if we're going to stay safe."

"Should we run for it?" someone asked in the crowd.

Remington shook his head. "No." He looked over at the others. "Listen, as crazy as it sounds, I think we can take this place over from the inside at this point. If we can do that, it'll be safer in here than it is out there. Trust me on that, I've been all over the country and it isn't any better anywhere else. Plus here in Alaska, you'd also have the elements to contend with."

"What chance do we have against all those guards?" a man asked. He was rail thin with a gaunt, haunted face. "There are humans…siding with them, and the zombies. Oh and the fu… the dinosaurs."

Remington explained how he interrupted the controlling pulses. "How many more of you are there down here?"

Someone explained that there were a couple dozen more people from their pod in the nearby holding rooms, but that they didn't have a good working knowledge of how many others there were outside of their pod.

"First thing we need to do is secure the Control Room." Remington pulled his spare pistol from his waistband and held it out butt first. "Who knows how to handle a gun?"

A younger man with eyeglasses and buzz-cut hair raised his hand.

"You military, son?" Remington asked, admiring the military-style barber work.

The man ran his hand over his smooth head. "No, just easier to manage my hair, but as for shooting? I'm from Texas, and—"

"Point taken."

A couple of people chuckled but all eyes were on Remington, who looked around at everyone, then leaned in toward his wife, whispering: "Is this person trustworthy?"

She nodded and the major handed the man his pistol and a few spare clips he had found. "Here you go. You'll be in charge of the control room and making sure that it stays under our control. The sooner we can set up fortifications, the easier the fight will be. You should have at least one other person with you. Who wants to volunteer?"

"What about the rest of us—what will be doing?" a disheveled woman wanted to know.

"After you tell me what you know about the rest of the layout, we'll make a decision on that, but I want to start right now on the control room to make sure they can't send anything else after us, reptilian or human."

"Sounds good to me," another man said, this one about Remington's same age. He had his left arm in a sling, but other than that seemed to be in decent shape.

"Okay, you, what's your name?"

"Aston."

"All right Aston, you're also on the Control Room team. Okay?"

Aston nodded and Remington turned to his wife, speaking to both her and the rest of them. "There are other weapons from guards I've killed nearby. Other zombie guards will be mentally incapacitated but not yet dead. Kill them all. Take their weapons and distribute them evenly amongst yourselves. Any humans that want to defect and join the winning team, well…we'll have to treat them on a case by case basis. Use your best judgment."

Then Remington and his two new recruits headed back out of the holding cell and over to the Control Room. It pained Remington to leave his daughter and wife after finally reuniting with them, but if they were to have a secure base from which to remain safe, he saw this step as imperative. They encountered almost no resistance on the way there; the only tense moment came when a brain-dead zombie came walking around a corner, arms outstretched in a hungry daze. Remington showed his two men how to make short work of the creature with his knife, urging them to both save bullets and to remain quiet whenever possible.

The major moved his budding new Resistance faction onward, aware that should these men live, they would be great heroes, hugely responsible for the continued survival of the human race. But personally, he didn't give that eventuality very high odds. DeKirk's hybrid technicians would be dispatched soon to see what was up with the control room, and when they did, if they couldn't deal with the resistance they met there on their own, then they'd surely call in reinforcements.

But he was getting ahead of himself. His job was simply to try. One step at a time. The fact that he was one of the few remaining people capable of even attempting to overthrow DeKirk only added to the pressure he felt.

They had reached the control room. Remington was glad to see his lead man (*soldier,* he told himself, *you've got to think of them as soldiers now, they're all you've got*) approach the door with his weapon drawn. The second man (*make him a lieutenant*) was quick enough to follow suit. Remington brought up the rear while his soldiers took either side of the doorway.

They cleared the room, finding no threats inside, and quickly got to work establishing a fortified zone. They locked the door, tested it from the outside. So far so good, Remington thought. He proceeded to give them a crash course in the facility automation controls, with a bonus lesson on neurological remote control of living life forms. He pointed out the various CCTV monitors, which identified many indoor points the new freedom fighters were familiar with. A pterodactyl flew across the screen, outside somewhere, and Remington told them to watch while he reacquired its control using the microchip signal, then deactivated it again.

The aerial beast reached the perimeter wall of the compound, but instead of the abrupt turns it had been making when it encountered the edge of the HABITAT, this time it continued flying straight out of the facility's airspace, toward the not-so-distant mountains.

"They're not patrolling the compound!" Aston stared in amazement at the monitor. The pteros had become such a way of life for him in recent months that he couldn't believe the flying dinosaurs had left.

Remington pointed to the controls. "So make sure you defend this panel and keep everything in the OFF position. I'm hoping that this is the only control center in this place, but I'm not sure about that."

Aston perked up. "I've heard many guards refer to 'the control center,' which suggests that there is only one."

"Let's hope so." Remington handed Aston one of the two-way radios he'd scavenged from a dead guard. "Use this to keep in touch with me. The main group inside will have one, too. I'm going to get back down there and coordinate." He could see slight expressions of concern register on the men's faces as the realized they were about to be left alone here, deep in enemy territory, effectively on their own.

He was about to leave the room when he heard an unmistakable noise. Series of noises, really, but altogether a sound that he had heard throughout his military career. *Beep-beep...beep.* High-pitched, staccato tones emanated from a speaker somewhere on the control desk.

Remington looked for the source, as did the other two men. Near one end of the desk he found a piece of equipment he had overlooked before, probably because it was obviously not any kind of automation control that could be used to open gates or control zombies. But that didn't mean it couldn't help them.

Remington's eyebrows rose as he moved to the device. A shortwave radio station, antenna wire leading from the box to the wall where it ran through a drilled hole presumably to a roof-mounted antenna tower somewhere outside. A microphone on a stand was plugged into the front of the unit.

"What's that noise?" Aston asked.

Remington turned up the volume on the set, but his eyes were riveted to the frequency display. *9870 KHz. That's the frequency I gave to CIA Agent Winters for emergency contact.* "Morse code.

Quiet. Get me a pen and paper if you can." He looked up from the radio as they both began rooting around on the control desk. "*One* of you look while the other guards the door. Get used to that kind of watchfulness."

Aston looked for the writing implements while Remington went back to the shortwave. Aston slid a pen and piece of paper over and the Major began writing down the sonic code, translating it to letters and words. His eyes widened when the message began repeating and he looked down at what he had written and actually read it:

CDC DR ARCADIA GREY TO MJR REMINGTON...REQUIRE URGENT GROUND SUPPORT ASAP...CLOSE TO BREAKTHROUGH....

An actual address in Colorado followed. Remington frowned. She was taking some risk in transmitting her location over an open frequency, although it was a little-used channel not normally used to send Morse code. But she must really be in a spot of trouble. But even through these thoughts, the single word, *breakthrough,* buoyed his spirits, and changed the entire direction of his strategy.

You've got to help her.

He looked for a Morse transmitter key but didn't see one. Although it meant he wouldn't be able to respond with Morse, he actually took it as a good sign, since it also meant that no one here was actively using Morse, and therefore they'd be that much less likely to pay attention to it.

He leaned over the microphone. He'd have to take a chance with an actual voice transmission and hope no one was listening; he had to let her know he had heard her. He knew what it was like out there alone in the darkness, knew that his response would be like a burning beacon of hope for the woman.

"Major to Grey, Major to Grey: I copy. Do not repeat specifics, over. Leaving for your location as soon as I can, over."

The reply was brief, but important nevertheless, since it told Remington she was now expecting him: *"Thank you. Please hurry."*

"Copy that, over and out." Remington pointed to the number on the radio display and said to Aston, "Remember this frequency, we can use it to stay in touch. If this station has to remain unguarded for any period of time, change the frequency to something else so they don't see it. Let them think you were on a different channel."

Aston nodded. "Will do, sir. So you're leaving to Colorado?"

Remington nodded. "We've got a chance at stopping this apocalypse once and for all. Gentlemen, you can do this. You have to do this. Good luck."

With that, the major departed the control room. Still seeing no one roaming about the halls, he made easy progress back to the holding cell, where his wife and the others now had visibly lifted spirits, strategizing with each other about how to best make use of this sudden and fortunate turn of events. Her eyes lit up when she saw Remington approach.

He hugged her again, even longer this time, causing her concern. "Is everything okay up there?"

He exhaled deeply. "It's okay for right now, baby. But no, things are definitely not *okay*. That fucking madman…" He trailed off in a reflective stupor as he contemplated the depths of depravity to which DeKirk had sunk, the extraordinary measures Remington had now been forced to take simply for a *chance* at a normal life once again.

She shook him gently by the shoulders. "Is it that bad out there—away from this place? The lower forty-eight?"

"It's bad everywhere. In fact, as terrible as this situation has been for all of you here, I have no doubt that most of you would not still be alive, not as humans, anyway, were it not for this strange whim of DeKirk's to build this…*facility*." The word evoked a bad taste in his mouth as he looked around.

His wife lowered her voice to a whisper, not wanting to panic the others, but they only leaned in even closer, as hungry for information about the outside world as the zombies were for flesh. "Then *what* are we supposed to do, Casey? Even if we win here and escape?"

He stared deep into her eyes as he gave his answer. Aware that the others were straining to listen, he raised his voice at the same time. "We took the Control Room. I've eliminated all the guards I could find down here, and some topside. I'll take out more on my way out."

"On your way out! Where?" His wife's voice sounded on the verge of panic.

He tried to soothe her. "Calm down. I've made radio contact with a CDC expert who thinks she's on the verge of coming up with some kind of biomedical solution for the outbreak…"

He told her—all of them—more, revealing bits and pieces of the struggle, and the hope, as best he could in a very limited time.

But his eyes never left hers, even though in his mind he was seeing something else: a hopeful future, a shining beacon of revival, and a world free of monsters.

20.

Colorado Springs, Colorado
Six hours later.

Dr. Arcadia Grey left her shortwave station and moved back to the main lab. She'd been working non-stop since her radio contact with Major Remington and she was exhausted, mentally and physically. But there were some perks to being trapped in a drugstore. She exited the pharmacology "lab." For Dr. Grey, the CVS lab was little more than a glorified drug dispensary, but it would have to do, and fortunately some of her specialized equipment and supplies had safely made the trip in her briefcase. Arcadia picked up another tiny bottle of Five Hour Energy and knocked it back. She went out into the main store and found a bag of Lays potato chips and tore into those.

Far from feeling refreshed, she was jittery with too much caffeine and not enough sleep, and although her spirits had been lifted by the contact with Major Remington, with each passing minute she grew more concerned that he would never arrive. What if he were killed on the way? She had monitored the radio closely following the exchange with him, but had heard nothing on their designated frequency. Other channels were highly discouraging, carrying both the cryptic communication of DeKirk's forces, still looking for her, as well as outright propaganda. *Attention members of the Resistance: surrender to the nearest federal facility or you will be shot and killed on sight. Rewards, including immunity from prosecution and incarceration, are being offered for information leading to the capture of Most Wanted individuals including Resistance leaders and rogue scientists...*

She made one more circuit through the store just to make sure she was still alone. All the windows were still intact, the front and back doors still locked. As she made her way back to the pharmacy, she wondered what had become of Veronica. Had she made it? No word of her on the radio. She kicked herself for not asking Remington about her, but knew he'd probably not want her to mention names if at all possible, so it was just as well. Reaching the lab, she eyed her laptop open on the workbench and forced herself to sit down. Again.

Something else was eating at her, too. What if the problem wasn't Remington, but her? What if he did get here only to find that her cure was ineffective? *I thought it would work. Sorry you had to come all the way from Alaska to find out I screwed up.* She cackled out loud like a madwoman. *That would be hilarious, wouldn't it?*

She had told him she had a breakthrough. That was true, but wasn't quite…correct. She wasn't sure yet how to use this breakthrough which had come from an entirely different line of experimentation.

She scrutinized the strings of genetic characters on her laptop again, searching for any anomaly that might hint at something she had overlooked. But no, she could detect nothing to indicate it wouldn't work. She swiveled around in the cheap lab chair to look at her test subjects: a male human zombie who she judged to have been in his mid-thirties when he died. Next to him, chained the same way he was with a jury-rigged assemblage of CVS bike chains and padlocks, was the female zombie who must have been in her fifties when she became one. She had found both of them walking side by side, just outside the store, oblivious of the other's presence. *Younger man, you go cougar.*

Littered around the floor of the lab were the carcasses of a dozen or so very small dinosaurs—about the size of turkeys—she knew to be *Compsognathus*, or "Compy's" for short. They were pack animals that had a mean little pecking bite and could overwhelm a human by attacking in coordinated groups. Not sure where DeKirk had found these little bastards, and still preserved, maybe in the depths in the tar fields, but she had captured them by using a fishing net sold in aisle seven.

After several modifications to the strain, she had hit on the one thing that had been staring at her in the face. Her old boyfriend, Xander Dyson…he was never one to mince words. He called a spade a spade, and what he left her on that thumb drive he had called a zombie *killer*.

Not a *cure*.

With that line of thought, her entire focus changed. No more looking to cure these things and remove the disease. With that line of reasoning, the answer fell into place. The answer was there the whole time. *Thank you Dyson, you crazy asshole!* It lay in going right at the prion's basic nature, keeping it intact but changing the genetic makeup slightly, working within its own framework. Enhancing the one aspect that was so integral to the thing.

Hunger.

#

The compys were the perfect test specimens.

Small and easily handled, kept in a closet with a window so she could observe from the outside: they turned on each other quickly after being administered a dose of her special serum, until only one remained—and, still starving, careening about in a pile of its mates' bloody, scattered bones, it literally began to eat itself. It chewed off its legs, then went to work on its arms and claws like they were buttery delicacies. What was more, in the initial attack, they seemed to know that to make their task easier, they had to go after the heads and brains first. All the others had their heads literally eaten, consumed, as if the beasts craved the tiny brain treat contained within the skull; they had sought it out. Afterward, Arcadia went inside to the mewling thing on the floor, snapping its jaws weakly, having consumed everything but the stump of a throat and upper abdomen. She crushed the sole survivor's head with the heel of her boot, then closed the door and heaved in the clearer air, away from the reek of gluttonous carnage inside the closet.

Now she glanced back at the human zombies, still bound in the back room. These were the last specimens she had before she would have to venture back outside again to get more, knowing that the zombie hordes had been thickening outside of late. Hopefully she wouldn't need more, but…if she used these two now just to make herself feel better that this *cure* had been successful for certain, then she'd have no test subjects to demonstrate to Remington when he arrived. He'd want to see that it worked, after all, before utilizing his resources to help her distribute it all over the place.

Also, the biochemist in her nagged that if she continued to fine-tune the adjustments to the code, tweaking it even more, that it would work even better, and take effect faster. The problem with the compys was that it didn't happen as fast as she would have liked. They just threw themselves at the door to get to her for a good five minutes until she noticed the change...and they went nuts and attacked each other.

Her time here in the store...she felt like Alice dropping into a rabbit hole on a strange and terrifying adventure fueled by a drugs and junk food; somehow she had come out the other side with two possible implementable solutions.

The first pitted zombies—both human and dinosaur—against each other, overriding the restriction against cannibalism of its own species. Instead, it made them crave the very prions present in the zombie blood stream to such a degree that they would kill an infected organism and consume its brain. At first she hadn't been convinced of the usefulness of this, but then it dawned on her, the same as it must have to Dyson's warped maniacal brain, that if enough of them could be infected with the agent, they would eventually all kill and eat each other!

Knowing it was highly impractical to inject each one of the thousands of dinosaurs now roaming the land and waterways, she had set to work on aerosolizing the serum, so that it could be air dropped on entire armies of these things.

She was satisfied with the prion-versus-prion agent at this point. *Zkillr indeed, Xander.*

Still, while she knew this was what could save them, the doctor in her, thinking back to the camps in Uganda, couldn't let go of something else.

While the zkiller would go a long way toward quelling new violence and new human victims, it did nothing to mitigate those who had already been infected. Unfortunately, those people who had been bitten and already turned into zombies would stay zombies. And sadly, there still wasn't anything she could do about that, or the dead that rose, reanimated by the prion. But there was something she could do about those who had been bitten but not yet transformed.

Much like a venomous snakebite victim who had a short span of time in which to administer an antidote in order to prevent death, she believed she had developed a second track of agent—a chemical compound that, if administered after a human bad been bitten but before they turned into a zombie, would prevent that transformation.

An antidote.

She sighed heavily while looking at a graph on the laptop screen. This was the initial serum she had tried out in Atlanta, and tweaked a bit here. It had yet to be tested on an actual specimen. She hadn't come across any other humans at all outside who weren't already part of DeKirk's military, much less one who was free and also had been recently bitten. She eyed her two captive undead specimens, shuffling and wheezing in their colorful PVC-coated bike chain restraints, and she gave in to a horrible thought:

I could let one of them bite me and then give myself the antidote to test it out.

This grim prospect was interrupted by a chime over the store's PA system and the announcement that Rewards Card holders could enjoy savings on vitamins all week! She hadn't figured out how to turn off the announcements, once she had the generator running and powering the place again, and in a weird kind of way she actually welcomed the sound of another human voice besides the propaganda over the radio, so she had ignored it.

How confident are you of this antidote?

She stared at the younger zombie's festering mouth. It would be so easy. Stick her bare wrist in there...wait, feel the pain, the shock when both of the undead would begin to get excited, to salivate at the sight and smell of fresh human blood, then to stick a knife into the thing's scalp to the hilt, feeling the rush of foul air against her skin as it gasped its last breath. Pull her wrist from its craggy maw while it slumped to the floor, stare at her own blood...

But that was akin to a type of half-assed suicide, wasn't it? Sort of a game of Russian roulette with biotechnology. Would the untested antidote work? She imagined Remington finally showing up only to find her lying on the floor under the fluorescent lights surrounded by a mess of dead chicken-dinosaur parts, zombies, and empty energy drink cans and candy bar wrappers. What an undignified way to go, but...whatever death awaited her on the outside was likely to be even worse than that, possibly much, much worse.

Do it, do it do it... If it didn't work, she'd have some time before the change, and before a knife into her own temple ended it. She could leave Remington the samples and some instructions and tell him good luck. *I've done what I can. Here's a batch of the 'cure.'*

In her caffeine-addled, sleep-deprived brain, a mind subjected over the last couple of weeks to intense and sometimes tedious bouts of concentration punctuated by startling rounds of horrifyingly brutal violence, it made perfect sense to Arcadia.

She got up off her stool and rolled up her shirtsleeve. Walked to the male zombie, which turned its head slowly toward her as she approached.

Ding! Attention shoppers...did you know CVS will offer flu-shots this season? Keep you and your family safe at no cost to Rewards Card holders!

"It's okay, Sam." She had named him Sam, no idea why. "Let's end this for both of us, okay?"

Sam snapped his jaws in response. Arcadia took a deep breath and closed her eyes. *Maybe I should just do it with a combination of pills, instead. I am in a pharmacy, after all...*

But the fascination with zombies had become an obsession. For endless hours she'd hypothesized, theorized and speculated on what the actual change must be like when one turns into a zombie. What do they feel, think, experience? Now was her chance to find out, her last exploration as a scientist. And then, of course, she would become one of them. *If you can't beat me, join 'em, right?* Then again, maybe the cure would work. Only one way to find out.

She was laughing hysterically while moving her wrist up to the zombie's mouth when she heard a knock at the store's front door.

#

Arcadia jerked her wrist back from the zombie's mouth. She had been ready, so ready. Her thoughts were in total alignment with what she was about to do, and this noise had jarred her from all of that. She slowly stepped away from the zombie.

"Sorry Sam, have to postpone our date."

She peeked over at the door from behind a display of deodorant. The major stood there, automatic weapon slung over one shoulder, a pistol held at the ready in one hand. He glanced around, scanning his surroundings. She looked past him to see if this could somehow be a trap, if he had been captured and was now being used as bait to lure her out without a fight. But she could detect nothing like that. She ran to the door and let him in.

He stepped inside, closed and locked the door, and then greeted her with a warm embrace.

"Dr. Grey! So good to so see you, and in one piece, and still...you."

"Likewise, Major Remington. You alone?"

"It's just me on foot but I have a pilot waiting in a helo about a mile from here, and I conscripted a local Resistance team upon landing. Pilot's waiting to take us back to Alaska, where we have a fortified compound that we took over from DeKirk's human breeding facility."

"Human breeding?"

"I'll explain on the way. Listen, it's rough out there, DeKirk's forces are looking for you, and they're closing in. Have you been outside at all?"

"A few times to collect specimens for my research."

He shook his head. "Very risky."

She nodded. "I think it was worth it, though." She briefly explained her two-pronged "cure" and then beckoned for him to follow her back to the lab. There, he balked at the two chained zombies but she told him not to worry. "They're secured. That one there is Sam." *I asked him to bite me and he said he would, but then you got here.*

She picked up a pink spray bottle. "Watch this."

She walked up to the two undead ghouls and misted them from the bottle containing the serum mixed with water. Remington appeared mystified.

"It's...it's going to turn them back into humans?"

"No, unfortunately I'm not *that* good, Major. But it will turn them against each other." She eyeballed her digital wristwatch. "Watch. Right...about...now!"

Suddenly, Sam lunged toward his neighboring captive. Although their movements were severely restricted by the chains, they could still reach each other.

"Notice how before they paid one another no mind?"

Remington nodded. "Now they're each other's worst enemies?"

"Yeah, but they don't just want to fight, they're programmed so that all that hunger and violence is directed at anything with the same prion."

She could see Remington was not only amazed, but processing this into a strategy. "I see where you're going with this…"

As they watched, both zombies bit each other's faces into ribbons. Arcadia walked to the captives.

Remington's voice was edged with concern. "What are you doing?"

"It's okay. I'm going to unchain them. To show you how single-minded they are at this point. We'll be safe, don't worry."

Remington raised his handgun at the zombies nonetheless. Arcadia reached over to undo one of the combination locks. The zombies ignored her while she set the numbers and slid the lock from the chain. She quickly repeated the process with the other locks until both zombies were unchained. Even though they were free and she was nearby, they paid her no attention at all, remaining focused solely on each other. As blood began to fly, she backed up until she was standing next to Remington, who still had his pistol aimed at the warring zombies.

"I'm rooting for Sam." Arcadia grinned. "Place your bets?"

Remington only shook his head, wide-eyed as he watched the spectacle. A few short minutes later, with the floor of the lab awash in rotten blood, Sam was burying his face deep in his foe's cranial cavity, making grunting and slurping sounds while he feasted. When there was nothing left, he stood, sniffing the air and snarling.

"Only problem now, which is good for us, too, is that he's going to chow down on himself unless he finds another suitable meal."

"Goddamn, that's…"

"Yeah."

Arcadia moved so that she was right in front of him, but still the zombie did not lunge for her. Its eyes tracked her, but only vaguely, as if she didn't even register as something that meant anything to him. "You see?" she called back to Remington.

"Hell of a job, Doc."

Remington lowered his weapon, convinced. "Does this effect wear off after a certain time?"

"I have every reason to believe it's permanent, although I can't say for certain what will happen. I think the frenzy of ravenous hunger continues until it eats everything in sight."

The sound of glass shattering made their heads snap toward the front of the store. Remington immediately crouched and began moving toward the front. "Gather your things, and that blessed serum. It's time to get the hell out of here."

#

Remington moved out into the main store and popped out from an aisle, squeezing off controlled bursts from his machine gun. More glass exploded, zombie voices rasped in emotionless pain, and when the commotion subsided, Arcadia heard Remington talking, but not to her.

"...keep it warmed up until we get there. Click and a half south. Tell 'em we'll provide air support on the way out if they give us ground support now. But I mean right *now*."

Another voice, male and sounding very frightened, responded over Remington's handheld radio. "They're pinned down seven ways from Sunday, Major. It's tough over here. Raptors, humans and zombies, pterodactyls dropping shit on us, dive-bombing in kamikaze missions, never seen anything like it."

"Hold 'em off best you can. This is it, I'm returning with the doc and our chances to end this. On our way now, out."

Arcadia placed her now precious antidotes and supporting equipment into her briefcase, as well as a separate backpack she'd taken from the store.

"Dr. Grey? Are you ready for hell?"

21.

Alex burst out of the bunker strapped to the back of a pterodactyl, gripping onto its conveniently exposed shoulder bones and steering while digging the points of his boots into the thing's rotting lower torso. The alien eyes stared back at him with complicit malevolence, yet Alex sensed something else, almost like a contagious thrill to be out, carrying its master—an alpha—out into the sky. No more suppressing its raging hunger, no more grounded days and nights. It was free—and so, at last, was Alex.

Alex was thrilled with the flight, but focused on purpose, one last mission. *Save Veronica, kill DeKirk.*

He had all the information he needed from the Shadow Government, from the remaining members and those left back there under the tacit command of the outwardly meek but soon-to-be leader of the new age, Charles Wilford. Like a Churchill or a Lincoln, reluctant and humble, he was about to be thrust into a role history would someday judge him as (Alex hoped) the perfect leader for the time, the only one who could unite the decimated survivors and rebuild civilization.

But in order to even give him that chance, the board had to be wiped clean of the ultimate enemy, the one obstacle to humanity's continuation as a species. Evolution be damned, Alex thought, and this thing—this prion which even now gave him such power and control beyond anything seen in a half billion years—already had its chance. Nevertheless, Alex would use it, embracing it like a rogue vampire in order to take down the master. This was real, and this was it. Everything literally riding on him at the moment.

Wilford and his team of techs, whiz kids most likely in the former life, recruited from MIT, hacked where they needed to hack: the remaining satellites DeKirk had kept in play, the military sites and the field command centers. They did their thing and intercepted and translated coded messages that revealed not only where DeKirk was hiding out, but that he had captured Veronica, and that Major Remington was in Alaska and causing some trouble up there.

As much as that last fact excited him, Alex focused on what the messages left out: *they didn't have Dr. Grey.* Not her, so the cure lived on. Hope lived on, and now he needed to buy the time she might need. Her, and Major Remington too. DeKirk must have been thinking that all the loose ends were just about wrapped up, and probably still felt overconfident.

Just keep thinking that, asshole.

He swooped low, then ducked under a bridge, veering west and away from civilization. He had the route calculated, the weather analyzed and the map studied for movements of the zombies, for soldier encampments and lookouts.

The War Room had it all at his disposal, but the army's condition was in a state of winding down, Alex realized. As if victory had been all but taken for granted and they were now in the mop up/containment phase, dialing back forces and defenses.

Alex shuddered as he realized what that would mean—that the human contingents would then become unnecessary and likely given over to the ravenous zombies waiting for their reward.

Hopefully it hadn't happened yet. The new government, should Alex succeed, was going to need every one of them.

He checked the GPS device strapped to his wrist.

Three hours to go at his current speed. He wished he had an F/A-18 Hornet or even his trusty Cessna, but this flying reptile was far more inconspicuous, if a bit revolting. Despite the wind and the air up here, he couldn't avoid the stench from the ptero's diseased flesh. But still, Alex could handle it; he had to, so he held on to the ancient bones and dug his boots into the decomposing gristle, and steered toward the Mississippi, the mighty river coursing its way toward the current seat of the world's power.

Toward the zombie lord.

And, Alex kept repeating, toward Veronica, who better still be alive. Safe, unchanged… His heart thudded and his pulse picked up. Hang on, Veronica.

I'm coming.

#

Two and a half hours later, as the clouds swept away from the horizon and the sun again hid from the horrors below and ducked behind a hilly range, Alex did his best to keep his grip on the pterodactyl. He and his steed both were failing. Both needed a break, needed to rest, and most importantly, to feed. These cells were supercharged, the prions enhancing muscle, blood, bone and senses, but that kind of performance required a lot of energy; it needed frequent replenishing. Hence the hunger.

Alex could sense prey. Below, there in a farmhouse. Scared souls hiding out. And there, in that trailer, a child, her dog and a baby that was almost dead from its own hunger. Over there…a larger group of humans…in the forest. He veered that direction *(or was it his ride with a mind of its own, sensing as he sensed…a buffet, a delicious meal for the taking?)*

Only…

Alex sensed something else. Not fear. No one was running. This group…

He reared up, yanking hard on the shoulder bones and tendons, trying to regain control and move away—but too late. Something streaked up from the copse of trees, just as the men burst out with guns blazing. Men in camouflage.

The Resistance!

Shit! Alex swerved and ducked out of the way of the RPG shell that whistled over his head, but then the barrage of bullets ripped through the ptero's wings and shattered cartilage. One shell fragment tore into Alex's thigh, and then they were plummeting. The farmland rose up fast and in the dying shadows of sunlight, Alex did his best to stand on the creature's spine, and launched himself off it at the last moment before impact.

He hit a patch of tilled earth, legs screaming, and then rolled. Continued the tumble, then jumped to his feet as the ptero reared its head up, looked back to Alex, and then turned and screeched a challenge at the men rushing ahead, guns firing. The wings spread out, one last effort to shield the alpha, to protect Alex even as it absorbed such damage. Its flesh and bone ripped open as the men took more care with their aim, preserving ammunition by firing directly into the ptero's skull.

Ten seconds and it was over, the dinosaur down in a bloody heap.

Alex stood, hands raised. He could see their pulses, sense their blood and their sustenance, waiting for his deliverance.

Again, with supreme will, he quashed that intense rage and desire, suppressed everything and bowed his head.

God I hope this works and they don't see how scaly my face is...

"Put down your weapons, men. If you want to win this, here and now, instead of hiding in trees all your life waiting to be eaten, listen to me."

A large man with a backwards cap and a vest full of ammo cartridges and pinned grenades stepped forward, barrel of his .45 trained on Alex's skull. He studied him, his face, and his eyes. "You look like one of them, but...you can talk. You're..."

"I'm something else," Alex said, then turned in the direction some of the soldiers were looking: back to the trees which were bending and shaking. The earth rumbled, men screamed and backed away, aiming guns behind them.

"Wait!" Alex shouted, stepping past the leader, past the others, approaching the shrouded forest, where leaves and branches fell in a tempest around the thing that burst from the trees, shattering bark and crunching through the earth in a rampage of hunger and ferocity.

A *T. rex*, larger than any Alex had seen, even back on Adranos Island. This one in surprisingly hideous shape, with masses of bloody connective tissue hanging loose from diseased ribs and exposed, half-chewed organs. But its jaws were intact, if teeth mostly shattered and uneven. Its eyes blazed and its snout turned up in a bellow of horrific intensity.

Before the men could shoot, Alex raised his hands higher. He had continued to walk, right up to within ten yards of the prehistoric behemoth, fighting the stench, feeling the wavering loyalty. It was the king of the dinosaurs, an arrogant monstrosity that likely hadn't felt DeKirk's touch yet, and knew no reality other than its own needs.

Now I'm in charge, Alex insisted, sending out the thought, the command, in as forceful and loud a thought as he could manage.

The *T. rex* roared, the men shouted something and the leader barked back something about restraint. They wanted to see what Alex was doing. Whether he was a complete madman, riding pterodactyls and believing he could control *T. rexes*—or whether he was truly something else.

I need that answer too, Alex thought—just as the monstrous dinosaur shrieked and thrashed its head and thrust its jaws down in a blindingly fast move, snapping its teeth shut within inches of Alex's body. Then it laid its snout on the soft earth, let out a murmur of submissive denial, snorted again, and its dead, cold eyes lined up with Alex's.

"Good boy," Alex said, forcing confidence to break through his utter terror, and then he reached out to lay a palm on the thing's spiny hide, right between its ocular ridges.

He finally broke contact, then spoke over his shoulder.

"Are you men with me? Together we are going to retake this planet, starting with a certain riverboat two miles to the east."

He glanced back to the leader. "It's time to use DeKirk's own goddamned weapons against him. It's time to assassinate the president."

22.

Veronica flinched. Again came the screams of some victim up on the main deck, cutting through the humming of the engines and the grumbling throats and shuffling feet from the things locked down here in the cargo hold with her. She had been promised, or threatened as the case might be, a date with DeKirk shortly, where he would send that horrific general—or the other one, the female Amazon-looking warrior—down to drag her to his quarters.

Hope was thin, but she couldn't think about her own fate. That was immaterial. Dr. Grey had to make it; she needed to get that cure to the world. Whatever happened to Veronica, she just hoped she made it long enough to see DeKirk melt down with fury at finally losing. He had to, he just…

A door slammed up above. Heavy feet crashing on stairs. Boots, not shoes. Veronica sighed. General Hecate was coming, dragging a huge bloodstained axe that echoed painfully down here and sent pulses of desperation through her soul. She struggled again with the wrist bonds, attached to a hot pipe, and again tried to avoid the blood stains all around her, the gore in the corners with crimson hues made all the darker by the engine room lights placed around the walls. She thought for a fleeting second about Alex, and for some reason the memory of first holding his hand on that plane, fleeing the burning island years ago, came to her mind, and the resulting smile banished her fear for a moment…

Until a huge, horned shadow fell over the floor, the axe rose and a voice from the grave called her to face her fate.

#

"Welcome to my office," DeKirk said, swiveling in his chair to meet the general and his favorite captive. He continued to relish how, despite everything he'd accomplished, this simple pleasure of capturing the one agent who had doggedly pursued him with such vengeance over so many years, was now his. His to taunt, terrorize and ultimately, to consume.

"It's a shithole, like you." Veronica forced herself to smile.

The general's hand shoved—hard, and down she went.

On her knees, Veronica looked up through a tangle of crumpled and coarse hair that once, ages ago, might have been beautiful. Still, she was grateful for the change of scenery. The windows up here were opened on three sides, providing a gentle respite, a cleansing blast of hot southern air to soothe her pores and clear away the stench of undeath and fear.

"Now," DeKirk said, as he waved back Hecate, who bowed her head and retreated just outside the doorway. "Where were we?"

Veronica tried not to look at those hideous eyes, his pallid skin, patched with scales and taut with flushed color as if he had just had an incredibly satisfying meal—or sex, or both. She had to try to drag this out, and as always, hold out for a chance at escape, or attack. "We were at the point where you gloat about how you've turned your back on your own species, and brought about the greatest mass carnage since the Black Plague."

His lips parted and a tongue slick with a recently-consumed bloody meal slithered along his teeth. "Ah yes. That. Or...we could have that meal I promised you. Share a last evening of civilized dining before the world changes forever."

"Can you even...eat? Like that anymore?"

DeKirk shrugged. "Why not? Might not be ultimately satisfying, not in the same way as picking this flesh from your bones while you're still screaming in horror, but...exciting in its own way. Like an exotic appetizer."

He snapped his fingers and the side door opened. A zombie with a torn throat and guts partially hanging from its abdomen lurched inside, carrying a tray.

"Oh really, you didn't have to..." Veronica suppressed an urge to gag, but then smelled what was in the bowl—a sumptuous scent of fried calamari, aioli base and Cajun spices. It had been so long, but her taste buds were going crazy, her stomach growling.

"Now you know how I feel almost all the time," DeKirk said, sniffing at the air as he motioned the zombie woman to set the tray on the captain's table. He cleared a few papers, a map and a book—one that Veronica recognized. Something her ex-fiancée had always been on her to read. *But why bother when I've seen the miniseries?*

"*The Stand*? A little light reading by Stephen King."

DeKirk smiled.

"So," she continued, moving toward the table and the food, almost salivating. "Which side are you on? As if I need to ask."

"I'm not the devil, Ms. Winters. As much as you'd like to paint me with that brush."

"You're certainly not the old lady hand-picked by God to save the world."

"Oh, but I'm certainly doing just that." He pulled out her chair, a real gentleman, then helped her sit before taking his own seat, then motioning to another zombie, a man dressed in a ratty, blood soaked tuxedo and carrying a bottle. "Tell me, how long do you think your precious civilization would have lasted if I hadn't hastened the end along a bit?"

"A bit?"

He shrugged. "You know it's sometimes better just to rip off the Band-Aid. We were destroying ourselves. Terrorism, economic inequality, climate change, war and massive resource depletion. Overpopulation. A reset was needed, but instead of a plague or a war, I ushered in a global improvement edict, an evolutionary leap that—"

"You tampered with something that had already come and gone hundreds of millions of years ago, unleashing some kind of...." She glanced at the King novel. "...evolutionary Pet Sematary. It didn't work then—for a reason. And it won't work now." She eyed the tentacles, breathed in the aioli and spices, and licked her lips. "You realize you might be alone in the whole world very soon, right? What are you going to eat when there's nothing left to hunt?"

A tentacle wriggled into his mouth, dripping with sauce. "Got that covered, my dear. Don't you fret. The cattle will survive, continue to breed, continue to serve the needs of those like me."

"So are you going to share? Let others be like you?"

His eyes darkened as he swallowed and fought back a grimace. "No one's like me."

She shuddered, but reached out and took the wine glass offered to her and held it with a shaking hand as the zombie did its best to pour.

"That's a neat trick you've got there, Mr. President. Can you make him roll over and play dead?"

The grin returned to DeKirk's lips. "I'm really going to miss you, dear Ms. Winters. Do you know about Alex?"

She swallowed, almost choking on the squid. *Don't listen to him. Don't believe anything he says.*

"I watched him die." DeKirk leaned in, fixing her with his terrible eyes, brimming with hatred, hunger and ancient malevolence.

"I don't believe you," Veronica said, sipping the wine. *Might be my last, better enjoy it.*

"Only regret is that I didn't get to rip him limb from limb myself."

"You can't have everything." Veronica downed the rest of the glass, then held it up to the zombie and shook the stem, asking for a refill.

"Apparently not, but I have enough, and I will take great pleasure in devouring you."

"So you've been telling me. It's getting old. You're all talk, no action." Another sip, then a gulp. "Known too many guys like you. Assholes right to the core." Another gulp. "Either arrogant bastards, or complete cowards." She finished the glass and then stared into his eyes defiantly. "I think you're both."

Now or never. That shit about Alex, she didn't believe it, couldn't believe it. Something unexpected happened, but it had DeKirk rattled, no matter how hard he was trying to hide it. Maybe Alex was dead, maybe not. She would hold on to the notion that he was alive. Even though the chances they would see each other again were almost non-existent, it was a hope she would cling to on the way to her death, which she imagined was imminent, but at least it would be on her terms.

"I think you're both," she repeated, "but mostly just an asshole." And with that, with his stupid confused look on his face, she yanked her empty glass away from the waiter, slammed it down on the edge of the table so it shattered just above the stem, and in a flash, lunged forward and thrust the jagged makeshift dagger directly into DeKirk's left eye.

A satisfying squishing sound, a grunt of pain, and then everything turned into a blur. Veronica thought the table might have been upturned and slammed against her as DeKirk backpedaled and kicked out, but then she flipped it aside, kicked the waiter zombie that rushed her, and fled from the door where General Hecate was on her way in, freeing the axe.

DeKirk screamed something that sounded like "She's mine!" and then she was ducking under the waiter zombie, punching with both hands and knocking her into the general's path—and the path of the axe which nearly cleaved her in half.

The door to the dining compartment and kitchen—she was in the doorway, and the stairs were clear, and that amazing smell rising from the stove. She only had to—

But then a hand gripped her by the back of her shirt and hauled her around. In a spinning blur, she saw the general backing away, again subdued by a thought. DeKirk was there, holding her up like she was a kitten by the scruff of her neck. Turning her until she was face to face. The glass stem still protruding from his eye, pus and blood oozing out of both the eye and his mouth as the other eye fixed her with a look of absolute anger.

"I—" she started, but got no farther.

DeKirk leaned in and sunk his teeth into her neck, and the pain and the shock drove her consciousness to the edge and spiraling over into blackness.

#

Later, DeKirk checked on her in the hold. Again he was amazed with his self-control. His eye was healing, and if he squinted he could make out features and shapes again without using the good eye, but he was also impressed he could check his hunger. One bite only, and when she had fainted, he pulled back. It was enough though, and she would change, and it would be a different sort of revenge he would savor.

Didn't like her taste anyway, he told himself. Or maybe, he wanted to keep her around a bit longer anyway, if only in a mindless, obedient slave sort of way. He could always break her into bits before the change, and feed her to the other dinosaurs later if he felt like it. Not that she would care so much anymore.

He had tossed her aside, hard, toward the general, instructing that she again bring her down to the makeshift brig, and at the same time he ordered up another captive and slaked the hunger that had been fired up with that one first bite.

He didn't have time to savor that meal, to savor her, or anything else.

News had come from Alaska.

Another test, another setback.

Another issue needing his direct intervention.

He sighed. Still, it wouldn't be long now, and he had to make sacrifices and get his hands dirty now and then.

He would return to his command center and check on the status of the special contingent of forces he had trained and ready, up in Siberia—where certain wondrous prehistoric specimens had been recently uncovered, to his immense satisfaction.

It was time to unleash hell upon the last remnants of the resistance.

23.

Colorado Springs

The undead mob outside was much thicker than the last time Arcadia ventured out. Streams of upright dead intermingled with the occasional zombified dinosaur, including a few pterodactyls jockeying for position in the sky above the area. Arcadia turned to Remington, who was reloading his machine gun after using it to blast the heads off of four zombies who ventured too close.

"Can't you just have the helicopter pilot land over here to pick us up? I'm not sure we'll make it."

Remington slammed in a fresh clip and fired off a short burst at a zombie that already existed only from the chest up, wallowing in a puddle of guts on the ground. He looked around briefly before answering. "Problem is he's camouflaged pretty well, under a radar cloaking device that I setup before he landed. If DeKirk's intelligence gathering sources get wind of that chopper, they'll put a missile on it. So I want to keep it hidden for as long as possible. If there's no other way for us to advance and I see a place for it to land, I'll call him in. Trust me, I wouldn't have made it from Alaska to Colorado without exercising that kind of caution."

Arcadia sighed, resigned to the trip ahead of her. Remington's radio exploded with chatter. "Rocky Mountain High Sector Leader reporting in. We're rolling into Colorado Springs now with a small armored convoy. Ready to kick some zombie fuckin' ass. Where do you want us?"

Remington grinned as he pressed the transmit button with a bloodstained finger. He felt like a military man again rather than some desperate survivor clinging to life, and that invigorated him. He rattled off a series of coordinates and explained he needed an open corridor to a designated location, without mentioning the hidden helicopter. The Resistance was a loose coordination of many groups, with some of the members coming and going at will, mercenary style. It wouldn't take much for DeKirk or anyone, really, to plant a mole, Remington knew. So he told them the bare minimum of what they needed to know.

Remington and Arcadia had a tough slog for the next two blocks, painful progress one zombie and one dinosaur at time, at a high cost of ammo and general stamina. But after that they noticed a change. The horde thinned. Heavy, large caliber gunfire erupted in the distance off to their right, and in the sky the pteros headed toward it.

"Your friends?" Arcadia watched as a gigantic lizard with a sail-like fin on its back skittered across the street fifty feet in front of them, its long tongue flicking rapidly in and out of its mouth. Remington stitched its side with his machine gun and it scuttled into the bushes, leaving a trail of bluish blood.

"Yeah, they're setting up a diversion a half-mile over there. Should draw the zombies off long enough for us to make that chopper, but we're going to have to run if we want to get there before some other incoming enemy horde finds us. You up for it?"

He glanced at her, but then felt he needn't have asked. All she'd been through, she was toughened, strong and in better shape than he could have hoped. Nothing was going to stop Dr. Arcadia Grey, not this close to unleashing a cure that could literally save the world as they once knew it. If they were going to undo the scourge, she would have to run, and she would run, that's all there was to it.

She nodded. "Lead the way, I'm right behind you."

Remington took off at a fast jog. He was burdened by fifty pounds of gear and heavy weaponry, but the conditioning bred into him from countless miles of military runs over the years paid off now as they threaded their way through the town. They encountered only the occasional zombie or dinosaur, the bulk of the horde having been attracted to the melee unfolding over at the approaching Resistance convoy. He dispatched the human undead with his handgun, reserving the automatic weapons for the reptiles.

When they reached an intersection, they looked right down a street lined with gutted buildings and could see explosions in the distance—in the air and on the ground. Remington glanced at a compass and then turned around to Arcadia, who trotted to catch up with him.

"Chopper's not far over this way." He pointed in the opposite direction of the battle unfolding, for which Arcadia was grateful. Remington read her expression.

"We'll miss the heavy action, but whatever enemies we do encounter, we'll be on our own to take care of them." He made direct eye contact with Arcadia until she nodded, then they set off toward the helicopter. After a block, a zombie stumbled out of a hedge between Remington and Arcadia. Both humans raised their pistols at the same time, pointed at each other across the undead threat.

"I got it!" Remington's warning was delivered in a fierce tone, his mind flashing on comrades lost to friendly fire in long forgotten conflicts. Arcadia stepped out of the way as the zombie tracked toward her, probably attracted by her sudden movement. Remington nailed it once in the brain. As it fell, he nodded to Arcadia and took off again toward the helicopter.

After a few more blocks, they came to a small public park featuring an open grassy area with a few trees here and there. A single human zombie lay face down, motionless on the lawn, but other than that the area appeared deserted. Remington started walking at a beeline toward a clump of trees. Arcadia couldn't see anything there but from the way he was moving so purposely while talking in a low voice into his radio she knew he must be closing in on something important.

Then they heard the thrum of an engine starting up, a powerful one. Remington waved Arcadia on toward the grouping of trees. She still couldn't see anything there, but she saw Remington reach up toward a low hanging branch and grab for something. A section of camo netting came down, and he began stripping it from the trees, revealing a military MH-6 "Little Bird," helicopter, a pilot the only figure inside the craft. Remington gave him the thumbs up before turning back to Arcadia.

"She's small but very fast." Arcadia worked with the major to rip away the camouflage that had kept the helicopter hidden. Then Remington climbed up into the trees and came back down holding an electrical device.

"Radar jammer—kept the satellites from spying it." He tossed it into the helo and extended a hand toward the aircraft and its open door. "Let's go, you take the back seat."

Remington climbed in next to the pilot, a taut, nervous-looking man who seemed as though he had committed himself to something way over his head. Nevertheless, his hands moved over the cockpit controls with practiced ease as he greeted the major.

"Glad you made it back, sir. Destination?"

It was clear that Remington kept his itinerary known only to himself, not risking compromise from any source. "Good to see you, too. Alaska, first refuel stop in La Grange, Wyoming. My contacts there are expecting us."

The pilot pecked at an electronic instrument on the dash while Remington turned around to address Arcadia, who stared fretfully out the window.

"How's it looking?" Remington asked, gaining her attention.

"Two raptors, I think, running this way from the edge of the park. And...ah, a couple dozen undead."

Remington slung his machine gun around to stick out the still open door.

"Lift off when ready, and it better be now!" he told the pilot, who gripped the collective in response. The Little Bird climbed through an opening between trees barely sufficient to let it pass. By the expression on his face, it wasn't an easy task, but the pilot had the 'copter airborne above the treetops within thirty seconds, and Remington was machine-gunning the human zombies below into pink shreds that littered the green grass.

"Pass me over the raptors."

"You got it."

The pilot banked the craft sharply toward the far edge of the park, where two velociraptors loped toward the bloody mess Remington had created on the ground. He let loose a fearsome volley with his automatic weapon, dissolving the heads and necks of the two reanimated dinosaurs until they stumbled and fell, dead again. In the distance, the convoy was visible, raining fire on the undead horde.

"Too bad," he said to Dr. Grey, "we can't test out that zombie killer of yours now and help our resistance men?"

She shook her head. "Not unless you've got some way to disperse it like a bomb or something. Or tranq guns."

"Nope."

"Sorry, we'll need time to set this up."

"You'll have it." Remington radioed the Rocky Mountain forces that their mission was successful and that they should evacuate as soon as they could. As promised though, he first had the chopper pass over the convoy on a strafing run, to give them some cover while they made their retreat.

Then the pilot leveled out the craft and followed the heading he'd set into his navigation equipment. Now safely underway, he turned to Remington, who had closed the door and was reloading his guns. "Major, I overheard. Does she..." He cocked his head back toward Arcadia. "...does she have the cure?"

Remington briefly explained the anti-prions that turned the zombies against one another as well as the untested antidote that would prevent a bitten subject from becoming zombified. Then he added, "When we get to Alaska, we'll figure out how to disseminate this stuff, see if we can air drop it or what."

The pilot perked up. "Air drop, eh? I'm up for that. You know, on the way back and not far from Nome is a private local airfield. Unless it's been shelled, and if we're lucky...if I recall correctly...they've got a pair of crop dusters in the hanger."

Remington's smile when he saw Dr. Grey's reaction was as big as his own.

We might actually have a shot at this...

"Sir! Another call coming in from the Alaska contingent."

Oh no.

"They're under attack. A massive force, a fleet it sounds like, heading their way from the Gulf of Alaska. Russian, maybe?" He listened, cocking his head. "Jesus... Loaded with zombies. Prehistoric mammoths, saber-tooth tigers and a fucking army...a couple hours out."

Remington swore right back and urged the pilot to gun the throttle, fuel efficiency and noise reduction be damned. Olivia, Hayden, all those valiant souls left back there to hold the position.

Have to get back in time.

24.

"Having trouble here," Alex said, on the back of the *T. rex*. The resistance members—forty-eight strong, although Captain Ryan Barrington said that number had just been diminished by thirty over the past week. Even then, they'd been lucky. They couldn't last much longer, running low on ammunition, low on sleep, low on hope.

Now they had one last chance with Alex, but something was wrong.

Not unexpected, Alex thought. "I'm losing control of this thing, which only means DeKirk is close."

He focused his mind, his control, and gripped the rope tighter, the makeshift collar he had encircled around the *T. rex's* throat to slow the beast. Its power was like nothing Alex had ever contemplated. For a moment, standing here holding this tether, he felt like the naïve adolescent he once was, ages ago, securing himself to a mighty redwood in defiance of corporate powers.

Even back then, he had known it was a one-way mission, likely resulting in his self-destruction, one way or another. Death in the eyes of his father at least; social and legal suicide. It didn't deter him then, and it wouldn't stop him now.

They were in a marshy land, not quite a swamp, but overgrowth running rampant. Sycamore and willows creating thick curtains and barriers that Alex barreled through, sensing the river close, and his quarry just a bit farther:

A riverboat with a great paddle wheel churning up the waters, propelling the zombie lord to the southern edge of his kingdom. The craft looked like some ominous floating fortress, dark and silent against the backdrop of spreading twilight. There on the prow...*was that him?* And who was that at his side? His senses reached out, past the pair of cryos on the riverbank, past the zombies—only a few by his notice—patrolling the deck, but then he sensed her, smelled her, felt her...

Changing.

Oh god, she's been bitten.

Not dead, but close. DeKirk was holding her in place while he surveyed the forest, likely reaching out and sensing their approach.

But he didn't know, couldn't know, not yet.

Alex had to keep it that way.

"Our enemy is close," he called down to the men behind him. They were alone, and Alex had patiently and with some difficulty sent another small herd of human zombies away. Rationalizing that his concentration would falter in the battle to come, he couldn't take the chance that they could be used against him or his own men. And if anything happened to Alex, the control would be gone and those things would have free reign, turning from allies to enemies in a heartbeat.

Captain Ryan, still wary of the dinosaur, kept his distance and his M5 at the ready. An RPG was strapped to his back, loaded and ready, and now Alex cursed his luck.

"Let me know when," Ryan said. "I think I see the boat. One shot and I can Titanic that bastard, then we take out any survivors when they float up."

"Damn right," said another, someone who might have been an ex-Marine, with biceps full of tattoos and scars.

"No," Alex said, his voice cracking. "He's got a hostage."

"Sorry mate," said Ryan. "One life is a shame but a damn acceptable loss, considering the alternative."

He's right, Alex thought. *And she's been bitten, infected. Unless Dr. Grey's figured this out, there's no hope.* She wasn't too far along, otherwise Alex would have been able to feel it, control her, maybe. Or at least communicate to her that he was still alive. Grimacing, Alex struggled again to regain control of the *T. rex*—which suddenly became easier.

"Hang on." Alex frowned, sensing, listening. Something wasn't right. "I think we've been spotted, and…the welcoming committee is—"

The branches shook and swayed, the wind picking up from nowhere and their view of the riverboat was lost in a burst of giant wings, and a hailstorm of broken tree branches and leaves.

A monolithic pterodactyl, eyes blazing and a beak the size of an F-18, slammed to the ground, screeched at the *T. rex*, then lowered its head, revealing a dark rider. Two-pronged helmet, like a Norse god, it raised its huge armored hands, holding aloft a scythe and an axe, and fixed its death-gaze on Alex.

"You…" said General Loki.

Alex reared back, feeling the control slipping again.

It's him, his voice, oh shit…

"Mr. President?"

But not him. Alex shifted his thoughts, reached back out to the river, and saw DeKirk was still on the prow, gripping Veronica about the throat…projecting his voice.

"That's some ventriloquist trick."

The general cocked his head, sniffing the air. "And you, that's some Lazarus trick. I wonder…my colleagues in Missouri…?"

"You'll have to ask them," Alex said, forcing the confidence back. *This is my show now. I still have the element of surprise, even though it's his turf.* But still, something didn't seem right. Why would the most powerful man on the planet put himself in such a vulnerable spot, a sitting duck on a river? Granted, no one knew it was him, but without any defense other than inaccessibility…

Was that it? Like a castle surrounded by a moat, he could see all threats and neutralize them before they gained access?

Whatever it was, it would have to wait. First things first.

"How does it feel, my boy? I sense…and can see by your mode of transportation, you did it. I'm almost proud of you. You drank the Kool Aid."

*I'm proud of you, Alex…*Alex snapped out of his mini-flashback and had to smile at the visual. "That I have."

"But you're newly changed. Raw, untested. Your hold is weak, your mind…not ruthless enough yet."

"We'll see." Alex made a motion behind his back to Ryan and his men: fan out, both directions. Then he reached out and tried to grasp the pterodactyl, testing DeKirk's control—and in an agonizing burst of pain spreading all the way through his skull, Alex shrieked and was thrust back—and off the rearing *T. rex* that roared at the sky. The great lizard turned and shook its head as if two warring factions collided and vied for its soul.

Alex grunted but forced himself up fast, pulling the M5 from his waist and reaching out first to steady and regain the hold on the *T. rex*.

DeKirk couldn't control both, not the ptero as well, not while another alpha wanted one or the other. "Now!" Alex shouted, and Ryan and his men didn't need to be told twice. They aimed for the ptero and the general, planning to end this now with superior weaponry and numbers.

Only DeKirk had other plans.

Too late, Alex sensed them: he had been focused in the wrong direction, all his thoughts and energies on the river, when the true menace had flanked them from behind.

Gunfire erupted at the same time as the screams cut the humid air.

Alex cried out in alarm, barking an order to Ryan—who didn't need one, already opening fire on the horde of zombies, seeking out the biggest threats, trying to protect his men—and also expanding his senses, feeling the immensity of the crowd, the two cryos, twins of the guardians at the shore. It was too much, all in the thrall of DeKirk. Couldn't wrest them away, not yet.

Not when the *T. rex* slipped out of his control, the general aimed his axe-hand and the ptero swooped into the air, and all three came at him at once.

#

Got to choose one, Alex thought, feeling like his own body was under attack and he could only pull one limb out of the fire.

Bigger is better...

You're with me, he insisted, and sent the thought like a barbed lance, directly into the ancient, malevolent *T. rex*, just in time. The great jaws and those chipped, gore-stained teeth snapped away from Alex, catching the ptero in its side, biting off a chunk under the left wing. *Protect me,* Alex insisted as he raised the M5 and fired at the general who leapt over the ptero and hurled the axe.

Alex ducked, faster than he would have imagined he could move, then strafed again where the general had been. The thing was faster, closing the distance and darting side to side. A few bullets struck—leg and side, sparking off armor. One struck the left horn and chipped it off.

DeKirk's voice came snarling back to him, and then the distance between them was gone in a heartbeat. Gunshots all around him, two dinosaurs thrashing and exchanging swipes. The ptero took to the air, swooped around and jammed its beak into the *T. rex's* jugular as it clung to the thing's back with its giant talons, and kept stabbing away.

In the half-second Alex thought he had before the general closed, he sensed the other zombies, tried to pull a few back, especially those in the front lines, closest to Ryan's men. Had to give them a chance to regroup, gain positions and take out as many as possible with headshots, while dealing with the cryos.

Alex turned sideways as a sword whistled just past his face, then he kicked out and swept the general's legs, knocking him down. Alex aimed and fired but the general rolled fast, again avoiding the direct headshots, bullets tearing through his biceps and shoulder plates.

The magazine clicked and the general got up, chuckling. "Time's up, kid." He brought back the sword and prepared to swing in a huge arc that might have lopped off Alex's head, but the space between them suddenly took the form of a dinosaur cage match, with the pterodactyl and *T. rex* slamming to the ground, rolling, each biting and nipping. The ptero held on, scraping and gashing with its talons, piercing with its beak and slapping the *T. rex's* face with its wings, keeping the teeth from finding a perfect target.

Alex rolled out of the way, grabbed a clip from his belt—his last—and slammed it home. On the other side of the twisting, grappling mess of tearing flesh and teeth and bone, the general glared back at him.

The screams of Ryan and his men cut the night, echoing off the gunfire and the hissing, screeching of zombies. This had to stop, or it was all lost. Veronica, Remington and Arcadia, all hope…

Alex focused his rage and his anger and let loose even his hunger in a primal scream, radiating it in all directions. The zombies were knocked back, the raptors disoriented and panicked. The infusion of another alpha into their brains threw the entire horde into confusion—and checked the pterodactyl just enough.

It lifted its head, pulling the beak from the *T. rex*'s throat. Blood spurted and splashed over the bird-creature's side, adding to its disorientation. Just enough, Alex thought, *time to change targets.*

He aimed and fired, unloading a dozen bullets into the ptero's skull plate, between the eyes and around the beak, centered on the head, nearly decapitating it. At the same time, Alex focused his command to the *T. rex*, still firmly in his control.

The great dinosaur shook the lifeless ptero off its back. It reared up, and before the general could react, since he was already disoriented himself with Alex's scream, it snapped its neck forward and clasped its great jaws down and around its prey. The general howled, almost ducked away but didn't get far enough. From his chest down, the great teeth broke through the armored plating, rib cage and muscle, and bit down. It shook its head and stood, upending its meal and devouring the entire mass.

On the ground beneath the great legs lay the grisly remnants— the armored head and the upper shoulders. And those eyes, still moving, seeking Alex out.

"Damn you, Ramirez. This wins you nothing. Come, try to save your Veronica, and try to challenge me." It laughed until the throat coughed up blood and wheezing air was all that it could muster.

Alex backed away, then nodded to the thing above—the *T. rex* that calmly lifted its powerful left leg—and brought it down hard with all its two tons of weight behind the step, crushing the head and flattening the remnants.

The beast roared, and Alex sent it on to its next meals: cleaning up the battlefield of the cryos.

Ryan came running out of the shadows. "That did it!" Raised his weapon and fired over Alex's shoulder, blasting a lumbering zombie as it stood, wavering in confusion. The rest of his men— maybe half of what they had started with, regrouped, reloaded and began picking off the others with a lot more ease.

The cryos, however, weren't so lucky to get a clean kill. One was already caught in the *T. rex*'s jaws, quickly looking like a huge wad of red and white chewing gum, its body demolished by the gnashing teeth and huge jaws; the other was trapped, wriggling under another foot, its bones broken, a threat no more.

Alex led Ryan and the others out of the battle zone, closer to the riverbank but still under the shelter of the swaying trees. The Natchez Bridge spanned over DeKirk's boat a good distance away: dark and looming, it crossed over a mile, connecting Louisiana and Mississippi. Alex considered it, then focused on his target.

"RPG would take him out right now," Ryan said again, hefting the weapon, already loaded. "Say the word."

Alex let the seconds stretch out, weighing his options, thinking again of a flight away from a burning island, of Veronica's touch, of her kiss. Of so many nights and moments since then. "Ryan?"

"Yes, mate?"

"Tell me about yourself and your men. Battle history, and especially...any sniper rifles?"

Ryan was silent a moment, following Alex's line of sight. "We've got three SEALs and ten Marines in our group. I did three tours. Afghanistan, Iraq. Max over there was trained with sniper combat, how many kills?"

A wry young man smiled with bright white teeth showing through crimson, his face covered in blood, the front of his flak jacket drenched with it. "Eight sir. Six high-ranking targets from over 400 yards."

Alex never took his eyes off the boat, the wheel that had now begun to turn, and above it on the top deck, the two figures still motionless. *Was he staring right back at me, cooking up a new counter attack?* It didn't matter though. With him out there, smack in the middle of the Mississippi, Alex knew why he had chosen this floating command center: archaic for sure, touching on whimsical nostalgia for a man who could and did buy everything he ever wanted. But from a strategic standpoint, it was perfect. Those braving the water for an attack could be picked off (assuming DeKirk carried armaments on board, beyond what Alex could see), and of course there were other possibilities.

Ryan cleared his throat. "We've got a rifle, but still, a shot from this distance?"

"I can do it," Max said, unslinging the long gun.

Alex turned to him. "Your chance to save the world, Max."

"I—"

He started, in the midst of preparing the weapon, when Ryan held up a hand. "Hang on, what's he doing?"

The riverboat was turning, faster than Alex expected. Likely, it was outfitted with powerful engines to go with the showy old-time wheel.

"Coming toward us?"

"Why?" Ryan asked. "He'd be giving up the defensible position. Is he nuts?"

Alex shook his head. "I don't know, but he's got something planned, for sure. Max, get ready, and...get out of sight, somewhere..."

"Just the spot," the sniper said, locating a thick sycamore and eyeing a higher perch in its branches with a clear sightline.

"Go, and be ready," Alex said. "You know what our president looks like, but now you know, it's not your true Commander in Chief."

"We all know the truth," Ryan said.

"And heck," Max replied, rushing to the tree, "I've played Xbox *Hitman* enough as a teenager, I live for this shit. And an evil president? Come on!"

Trying not to smile, Alex returned his attention to the boat rushing toward them, now with its bow directly facing them, and DeKirk and Veronica—if they were still on deck—were at the aft, beyond their view. *What are you up to?*

"Let's get ready, men." Ryan directed the remnants of his team to fan out, find positions behind trees and boulders.

Alex, standing beside the hulking *T. rex*, covered by all those weapons, stepped out of the forest and onto the marshy hill toward the riverbank, where the boat began to angle again, coming in for a closer view—or a docking.

The balcony was empty, as Alex feared. The sniper shot would have to wait, but Alex might be able to draw him out. If not, he'd have to find a way onto the boat, and...

"What the hell is *that?*"

He heard Ryan's voice, but using his other senses, he knew what it was long before the bubbles in the wake of DeKirk's vessel frothed over in a massive explosion, releasing the thing that had been hidden deep and far behind the boat before.

Spinosaurus—Alex recognized in an instant, seeing past the froth and the Mississippi muck and the blood and exposed bones of the ancient Cretaceous creature. He reached out with his zombie control, but didn't have far to go: it was right there, massive, alien and so beyond his reach.

Completely under DeKirk's power, this was like a phantom limb, something that a mad scientist had attached to his torso, something that didn't belong and had a true mind of its own.

And what's worse: it had well-developed, if small, forearms and legs. Its enormous maw opened and shark teeth the size of great whites themselves glittered in the sickly moonlight. The *T. rex* screeched in challenge, but it was still too far away, and with the water…could it even fight in that? His control slipped, too much sensation, too much…

Alex was about to scream "RPG" and hope Ryan was ready for this, at the same time thinking he had severely miscalculated everything. The boat could have been burning and ready to sink, carrying DeKirk to the depths with it, had he been willing to sacrifice Veronica—who was likely already dead, or almost there.

Now I've killed us all, he thought, still clinging to the belief that this wasn't the end, only another obstacle. DeKirk had erred, coming to land, relying on one more monster that could be dispatched—especially an aquatic one with limitations.

He still had a powerful chess piece in the *T. rex*, just had to keep control. Use it properly…

But again his senses failed him, and he didn't notice the secondary assault. The strategic backup that made the riverboat fortress even more secure.

The creature lowered its spiny head, dug in the muck for purchase, then up came its tail in a high arc, catapulting something out of the waters behind it. Alex saw a huge chain uncoiling, unspooling, and firing something box-like into the sky. In the twilight gloom, it was hard to see what it was. Then he noticed bars and a mass of figures inside.

A cage, an enormous cage. Dragged through the waters behind this creature for hundreds of miles. A cage submerged with all those inside it.

Close to a hundred waterlogged, drenched but very much alive and hungry zombies.

The cage slammed down hard twenty yards behind Alex, right in the middle of Ryan's concealed men.

The bars shattered, bent and split. The cage rolled and spun and cracked open the rest of the way, spilling out its hungry, maddened cargo.

And the battle was begun again.

25.

President DeKirk, watching from back inside his cabin, gave himself a moment to relax. It was done. Alex was finished. The pitiful militia's attack...he had sensed them in the woods for days, tracking him. They were nothing. He could have taken them out at any time, but this was far more satisfying.

"Life's little pleasures," DeKirk said, glancing back to Veronica, who was lying on her side now. So pale, his bite wound a deep red, with purple veins spreading out down her side. "I thought I had been denied the joy of watching your little pest of a boyfriend be torn apart, but now I have another chance."

Veronica lifted her head and a wheezing sound came from her lips. "Fuuuu..."

"Yes, yes, save your profanities. And your strength. It will aid in your change, and your transition will be ever more seamless. You'll join me in power and hunger, and we will truly dine together as I intended."

He turned his attention back to the shore, to the chessboard as he imagined it. His opponent had but one powerful piece beside the king, himself: the *T. rex*.

Admirable that Alex could control it, and perhaps a bit of luck, or experience. The boy controlled his terror for sure, having been familiar with the beast from Antarctica, up close on the island as well. It surely helped, but he was still untested, lacking in discipline and focus.

And DeKirk had what Alex truly wanted, right here. He studied Veronica. Emotion would be Alex's end, if something out there, one of DeKirk's many pets, didn't do the job first.

He breathed easier. It was nearly over. Now to focus on two other threats—annoyances, really, that needed his attention. Needed fixing, soon.

First, Alaska...

He closed his eyes and when he opened them, it was to see through one of his minion's eyes. Standing on a glacier, a tall Russian juggernaut of a zombie, winds whipping about him. Still an hour or two of daylight from a weak, fading sun over the ice-capped mountains to the east. To the west, he surveyed the churning green waves, the frozen chunks of ice nudged aside by the fleet of trawlers, tankers and freighters coming fast, having made the trip from the Bering Strait loaded with his Siberian army. Russian zombie soldiers...bringing back thoughts of Antarctica again and how this all began. He focused closer, and saw ahead, onto the first of the freighters, the one loaded with more exotic soldiers. Recent finds dug up and thawed from deep layers of permafrost.

A wooly mammoth, huge and diseased, shedding gristle and gore with a portion of its left flank exposed and raw and one of its huge tusks broken off just past the midpoint. One eye full of pus and crusted with ice, the other nearly opaque with yellow film and a monstrously alien gaze. At its feet were three hulking saber-tooth tigers in equal states of frosty undeath.

On the docks, other transports were waiting. The general shifted his gaze to the east again, following the short highway to the walled settlement. He saw the pathetic preparations and defenses.

Remington. It had been a mistake to try to turn him, to barter for his compliance, but this was only a setback. There were other settlements, and after this assault...perhaps the breeders could still be saved. There would be some survivors he could permit to live while he slaughtered and turned the defenders.

He raised the general's arms in welcome, and shouted a war cry of preparation. Then he closed his eyes and reopened them. The monitors showed his triumphs across the world, so much perfection, the evolutionary paradigm spreading and taking root everywhere.

It had to be preserved, and he...he had to rule.

Next, he directed his attention to the bunker. Had to check on the cabinet and the situation there. He had a bad feeling.

Nothing.

Darkness.

He tried several possibilities—infected soldiers, raptors...

Nothing.

Grumbling, he pulled back and sat at his massive desk, checking the monitors. Called up the Cabinet room video feed, and wasn't surprised to see the room full. What he was surprised at was who was missing.

He clicked the audio. "Secretary Wilford."

The little man jumped in his chair, then looked up to the wall-screen.

"Mr. President. I—"

"Where the hell is Norris? Why are you in my chair?"

Wilford stood up on what must have been shaky legs. He was surrounded by soldiers and administrators. "Sir, she and the general are...indisposed. We waited to hear from you. Is there anything—"

"I believe," DeKirk said, "you know full well everything isn't the way it should be. In moments, you miserable shit, I will be sending an elite force of particularly nasty predators to eat your children and disassemble your wife, limb from limb, if you have failed me."

He swallowed hard, and DeKirk could sense his fear.

But somehow the man found an ounce of courage and raised his head. "I'm sorry, sir. But... I don't know what you want to hear. I will have the others contact you shortly. We are...having technical issues here."

A chuckle from Veronica on the floor. Her eyes were open and her teeth showing in a struggling smile.

"Shut up." He glowered at the screen, considering his options. Again he focused on his senses, reaching out to the zombies that had to be there. And again, only sensed darkness, but this time—a sense of an open space, many others in here too.

He opened his eyes. "The arena?"

Wilford blinked, a tell.

"They're locked in there, aren't they?" DeKirk leaned forward. "Which means... Alex. Now I understand. Our doctor...he had his own designs on my power, didn't he? All those experiments? A little extra-curricular activity and ulterior motives. And what, your little coup didn't go as planned, but he took what I designed? And you? Now you're backing another horse?"

Wilford looked down, turned and motioned to a young aide. Someone DeKirk barely remembered. He focused, trying to hear what they were saying. The kid was shaking badly, but nodding assuredly.

Wilford turned, after first setting his hand on the young man's shoulder. "Mr. President, I'm sorry to say we have invoked the rules of succession as laid out in Constitutional Amendment XXV. You are infected with a disease that has rendered you materially incapable of fulfilling your duties as Commander in Chief and president of this country."

"What the hell are you—?"

"In accordance with said Amendment, you are hereby relieved of duty."

"And you're signing your death warrant, Wilford, along with everyone in there. All your families. I will consign them to unending hell."

Wilford nodded grimly. "Do as you will. We all have our sacrifices to make."

"And then," DeKirk spat, "I will nuke all of Springfield and annihilate your bunker and incinerate every one of you traitors!"

"Do your worst," Wilford said, forcing a smile, and again nodding to the youngster. Then he reached forward and clicked off the virtual feed.

As the screen went dark, DeKirk howled in fury. The hunger raged, his control slipped a notch, but it didn't matter, he sent out waves of anger and aggression to his troops outside, urging extreme violence, an end to the annoyance of Alex and his friends.

But first things first. He called up on another screen, the missile command and silo centers. He had been briefed on all the workings of military response, for the last three years training for such unthinkable scenarios. His command center here was fully equipped with all the necessary features, controls and codes. Wilford was full of shit. He had no power, not yet. All show.

DeKirk entered the target, chose Springfield and armed a warhead from the nearest silo.

"They don't know how inconsequential they are," he said to Veronica, as if she had been following any of this, in her state. "I have backups for my backups. Alternatives, as if we actually need a governmental system. Depending on what's left, what I allow to exist, this is nothing. Others are in line, waiting for their turn."

Veronica made a coughing sound, and again a laugh escaped her lips. "You...are wrong. Again."

DeKirk turned the keys in the mobile launch unit after entering the codes and the coordinates, and then sat back, a smile of satisfaction on his face.

One that turned to confusion and then rage.

ACCESS DENIED—INVALID RESPONSE

Now he remembered that kid, the teen from the bunker.

A whiz tech recruit. Expert hacker and computer expert. That exchange?

"Son of a bitch!" They did it, blocked him out.

He was president no longer.

With Veronica's laughter echoing in his ears, DeKirk stood and threw the first monitor across the room, shattering it into a thousand pieces. He was about to give in to the rage and slake his hunger on the only target in view, when the ship rocked, tilted and everything went sliding toward him.

He fought for leverage, caught a rail, and as he hung sideways before the ship righted itself in a massive slap onto the waves, he saw what had happened.

A giant draconic visage peered right into the window.

The *T. rex*!

Its jaws clamped onto the great wheel as its hind legs scraped through the lower decks to find purchase and elevate it—and its rider—onto the deck.

26.

Alaska

Dr. Grey was on the ground, a successful landing inside the compound, and then Remington—after escorting the refueled chopper in his Thrush 710P crop-duster—was back up in the air. He banked around the central tower and straight out into the dying sunlight setting over a massive force converging on their tiny settlement from the south. Tankers and transports, fortunately moving slow due to the ice and the need to wait for the huge ground force proceeding on foot. Fast, though—Remington gave them that. These boots on the ground would never fatigue, never wear down, and their bloodlust knew no bounds.

Fine with me, Remington thought, signaling to the other plane to prepare. If Dr. Grey's solution worked, if the aerosol mix-bomb she created back there could indeed drop over those bastards, or enough of them to make this work, they would switch sides and take care of everything. DeKirk's assholes wouldn't know what hit them.

The tanks were loaded. They only needed a small solution applied to the canisters, which Dr. Grey synthesized with the materials and supplies found back in the hangar. They had enough for two strafing passes, and with the way the force was bottled in, converging with all the arrogance of DeKirk himself, believing that brute force would be sufficient to retake the facility, it might just be enough to hit a majority of the invaders and infect them right back with this zombie killing super weapon.

Please let it work.

And in that moment he could see it, could see the future now in their grasp: the world cleansed of this ancient curse, civilization granted a second chance; Olivia in his arms again and Hayden growing up to a hopeful future.

Only problem he could see?

If the invaders had air support.

"Shit!" his radio flared. The other crop-duster's pilot, up ahead, dove low just as something rose up from one of the open tankers, and another blip appeared from below a distant hill.

Here come those goddamned pterodactyls!

#

No hope to fight them, no armaments on these planes. Only one possibility…

"Nate! Evade and head back, then do a pass over the central compound!"

He radioed ahead and told the gunners to get ready.

As he watched with admiration, Nate—living up to the arrogant promise he'd made about his flying skills—spun and looped, banked hard and avoided the first ptero and nearly got them tangled together as they both converged on his plane at once. Then he swooped over a mammoth's head as the trunk reared up. He turned and raced back toward the compound.

Speed was their advantage, the little planes easily outpacing the pteros.

Remington stayed low, dipping under the tree line and around a series of glacial hills, keeping his eye on the enemy. The pteros were both following Nate, which meant…

It was now or never. He had to risk it.

The force was too close. The mammoths would take down the makeshift fencing in seconds and the zombie horde, once in, would be unstoppable. Olivia, Hayden…everyone in there, they would all be dead or worse in the time it took him to land the plane.

No, he had to do this now, and had to hope one pass, unloading the contents of his duster, would do the trick.

He pulled back on the stick, rose over a concealing section of snow-capped trees, and set his thumb on the payload solution release knob as he soared down toward the front flank of the invasion force. Two huge prehistoric mammoths roared at his approach, and a legion of red-eyed, yellow-scaled human zombies shrieked with remote-fueled bloodlust.

"Welcome to Hell, assholes." Remington clicked the switch and released a stream of deliverance upon their ranks.

27.

Alex had a moment on the beach, when the major events of his life all did more than flash before his eyes. They floated, juggled and revolved like planets through his mind's vision, a rapid-fire montage of everything that mattered: his father carrying him on his back, teaching him to hit a line drive; Mom teaching him to ride a bike, then how to hot-wire a car and post bail; then how he held her hand through chemo, and then, watching her change, her death. His dad's; Veronica stepping into the void, taking the emptiness and filling it with adventures of passion. He took them all, the good and the bad, and embraced his past and accepted his fate, whatever it would be, once he set it in motion.

Then he realized he already had accepted it. His decision was made, through the screams and shouts, the gunfire of Ryan's men fighting valiantly against the overwhelming odds, the vicious, waterlogged monstrosities, the pair of cryolophosaurs, and the *T. rex* and the spinosaurus battling on the bank. Alex realized he was running, leaping over the *T .rex's* tail, then onto its spine. Two more steps, even as he willed his champion into motion, toward a different course of action, but one that lay open to him now.

A long shot maybe, but the sea creature, after ducking its head out of the way of the *T. rex's* jaws, offered an inviting ramp, and Alex, thrusting his fists into the eternally rotting muscle of the *T. rex's* powerful back so he wouldn't fall off, kicked and charged the beast ahead.

Onto the sea dinosaur's spine, trampling on its fin and pushing it down into the muck, two more steps toward the boat, and then it pounced, flexing its great legs and launching itself and Alex toward the red and white wheel boards. Alex had hoped even for just a collision that would cripple DeKirk's naval center and root him here, but was thrilled at the actual outcome.

He knew the hind legs were massive, and had often asked his father if *T. rexes* could leap and knock prey out of trees or grab pesky pterodactyls, but in all honesty, no one knew. His father could conjecture based on the size of the bones and the weight of the creature, but really, with this prion and its enhancements to physiology, all bets were off.

Its feet launched off the ridged back of its aquatic adversary and then crunched down into the middle of the great paddle wheel, cracking its axle and snapping half the boards, and for a terrifying second, Alex thought that they were going to tumble backwards into the rising maw of the raging spinosaurus. But the *T. rex* had other ideas. It thrust its neck out and snapped its huge jaws onto the top deck, teeth crunching through the railings and the metal floor and lodging hard in the buttresses.

Alex released his hold and didn't wait for anything. This was it, he had to end it before Ryan and his men were overrun, before DeKirk had a chance to kill Veronica or unleash whatever other defenses he had at the ready.

If I fail... He couldn't think that, but he was prepared. Before the final assault, he had given Ryan and several of the militia the coded frequency to the Springfield bunker control room. They could reach the Cabinet now, reach Wilford and mount some sort of backup response if Alex failed; coordinate with Major Remington and Dr. Grey. Hopefully there was a chance from that part of the resistance and this all wouldn't die with Alex.

But he wasn't thinking about any of that now, not as he scaled the *T. rex's* arched back, gripped its horned appendages, and vaulted over the great head and onto the boat's deck.

He landed on a shaky section of the floor, directly facing a window with a long crack in it, but he could still see inside. The command room. Veronica on the floor, and lurching into his view, recovering from his surprise...

DeKirk.

#

The glass shattered and his enemy flew through the window at a pace that nearly knocked Alex back into the gnashing teeth of the king of dinosaurs. Alex slipped on the wet deck and got one hard jab into DeKirk's side and then regained his balance, facing his adversary as the giant eyes of the undead *T. rex* watched on.

"Welcome aboard," DeKirk said, spreading out his arms, and then making a motion with his left hand.

Alex sensed it, a wave of challenge from the other alpha. "No you don't," he hissed, reasserting his hold on the *T. rex*—but failing to realize what DeKirk was doing until too late.

"Stupid kid," DeKirk laughed, backing up. "Shortsighted, just like your father."

The boat lurched suddenly, hard, banking down. Something had caught the *T. rex* in a death grip. A huge splash, a screech of unholy pain, and the *T. rex* released its hold to defend itself. Alex caught a glimpse, between the river spray, the massive tilting of the boat and the eruption of wood, bone, blood and glass, of the spinosaurus, fully in DeKirk's control, with its shark-like jaws clenched around the midsection of the *T. rex*. It savagely shook its head as it tore the land nemesis free and down into the waters.

The boat tilted precipitously toward the shore, and Alex and DeKirk slammed together against the railing. More glass shattered. Three human flailing zombies hurtled out and down over the side, and then another figure rolled through, hit the wall beside Alex, and then rolled over. He caught a glimpse of auburn hair and a mouth open in a desperate scream.

"Veronica!"

With reflexes enhanced and a speed that astonished even him now, Alex shoved DeKirk back, then reached over the railing and just caught one of Veronica's wrists. He gripped hard and held on as the boat groaned and complained and then righted itself.

"Hang on!" he screamed over the side, his shoulder strained and the agony flaring as the boat came careening back down, slammed to the water, tilting the other way now.

DeKirk took a swipe at Alex, but his massive swing missed as he lost balance and slid backwards, crunching his back against the far railing.

Another tilt and the boat rocked down again, nearly back to level. Alex and DeKirk faced each other now from the opposite edges of the vessel. It looked like they had just survived an initial volley from a pirate fleet. The command room was a smoking ruin, with a fire raging from one of the lower compartments. The wheel was still trying to turn, but jamming and throwing off sparks and breaking more and more pieces as the levers struck the water.

Alex struggled against the pain, but now his arm couldn't move. Couldn't lift her.

"Don't drop me," he heard from over the side, over the splashing and biting and tearing sounds from the river. The two undead behemoths were locked in an epic water battle, and there too, Alex couldn't help. His attention was faltering, his focus on saving Veronica. He was helpless before DeKirk, who had pushed himself off the railing and now came with careful steps over the ruined deck to stand over him.

"Here we are," DeKirk gloated. The moon slipped free from a heavy cloud at his back, shining over his shoulder and casting the president in an eerie silhouette that made him look like a newly-risen vampire lord. "Not bad, A for effort and all that. You messed me up, kid. You and this persistent agent, but honestly, I couldn't have done any of this without you. Back in Antarctica. You and your good old dad. Dyson, all of it. You showed me the way, and here we are."

"Said that...already," Alex managed. Had to focus, had to think. Too much shadow, couldn't see clearly. All the lights sparking. What was happening on the shore? Down below?

He sensed movement on the boat still. Another zombie lingering in the cabin, this one female, looking like a Norse goddess with gold Kevlar armor, a horned helmet and long locks of hair. But there was something else, something scrambling fast up the side of the deck. What was it: ancient, undead and speedy...?

It didn't matter. Alex could barely maintain any control on the *T. rex*, much less an enhanced zombie human warrior, and raptor or whatever was joining them, heeding DeKirk's call. He couldn't move his own limbs much less those of someone else's. He shifted his weight, forced more motion to his shoulder, and started to lift Veronica. *First things first...*

"Look at you," DeKirk said in a calm voice, taking another step closer. Something scrambled behind him, large teeth scraping for purchase on the railing, a small fan-crowned head. "Still trying to save the world. First it was the redwoods, then the poor little prehistoric amoebas in the ice." He laughed. "Remember how that turned out?"

"Yeah, we're both living examples of that."

"True, my boy, although one of us won't be living for much longer." Another step, and a light from the edge of the shattered roof briefly caught his features—and for an instant Alex noticed it. *A red dot!*

And then DeKirk was out of the light and back in the shadow.

But it was enough, it was hope. *Max...*

DeKirk, mind fully engaged attempting to control massive beasts, raised one hand and motioned with his fingers. The thing behind him slipped over the edge, scrambled for balance on the slippery deck, then loped forward. *Definitely a cryo*, Alex noted, rapidly processing that fact along with several others.

Something huge jarred the boat from Veronica's side, the fight still raging there. Gunfire on the shore, and more screams. Alex closed his eyes and reached out: to the *T. rex*, the spinosaurus, the zombie general in the cabin heading for the broken window, and the cryo behind DeKirk, coming this way.

Alex saw them all, viewed out through their eyes...saw up through the bloody river spray that Veronica, although helpless, was never quite powerless. She had a huge dagger-like piece of the window glass gripped in her right hand.

Alex smiled. *Love you,* he thought.

DeKirk was still muttering something, talking about the power and the privilege that came with this augmentation. "...if things had been different, I'd welcome you as a partner, but..."

Blah blah blah.

Alex lifted Veronica up suddenly, standing fast, letting the momentum do his work for him. Some part of his viral connection touched Veronica's, and they shared one mind for an instant, and it was just long enough. He gave her a burst of energy, unlocked some of the potential in the disease that was killing her. With her new strength, she hurtled over the side, thrown by Alex's motion. Feet together, she landed hard on the deck between them, deposited in a perfect position to reach up, thrusting with the shard, a veritable sword point.

"Eat this, asshole," Alex heard her say, and the shard impaled through DeKirk's left cheek.

He backhanded her into Alex's arms as he staggered, shaking his head. Grabbed the shard and leaned down, then up fast, ripping it out. The three-inch wound, almost to his eye, spurted, and Alex got a clean look at the hole, the exposed upper molars and the white fractured sinus cavity as DeKirk stumbled back into the shaft of light.

Did she get the brain? Alex didn't know, and wasn't even sure that would have been enough in DeKirk's case. And suddenly DeKirk knew it too, saw the smile on Alex's face—the mirror of Veronica's who had seen it as well: The red dot was back. Dancing in a calm, perfect circle in the center of DeKirk's forehead.

He opened his mouth to shout, and he moved, lightning fast, but not fast enough.

The burst of blood, bone, brains and yellow pus exploded out the rear of DeKirk's skull at the same time the distant shot echoed over the water.

President, CEO and zombie lord DeKirk rocked backward, staggered, arms flailing, eyes rolled up in a mask of white.

Whether or not he was dead, again it didn't matter. The endgame was to release control, which happened at once—a break in the chain of his alpha stronghold.

Ready for this, Alex stepped in to the vacancy. Reaching out to his phantom limbs: his allies in the water, on the land, on the boat, in the cabin coming out now, and on the floorboards right behind DeKirk.

The ex-president staggered and shook his head as if trying to will the synapses and muscle and bone to heal and re-graft and connect, and for a moment Alex felt the challenge reasserting itself.

No way, no way...come on, strike!

And they did.

First the cryo, the ten-foot 'baby,' a runt by Antarctica standards and some of the others Alex and Veronica had faced, this one more than made up for its size by its feistiness and rabid hunger. It leaped and caught DeKirk in a deadly embrace, reared back its fan-tipped head and then snapped it forward in a gouging attack, chomping onto the side of DeKirk's neck. Howling and flailing, DeKirk slapped at the pesky dinosaur, and soon the two were doing a mad dance of desperation, of hunger and attempted escape. Bite after bite, the cryo took out chunks of flesh, shaking its head and tearing, rending, splitting, the tail whipping about. And then, when DeKirk finally managed to get his hands on the thing's throat and push back slightly, the general, Hecate, crawled out of the broken window and leapt into the fray.

She fastened her jaws on DeKirk's abdomen and went to work.

Again Alex fought off DeKirk's desperate attempt to regain control, slamming it back fast.

"I'm the alpha now." He stood and helped Veronica to her feet. A thought came to his mind, an image of how this should end, and with it, the prion elements acted on his desires.

The cryo found its legs and dug into the deck. It clamped onto DeKirk's shoulder with its teeth, its talons, and lifted, taking the general along as well while it charged the broken section of the aft railing—and leapt over the edge.

A glimpse of DeKirk's left eye in his ruined face, his one arm flailing, was all Veronica and Alex saw in the shadowy light as the zombie-dinosaur-human pile tumbled over the edge—and into the waiting open maw of the *T. rex*.

Rent flesh from the shredded spinosaurus still clinging to its teeth, the *T. rex* snapped its jaws shut on the morsels falling into its gullet. Shook its head as feet and a tail wriggled outside the mouth. The river spray splashed in all directions as the dinosaur chewed and ground up its meal into a shredded, pulverized bolus. It sucked in the remainder and devoured every last bit.

"Holy *shit*." Veronica clung to Alex, then pulled back, intently looking into his eyes.

He nodded. "Later. We still have work to do."

Turning to the shore, he quickly sent out his feelers, caressed and caught each of the remaining zombies. Saw through their eyes and sensed the situation.

Max the sniper was in the tree, picking off those he could, assisting the reduced force below—Ryan and maybe six others.

Good, Alex thought. *Now...*

He calmed the zombies, made them turn and face him. Drop to their knees, bow their heads.

Your service is done, he whispered. Let Ryan take it from there.

The gunfire silenced, only one thing remained—and it pained Alex to have to do it, to end such a magnificent creature, an ally that saved the day, saved the world, ironically, after another of its kind had been the first to start this madness, hauled from the subterranean depths of an Antarctic lake. A lake where it should have remained for untold millennia, resting in peace, but where DeKirk had instead chosen to revive it.

But that was over now and Alex didn't wait long. Keeping his control on the *T. rex*, he sent it out a little farther into the depths of the Mississippi until only its bloody, well-satiated jaws were above the water and its dead, ancient eyes stared back at them. Then he let Ryan do the honors, firing the last RPG shell, ending the dinosaur's existence once and for all, a personalized meteorite to bring about a second extinction.

#

Moments later, Alex carried Veronica out of the water, struggling on pained legs up the shore, to where Ryan and Max waited beside a pile of zombie corpses. They helped him take Veronica and lay her down on a dry patch of earth.

"Nice work up there," Ryan said.

"Thanks to you. And you, Max." Alex nodded to the sniper, and to the rest of the men. Blood-soaked and shaken, but with hope glinting on their eyes in the rising full moon.

Alex glanced back to the river. DeKirk's boat looked like a model version of the Titanic, it's tip pointed up under the silvery disc of the moon as it sunk and then lodged in the sediment. Alex imagined it might one day become a landmark tourist attraction: the place where it all ended, the last stand where salvation was returned. A *Remember the Alamo* for the New Age, the Second Chance, as Alex had come to think of it.

But was it?

"The radio," Alex whispered, his voice giving out.

A man came running over, unslinging his pack and holding out a satellite phone. "While you guys were dealing with this mess, I called like you said. Mr. President now, I guess... President Wilford, he has a message for you."

Alex licked his lips, then looked at Veronica, who was pale, and fading. She reached up to him and he held her hand. He focused and reached out into her brain, felt the prion's cells spreading, invading. Couldn't stop it...

I can slow it down, though, if there's hope.

He took the phone, held it to his ear.

"Tell me, Wilford. Tell me there's hope."

Epilogue

East Rutherford, NJ—two months later

Alex coordinated this last effort from the helicopter, watching along with the pilot. Viewed the carnage below. It had been a long day indeed, from dawn until dusk, refueling three times as they flew over the zombie horde, shepherding them toward the stadium, filling it slowly and methodically. Multiple runs, each time Alex calling the surviving zombies, ordering them to follow. He was fairly sure now they had gotten them all, all of the undead that were left in the tri-state area.

He herded them inside, gave the signal and then unleashed the aerosol component into their midst. What followed was quick, brutal and intense. Faster than any two two-minute drill back when this stadium had seen its share of thrills and heartbreaks.

"We're done here," Alex told the pilot. "Take me home."

\#

Monticello, NY

They touched down with the sun's final descent, and in minutes Alex was back in the mansion that once belonged to Thomas Jefferson, and was currently the new seat of power in the restored Republic. It was also currently his residence, having been provided with the master suite on the second level. Of course, he didn't mind being this close to the action—or to the woman he loved, who remained at the center of it all.

Veronica Winters stood up first upon his arrival, and all the others followed suit out of utmost respect. Alex, however interested in what had been going on in this new strategic and command center, only had eyes for Veronica. She looked radiant, even with the stitches and bruising on her neck—what would be a permanent scar and constant reminder of DeKirk's wrath. They embraced while the others looked on with appreciation.

"Is it done?" she asked, finally pulling away. He knew she asked more for verbalization of closure than certainty. They all knew. They'd been watching this latest round, just as they had monitored all the other missions during the past two months. Not just these men and women—the inner circle and new Cabinet—but gradually more and more viewers around the country and the world watched with rapt attention. As the electrical grid was steadily restored, broadcasts resumed and the frightened survivors gathered in town centers and zones freed by the Resistance, congregating to watch, to heal and to feel the power of hope once again. There were celebrations as each zone joined in liberation, and what came about was an unprecedented amount of cooperation, a coming together of different races, faiths and backgrounds, all united against the common scourge that had nearly brought annihilation to their species.

The cure worked, but it was slow going. Fleets of crop-dusters and fire-planes crisscrossed the most populated areas, but with the threat so spread out and the aerosol delivery problematically dissipating quickly with wind and time, that's where Alex's skills were still needed. The Alpha did his job, however reluctantly, and with precision planning from some of the best remaining minds in the country and the world. Alex used his powers of persuasion to speed things along, to move the undead and the remaining dinosaurs into position, and just like in Alaska where Remington and Dr. Grey had the first great victory, the cure did the rest. The disease destroyed itself, zombies consumed each other in an orgy of violence and all-out brutality, quick and sudden, and it was finally done. Stadiums made efficient arenas for the final end to this scourge.

There would certainly be stragglers, isolated pockets of zombie survivors, but that's where Remington came in.

Veronica stepped aside and Alex could see the major on the main view screen at the head of the conference room table. He stood, apparently in the midst of a briefing report from the field. He was watching appreciatively, like the others here: President Wilford, Dr. Grey—who had accepted the new hybrid role of Surgeon General and Health Czar, several other politicians, scientists and intellectuals, and a select group of heroes who had proven their leadership in the past few months.

This country would need them all. Rebuilding had already begun. It would take time, but there was a great sense of anticipation, not only here in this room, but across the country, even the world—where the cure had been quickly adopted, and other countries began their own brand of heroic liberation, recapturing their lands slowly but tenaciously.

Glancing at the screen, Alex was happy to see a familiar face. "Captain Ryan Barrington?"

The man, who had fought at his side at the now-legendary battle of Natchez, came up beside Remington and offered a salute.

"Followed your recommendation," Remington said, "and Captain Barrington here has been a great addition to the force. I was just briefing the cabinet on the Liberation status."

Alex nodded, noting the view of the St. Louis arch in the background. He wanted to ask about Olivia and little Hayden, who he and Veronica last saw during a brief Christmas visit, where Hayden was not just walking, but running circles around the tree. But he knew this was a professional meeting, no doubt concerned with incredibly serious matters.

"*General* Remington is too modest," Veronica said. "He's just been promoted, again, and has accepted the role of Commander of the Joint Chiefs. He will be flying out to the restored NATO headquarters in Geneva next week."

Remington rolled his eyes. "No rest for the weary."

Veronica leaned in to Alex and said in a whisper, "There's no doubt from anyone in this room that Wilford will be a one-termer. Remington will be the first elected president of the new republic, and with good reason."

Alex smiled, saluted Remington and addressed the room. "I, for one, am exhausted. You good folks carry on." He put a hand to his head and backed out of the room, Veronica following.

But as the doors closed, Dr. Grey slipped through. She met the couple in the sitting lounge, beside a small lamp and a leather sofa where Alex reclined, head back, breathing hard.

"It's getting worse," the doctor said. It wasn't a question.

Veronica looked at her with concern, but Alex just sighed. The headaches, the pain, the hunger, it was all taking its toll, and his body was reacting badly to being deprived of its needs. He couldn't last much longer, and truthfully Dr. Grey had no idea what could happen if they didn't reverse what he had done to himself in that bunker. If they didn't cure him.

"I'm almost done. Just...need to be sure there are no more of them around. Nothing else that..."

"Remington can handle it from here," Veronica urged. "The army—now that they are united again and in his control after the amnesty and court martials and everything else—they can do this. They *will* do it. Mop up anything and everything that survived."

"And if it spreads again?"

Dr. Grey knelt beside him, put a hand on his. "Then *I'll* stop it."

He met her eyes, then Veronica's. "I'm so tired."

"You deserve a rest." Veronica held his other hand. "You've done it. You've sacrificed, you've avenged your parents, all of our lost friends, and you've done more than you needed to for everyone else. Now, do this for me: Let her cure you and take this away."

Alex closed his eyes tight, squeezing her hand, deliberating within himself. He knew she was right, and yet—maybe it was the prion, maybe it was the ancient biology itself which had integrated into his personality now—but it didn't want to give up. Still protecting itself.

"I need you back," Veronica said. "It's time."

Alex started to shake his head. He thought up rational arguments as to why he shouldn't accept a cure, why he should remain as he was—all-powerful, near-immortal, the ultimate Alpha. He wanted to argue they should find more surviving zombie dinosaurs, that they could establish a refuge, an island even, where he could remain as their leader. They could study and learn from him, and from them. Maybe synthesize new biological remedies, make strides in defeating human diseases, modify this thing to...

"Enough," Veronica said, as if reading his mind. Then her lips were at his, her breath warm and soothing against his face, her eyes seeking out his. "Nothing is worth what it's doing to you. To us." She kissed him and he felt the hunger rise, just as he pushed it back away, like so many other times.

Pushed it—and the fiercely ravenous prions—away.

Kissed her.

When he opened his eyes again, he looked toward Dr. Grey.

"I'm ready," he said. "But first I need to make one more trip." He met Veronica's concerned look. "Where it all began for us. We need to go back there. I want to see it finished. For good."

#

Lake Vostok, Antarctica

They stood on the deck of the *USS Triumph*, bundled in heavy parkas and thick wool hoods, holding each other for added warmth as they watched the sky over the demolished site of the former drilling operation and research center. This was the place where it all began, where he had once dared a reckless stunt to try to protect an ancient, microbial life form from greedy multinational interests.

"Hard to believe," Alex said, "that I had been so in favor of reducing overpopulation, fighting the unchecked consumption of natural resources and fiercely protecting the environment, that I got my wish—in the most horrible way imaginable."

"It'll take a while to get back to those population levels," Veronica said, hugging him closer, her teeth chattering. An aurora swirled overhead, brilliant indigo and muted jade ribbons undulating against the dim stars. "So you don't have to worry about that, at least." She sighed. "Do you…sense them?"

"Oh yes." Alex focused ahead, narrowing on the ridge of an icy glacial wall, and beyond. This whole area had been leveled by DeKirk right after he had mined what dinosaurs he could and siphoned out enough of the prion-laden prehistoric lake water to infect the world.

"They're still down there," Alex said. The lake was a mile or more beneath the surface, heated by a pocket of geothermal gases and sheltered from the cold. The microbes thrived still, mindless and ever in search of new hosts.

"They have no idea what's coming."

Alex focused again, this time with his eyes—seeing the grouping of lights beyond the shore. The drills and the cranes, the excavators. A skeleton crew, moving swiftly and under Alex's supervision to ensure that nothing came out of that lake. They drilled through the rubble, creating several cavities down to the liquid water. Cavities which were then filled with nuclear explosive devices.

The team returned to the *Triumph*, and now they were retreating, back to a safe distance.

"I'm in touch with their primitive instincts," Alex said, trying to find another word for 'mind.' It was definitely like a group consciousness that he sensed down there among all those molecules, the prions swimming with urgent, gleeful abandon. "I'm bringing them together, all together in one last communal celebration..."

The loudspeaker crackled. *"Detonation in Five..."*

Alex and Veronica donned their tinted goggles, held each other tighter, and watched the show, anticlimactic as it was, being an underground explosion. Alex, however, could feel it. He doubled over in agony as he sensed the collective death gasp of a billion or more tiny, deadly, lives.

Veronica gave him time to recover. As she always would be, she stayed at his side until he was ready. Together they went inside, to the warmth, to the cure, to each other.

END

 SEVERED**PRESS**

CHECK OUT OTHER GREAT DINOSAUR THRILLERS

THE VALLEY
by Rick Jones

In a dystopian future, a self-contained valley in Argentina serves as the 'far arena' for those convicted of a crime. Inside the Valley: carnivorous dinosaurs generated from preserved DNA. The goal: cross the Valley to get to the Gates of Freedom. The chance of survival: no one has ever completed the journey. Convicted of crimes with little or no merit, Ben Peyton and others must battle their way across fields filled with the world's deadliest apex predators in order to reach salvation. All the while the journey is caught on cameras and broadcast to the world as a reality show, the deaths and killings real, the macabre appetite of the audience needing to be satiated as Ben Peyton leads his team to escape not only from a legal system that's more interested in entertainment than in justice, but also from the predators of the Valley.

JURASSIC DEAD
by Rick Chesler & David Sakmyster

An Antarctic research team hoping to study microbial organisms in an underground lake discovers something far more amazing: perfectly preserved dinosaur corpses. After one thaws and wakes ravenously hungry, it becomes apparent that death, like life, will find a way.

Environmental activist Alex Ramirez, son of the expedition's paleontologist, came to Antarctica to defend the organisms from extinction, but soon learns that it is the human race that needs protecting.

CHECK OUT OTHER GREAT DINOSAUR THRILLERS

LOST WORLD OF PATAGONIA
by Dane Hatchell

An earthquake opens a path to a land hidden for millions of years. Under the guise of finding cryptid animals, Ace Corporation sends Alex Klasse, a Cryptozoologist and university professor, his associates, and a band of mercenaries to explore the Lost World of Patagonia. The crew boards a nuclear powered All-Terrain Tracked Carrier and takes a harrowing ride into the unknown.

The expedition soon discovers prehistoric creatures still exist. But the dangers won't prevent a sub-team from leaving the group in search of rare jewels. Tensions run high as personalities clash, and man proves to be just as deadly as the dinosaurs that roam the countryside.

Lost World of Patagonia is a prehistoric thriller filled with murder, mayhem, and savage dinosaur action.

SAVAGE ISLAND
by Alan Spencer

Somewhere in the Atlantic Ocean, an uncharted island has been used for the illegal dumping of chemicals and pollutants for years by Globo Corp's. Private investigator Pierce Range will learn plenty about the evil conglomerate when Susan Branch, an environmentalist from The Green Project, hires him to join the expedition to save her kidnapped father from Globo Corp's evil hands.

Things go to hell in a hurry once the team reaches the island. The bloodthirsty dinosaurs and voracious cannibals are only the beginning of the fight for survival. Pierce must unlock the mysteries surrounding the toxic operation and somehow remain in one piece to complete the rescue mission.

Ratchet up the body count, because this mission will leave the killing floor soaked in blood and chewed up corpses. When the insane battle ends, will there by anybody left alive to survive Savage Island?